PRAISE FOR THE DCI RYAN MYSTERIES

What newspapers say

"She keeps company with the best mystery writers" – *The Times*

"LJ Ross is the queen of Kindle" – *Sunday Telegraph*

"Holy Island is a blockbuster" – *Daily Express*

"A literary phenomenon" – *Evening Chronicle*

"A pacey, enthralling read" – *Independent*

What readers say

"I couldn't put it down. I think the full series will cause a divorce, but it will be worth it."

"I gave this book 5 stars because there's no option for 100."

"Thank you, LJ Ross, for the best two hours of my life."

"This book has more twists than a demented corkscrew."

"Another masterpiece in the series. The DCI Ryan mysteries are superb, with very realistic characters and wonderful plots. They are a joy to read!"

BOOKS BY LJ ROSS

THE ALEXANDER GREGORY THRILLERS:

1. *Impostor*
2. *Hysteria*
3. *Bedlam*
4. *Mania*
5. *Panic*

THE DCI RYAN MYSTERIES:

1. *Holy Island*
2. *Sycamore Gap*
3. *Heavenfield*
4. *Angel*
5. *High Force*
6. *Cragside*
7. *Dark Skies*
8. *Seven Bridges*
9. *The Hermitage*
10. *Longstone*
11. *The Infirmary (Prequel)*
12. *The Moor*
13. *Penshaw*
14. *Borderlands*
15. *Ryan's Christmas*
16. *The Shrine*
17. *Cuthbert's Way*
18. *The Rock*
19. *Bamburgh*
20. *Lady's Well*
21. *Death Rocks*
22. *Poison Garden*

THE SUMMER SUSPENSE MYSTERIES:

1. *The Cove*
2. *The Creek*
3. *The Bay*
4. *The Haven*

POISON GARDEN

A DCI RYAN MYSTERY

POISON GARDEN

A DCI RYAN MYSTERY

LJ ROSS

ISBN: 978-1-912310-72-2

First published in November 2024 by Dark Skies Publishing

Cover artwork and map by Andrew Davidson

Cover layout and typesetting by
Riverside Publishing Solutions Limited

"It is not death that man should fear, but rather he should fear never beginning to live."

—Marcus Aurelius

PROLOGUE

University Halls of Residence
September 2005

Emily heard him moving around her room, dragging on pants and jeans, and then looking for his wallet and keys. She continued to lie on the bed in the foetal position, facing the wall, eyes tightly shut.

Everything hurt.

Her head throbbed, blood hammering against the optic nerve, sending waves of pain across her eyes. Her lip was cut and swollen, while her arms and breasts were bruised from rough handling. Her inner thighs were scratched and torn and—

And—

She began to cry silently, tears running down her cheeks and onto the pillow.

He wondered whether he should say something, then decided to leave her to sleep it off. *Fresher girls were all the same*, he thought, from his lofty position as a final year student.

They gave out green light signals all night long, then changed their mind when he was primed and ready to go.

Tease, he thought, with a curl of his lip.

Maybe she'd think twice about offering it up on a plate, next time.

Maybe she'd say it was 'rape', his mind whispered.

He'd put it about that she was up for it with anyone, and his mates would back him up—he'd done the same for them, plenty of times. That should pre-empt any awkward questions, if she decided to get bitchy about it.

Yes, that's what he'd do.

He cast one last look at her slim back, and decided she was one of his better conquests. Pretty, with a nice little body. He'd managed to take quite a few pictures during the night, which he could hardly wait to share with the lads.

He blew her a kiss, and let himself out.

Emily heard him whistle as he made his way along the corridor, but didn't move until she heard the distant slam of the outer door that led onto the quadrangle outside. Then, very slowly, she rolled onto her back, gasping as fresh pain rocketed through her body. She'd strained her muscles while fighting him, and there was a lump on her head, where he'd smashed her skull against the wall in the struggle. She was afraid to look at herself and see the full extent of the damage, but she didn't need to see some things to know it was bad.

The delicate area between her legs burned.

Emily forced herself to roll off the bed, where she collapsed in a heap on the floor. She stayed there for long minutes, crying without a sound, eyes streaming as she rocked her naked body back and forth. Eventually, when tears subsided, she crawled over to the sink in the corner of the room and grasped the edge of it. Dragging herself up, she leaned heavily on the porcelain and then, in an enormous act of bravery, looked at her face in the mirror.

The first thing she saw was the beginnings of a black eye, from where he'd levelled a back-handed smack and thrown her onto the bed.

The next thing she saw was the crusted scab on her upper lip, where he'd bitten her. There were further bite marks on her neck. Her hair was in disarray, and her eyes looked hollowed out and fathoms deep in misery.

Emily looked down at her body, and saw the dried blood against her thighs.

She began to shake as memories flooded in from the night before.

You want it, don't you?

How'd you like that?

A sudden wave of nausea made her violently ill, and she threw up the contents of her stomach in the sink, heaving until there was nothing left, not even bile.

Then, she grasped a flannel and began to scrub herself with soap and water, uncaring of the fresh pain it brought. If she'd had any bleach, she'd have used that, instead.

She needed to be clean.

She'd never be clean again.

Newcastle Crown Court
One year later

His Honour Judge Alan Golightly leaned forward and faced the jury of twelve men and women.

"Have you reached a decision upon which you all agree?"

The foreman stood up and nodded. "Yes, Your Honour, we have."

Emily held her parents' hands and said a quiet prayer.

"We find the defendant, Edward Delaney, not guilty."

Emily jerked once in shock, while a cheer rose up from the other side of the aisle, where Eddie's parents, their expensive legal team, and a gathering of his friends and acolytes had taken up half of the courtroom.

"I don't believe it," her father whispered, angrily. "This is a *disgrace*—" He stood up, and pointed a finger at the jurors. "You should be ashamed of yourselves!" he cried. "What if this was your daughter, eh? How would you feel *then*?"

"You will sit down or be held in contempt of court!" Golightly warned him.

"Kevin," his wife said, tremulously.

"As for *you lot* over there," he said, turning to Delaney's family. "You should be hanging your heads! If I knew what my son had done to a young woman, I wouldn't have the audacity to show my face in public!"

"You just watch your mouth or you'll get a writ for slander! It isn't Ed's fault that your girl's nothing but a little *slut*—"

4

Kevin saw red, and crossed the aisle before his mind even knew that his legs had moved. He landed a hard punch squarely on Delaney Senior's jaw before the court security guard had even made it halfway down the central aisle.

"*Scum*," he said, and spat on the ground beside Delaney. "You, *and* your offspring."

The guard fell upon him then, and Kevin was taken to the cells on the judge's order, following which he dismissed the court. His wife held Emily close, felt the uncontrollable trembling that had been a constant companion since her ordeal, and told herself to be strong.

She had to be.

"Come on, love," she whispered. "Let's go—"

Emily nodded, defeat etched in every line of her body.

"I won't leave here without saying my piece," Eddie's mother accosted them, as they turned to leave. "It's thanks to *girls like you*, that good, hardworking boys like *mine* have their lives ruined by false accusations—"

"Ignore her," Emily's mother said, between gritted teeth. "Come on."

But every word was a poisoned dart.

"Changing your mind in the morning isn't the same as rape!" Mrs Delaney threw at their retreating backs. "I'll be telling everyone what you are…a *liar*!"

Emily's legs threatened to give way, but somehow she continued, flanked by her mother and the tired-looking barrister who'd given the trial her best effort.

"I'm so sorry," she said, as they left the courtroom. "I wish the outcome had been different."

There was nothing else to say and so, with a heavy heart, she bade them farewell.

"I want to go home," Emily whispered. "I just want to go home."

One week later

"Emily! Dinner's on the table!" her mother called up the stairs, one hand resting on the newel post. "Emily!"

She hadn't been eating lately...well, that wasn't quite true. Emily hadn't enjoyed a proper meal since her attack, and that was over a year ago. Her slim, athletic figure had wasted away to something skeletal, and her fine bone structure was now a collection of bony angles and pale, shadowed skin. The anti-depressants had helped for a while, giving her a false appetite when she needed it most, but that particular side-effect had worn off. *Breakthrough depression,* the psychiatrist called it, when they'd taken her to see him. Emily's body had learned to override the drugs or, to put it another way, her mind was stronger than the pills.

Would Emily ever be able to begin her life again, at a new university? She was so intelligent, so *kind*, it was a tragedy that she'd been forced to drop out.

All because of him...

Her mother grasped the banister and headed upstairs, her bare feet padding softly against the carpet runner as she fought the familiar tide of anger.

It did no good to dwell on the past.

She knocked on her daughter's bedroom door and, when there was no reply, tried the handle.

It was locked.

That was highly unusual.

"Emily? Can you open the door, please?"

Still, no answer.

Her mother rattled the handle again, turning it this way and that.

"Kev? *Kev!*" she called downstairs to her husband.

"What?" he called back.

"I—I can't open Emily's door, and she's not answering!"

A creeping feeling began to crawl over her skin; a terrible, prescient knowledge of what she would find behind the plain white door.

She stepped away from it, breathing fast.

"What's wrong?" Kevin said, huffing his way upstairs.

"The door," she whispered. "It won't open."

He frowned, and she watched him repeat the steps she had taken; knocking and calling out to their daughter and then, when there was no reply, turning the handle.

They exchanged a silent look which spoke volumes.

"Stand back, love," he said, in an odd, emotionless voice. "Turn away."

"No," she said. "I won't turn away."

Kevin steeled himself, and did what no father should ever have to do. He broke into his daughter's room with a couple of hard kicks and found her lifeless body hanging there, from the light fitting in the centre of the room. He let out a long, keening sound, like an animal in torment, and rushed forward to grab her legs.

His girl.

His little girl...

"Get an ambulance!" he shouted. "For God's sake!"

But she was gone. They both knew that.

Emily was long gone.

CHAPTER 1

Newcastle Central Station
Sunday, Eighteen years later

Detective Sergeant Frank Phillips tended to avoid train journeys, especially after a memorable case in which he'd almost been blown to kingdom come by a deranged bomber while on a train—not a hundred yards from where he was now seated.

He fidgeted, and checked the aisle again for any suspicious looking bags.

That suitcase looked a bit dodgy, the way it was sitting on the luggage rack as if it belonged there—

"Relax, Frank," a woman's voice said. "We'll be in London before you know it."

He looked across the table at Chief Constable Sandra Morrison, who appeared entirely at ease while reading a copy of *The Sunday Times.*

"Easy for you to say," he muttered.

She smiled to herself. "Why don't you get yourself a bacon stottie from the café?" she said. "That'll cheer you up."

His mouth watered at the very mention of it, but there was one problem. "I'm on a diet," he grumbled.

Sandra eyed him over the top of the newspaper. "I'm sure I saw you round the back of the Pie Van, the other day, scoffing a corned beef pasty."

"You must've mistaken me for someone else," he said, sweetly. "Eyewitness accounts can be very unreliable, as you and I both know."

She snorted, and resumed her reading.

"D' you think they have anything healthy?" he wondered aloud.

"Frank, this is a standard class train carriage," she said. "They're not dishing out quinoa and beetroot salads."

"I thought you could travel first class, anyhow?" he said.

Sandra nodded. "I can," she said, a bit smugly. "Technically, anyone of the rank 'superintendent' or above is entitled to, but I always travel standard class. It sets a good example to the likes of you."

He rolled his eyes, and turned to watch the passing scenery. "I still don't understand why you're bringin' me along," he mumbled. "It's a bit above my pay grade, isn't it?"

Behind the cover of her newspaper, Morrison chose her words with care. "As you know, we're setting up a nationwide task force," she said. "It's clear that the organisation responsible for facilitating the murder of numerous people has been operational for some time, and we have no reason to doubt it has reach far beyond the North East. Whilst I'll certainly deal with any high level matters to do with cooperation and funding, I want you to be the main point of contact."

She paused to look at him again.

"You have a detailed knowledge of the investigation, so far," she reminded him. "Besides, with Ryan gone, we've got a shortage of senior officers."

A heavy silence followed the mention of their friend's name. Phillips turned to stare out of the window again, but, this time, he saw nothing of the scenery.

"Sorry," she said, belatedly.

"It's alreet," he said, and then cleared his throat. "How come we're meetin' everyone on a Sunday?"

"It's the only day everyone could do, at short notice."

"It still doesn't feel real," he said, and she knew he wasn't speaking of the meeting. "I can hardly believe he's gone."

Morrison reached across the table to pat his hand, before thinking better of it. "This trip might be just what you need," she said, and left it at that.

———

Three hours later, Phillips was reminded of why he'd never had any desire to live in the Big City. King's Cross station was awash with people jockeying for position.

"Chief Constable Morrison?"

They looked up to find a tall, good-looking man waiting for them. He bore more than a passing resemblance to the actor Idris Elba and, judging by the cut of his jib, was not unaware or unhappy about the fact.

"DCI Hassan? Good to see you, again," Morrison said, and shook his hand. "You remember Sergeant Frank Phillips?"

"How could I forget?" he said, with a broad smile. "Good to see you again, Frank."

Privately, Phillips seethed. He'd liked John Hassan, the last time they'd met, but, considering the man claimed to have been one of Ryan's old friends from his Met days, he considered it an insult that he hadn't so much as attended his memorial service.

"Aye," he said, and left it at that.

Hassan frowned, then suddenly his brow cleared, and he smiled at Morrison. "Right, well, we'd better get going," he said. "I brought a car."

"We'd have happily taken the Tube," Morrison said, and Phillips looked at her as if she'd grown two heads.

Speak for yourself, he thought.

"It's only right for a visiting Chief Constable to be collected," Hassan said, with charming deference.

They made their way out into the autumn sunshine, then on towards a dark saloon car parked illegally at the end of a taxi rank.

"Parking is a nightmare around here," Hassan said, and held the door open for Morrison. "After you, ma'am."

Smooth operator, Phillips thought to himself.

Presently, they caught a gap in the traffic and Hassan accelerated from the kerb with the kind of reckless abandon that reminded him of Ryan, and almost brought a tear to his eye, while his hand gripped the edge of his seat.

The offices of New Scotland Yard were based in the City of Westminster, overlooking the River Thames. Constructed during a period of roaring Art Deco architectural design, the headquarters of the Metropolitan Police were a far cry from those of the Northumbria Police Constabulary, whose employees were happy simply to have a roof over their heads and a toilet that flushed.

Phillips gave a long whistle as they entered the hallowed walls. "Not bad," he said.

"Don't get any ideas," Morrison warned him. "I've already stretched the departmental budget to accommodate your biscuit habit, let alone anything else—like putting more bobbies on the beat."

Hassan laughed, and led them through the security barriers. "I can procure some digestives," he offered. "I don't want you suffering from withdrawal symptoms during the meeting, Frank."

Phillips managed to look down his nose at the man, who was significantly taller than himself. "That won't be necessary," he said, with dignity.

"There's a vending machine down the hall, if you change your mind," Hassan said. "The meeting room's just down here. We're a bit early, so the others might not have arrived, yet."

They were due to meet with Morrison's corollary at the Met, Chief Constable Steven Porter, as well as the heads of several of the twenty-four murder investigation teams that made up their Homicide and Major Crime Command. When Ryan had cut his teeth at the Met, he'd been based in one such team and worked out of the Command's 'Central' unit, which covered most of the city centre.

Hassan led them into one of the smaller conference rooms, and turned on the lights. "Shouldn't be too long," he said, checking his watch. "Most of the senior staff live outside of London in the suburbs, so they're probably battling the M25. There's time to grab a coffee or a snack, if you want?"

They agreed that some caffeine was in order, and, while Hassan took himself off to the break room to procure three strong cups of coffee, Phillips excused himself under the pretext of needing the gents and went in search of the fabled vending machine. After a harrowing few minutes spent wandering the clinical, white-painted walls of The Yard, Phillips found the machine tucked in a shadowed corner where only the most determined sugar addict could possibly have found it.

"Thank God," he muttered, and then promptly swore at the inflated price of a Kit Kat in London.

Daylight robbery.

He fished around for several coins, fed them into the slot and pressed the code.

Nothing happened.

He tried the code again.

Still no chocolate.

14

"Howay, man," he said to the machine, as if it could hear him.

"You need to give it a good kick," a voice said, from behind him.

Phillips froze, and thought that he must have finally lost his last marble, because he was obviously hearing voices.

He turned, and saw a man who looked remarkably like his friend, Ryan.

Only, it couldn't be him, because he was *dead*.

Phillips let out a funny sound in his throat, and turned back to the machine. "You're tired," he told himself. "That's all it is." But his hand shook as he keyed in the code for a third time, and, if he wasn't mistaken, he could see the outline of a man's body reflected in the glass.

He squeezed his eyes shut, and counted to five.

"Well, I have to say, I was expecting a warmer welcome than this," Ryan said.

Phillips' eyes flew open again, and he turned around slowly to find the man still standing there, living and breathing—all six feet, four inches of him.

"You—" he whispered, and flattened himself back against the vending machine.

"I'm alive," Ryan confirmed.

"You—" Phillips repeated, and took a tentative step forward. "You lyin' git!"

Phillips planted his prize-fighting fist squarely on his friend's handsome jawline, and heard a satisfying *crunch*.

CHAPTER 2

"What've you got in here—a dead body?"

Hundreds of miles further north, Detective Constable Jack Lowerson heaved a cardboard box from the back of his friend's car.

"Foiled again," Charlie quipped, and led him inside the new apartment she'd found for herself and her young son, Ben. Since she could barely afford the downpayment as well as food that month, she was eternally grateful to Jack for the free labour he'd offered in helping her move.

"Time for a tea break?" she said. "I think the kettle's in that box, over there."

"I won't say 'no' to a cuppa," Jack replied, and surreptitiously wiped sweat from his brow. "Where's Ben?"

"He's with my mother for the weekend," she replied, her voice muffled as she rooted around for a couple of mugs. "This way, I can get his room ready, put his bed back together and all that."

Lowerson came to stand in the little galley kitchen beside her, and leaned back against the counter. "I'm pretty handy with a screwdriver," he said, and hoped it was true. "If you need any help putting furniture back together?"

Detective Constable Charlie Reed was used to being independent. As a single mother and unofficial carer for her own mother, who'd been diagnosed recently with multiple sclerosis, she was no stranger to DIY or any other domestic task, for that matter. Help had seldom been offered, so it always came as a slight shock when anybody held out their hand to her. "I—thanks, actually, that would be really kind," she said, and turned to smile at him. "It's hard to put bed frames back together, when you're on your own."

Jack nodded, and remembered a time when he and Melanie had put their bed together. He still slept in it, each night, while she was somewhere else in the world. He turned away, looking for a distraction so that he wouldn't think of it, or of her.

"Um, it's a nice place," he said, and meant it. The flat was small but perfectly proportioned, in an area of Newcastle known as Gosforth. It occupied the entire ground floor of a large Edwardian house, with a small garden leading off the back which would be perfect for her son to play in.

"Thanks," she replied, and poured milk into their tea. "I was starting to worry, because there wasn't much on the market, but when the agent rang to tell me about this place, I knew it was 'The One'."

"Sometimes, you just know," Jack agreed, and she gave him a lopsided smile.

"Yeah," she muttered, and handed him one of the mugs. "It's a bit more than I wanted to spend, but it has three bedrooms and it's on the ground floor, which means my mum can come and stay with us whenever she likes." Charlie took a sip of tea, and shrugged. "To be honest, I'm hoping she might decide to move in with us. It would be easier, all round, because it's going to become more and more difficult for my mum to look after her own place as her illness progresses. I'm struggling to help her as much as I could if we lived under the same roof."

Jack found himself admiring his new colleague very much. It wasn't easy to progress in the ranks, do a stellar job at work, run a household, bring up a little boy and look after an ailing mother, but she managed to do it all with a smile.

"Would your mum accept help from a nurse?" he asked.

"She's very proud," Charlie said. "There's some care available to her, but she's refused it, so far."

They drank their tea, each comfortable in the silence and enjoying the rays of sunshine filtering through the kitchen window.

"How's Frank holding up?" she asked him, after a moment. "It only feels like yesterday that we lost him."

"Frank?"

"No, since we lost *Ryan*."

"Oh, right. Yeah."

She frowned at him, and wondered if brain fog was one of the unofficial stages of grief.

"Um, you know, he's holding up as best he can," Jack said.

If she hadn't known better, Charlie might have thought he was keeping something from her, but she told herself not to be so suspicious. She wasn't on the clock, after all.

"He said something about going on a trip down to London with Morrison today," she said, and waggled a packet of biscuits, which he refused. "I wonder why?"

"Something to do with the task force that's being set up," Jack replied. "Better him than us."

She grinned, and then set her empty cup aside.

"Well, c'mon," she said. "Let's get moving—those beds aren't going to put themselves up."

"Aye, aye," he said, with a mock salute.

"Jack?"

"Mm hm?"

"I really appreciate this," she said, quietly. "Thank you."

"Don't mention it," he said, and headed off in search of some tools.

Charlie smiled wistfully. *There was no future there*, she reminded herself.

Jack's heart was already taken.

———

The historic market town of Alnwick was bathed in early afternoon sunshine, which spread over the surrounding countryside and sturdy, stone-built houses that clustered around an impressive Mediaeval castle in the centre of it all, which had been home to the Dukes of Northumberland for generations since the Norman Conquest.

George Masters had been born and bred thirty four miles further south, in Newcastle. However, he'd often visited Alnwick as a child and so, when the opportunity presented itself to open another site for his estate agency, he'd taken it as a sign to make a more permanent move. For the most part, he'd never regretted the decision, although country towns weren't half as quiet as city folk were led to believe. He thought of all the gossip that flowed through his shop door, which often meant that he knew exactly which houses were going to be coming up for sale, even before the owners realised it themselves. There was an art to salesmanship, he thought, and it wasn't all in the selling; sometimes, it was in acquiring the right stock, at the right time.

George thought this as he warmed up for his usual five-kilometre circuit around the town.

He began to jog along the high street, dodging pedestrians and waving to anybody he recognised. He liked being *seen*, especially by the younger, better-looking female members of his local community. George could admit that he hadn't always looked as good as he did now; in the old days, he'd been downright flabby, with a taste for carbohydrates that would probably have precipitated an early stroke, if he hadn't taken himself in hand. When a new gym opened up on the edge of town a few years back, he'd plucked up the courage to go along and try out its new, industrial-looking facilities and it had changed his life. He ran a hand over his six-pack, and smiled.

"Not bad," he said to himself.

Masters ran at a steady pace and cut through the old market square along Narrowgate, where he passed by a statue of old 'Harry Hotspur', which was the nickname given to Sir

Henry Percy, an English knight and ancestor of the present Duke. He continued north, planning to skirt the perimeter of the castle walls towards Lions Bridge and the River Aln, which afforded a particularly arcadian view of the castle that had graced numerous oil paintings and postcards over the years. From there, he'd run along the riverbank for a while and loop back around, in time for a shower and some dinner.

Very suddenly, he began to feel unwell.

It started as a mild cramp in his abdomen, which he mistook for a stitch. However, the cramp soon became a severe pain that spread up into his chest, tightening the intercostal muscles so that he could hardly breathe. He was forced to stop and throw out a hand, leaning heavily against the castle wall as he doubled over in agony. He felt numb, a tingling sensation that crept from his fingers and toes and upward into his arms and legs.

His vision blurred, and he cast around for somebody— *anybody*.

"*Help*," he gasped.

His legs gave way, and drew the attention of a woman passing by. "Oh, my God!" she said, and hurried to his side.

Lisa Cookson was an experienced first aider, having been a volunteer with the St John's Ambulance Service for many years, but that was a far cry from being a paramedic, and even a cursory glance at George's contorted face told her that he needed urgent clinical care.

"Where does it hurt?" she said, and shrugged off her coat to keep him warm. "What happened to you?"

"Chest," he wheezed. "Can't—can't breathe. Stomach. Stomach cramps. Feel—feel numb—"

His eyes rolled back in his head.

"Stay with me!" she said urgently. Lisa fumbled for her phone, but his pale face warned her that even the fastest ambulance might be too late. On the other hand, her car was parked only a few feet away and the small hospital in Alnwick was less than a two-minute drive from there, particularly if she floored it all the way. It might not have an emergency department, but it would certainly have doctors and nurses, and was far closer than the nearest major hospital with a dedicated A&E unit.

She made a split-second decision, and grabbed the car keys from her pocket. By then, another couple had arrived, crowding around Masters' collapsed body with open curiosity.

"What happened?"

"Help me get him into the car!" Lisa cried. "I think he's having a heart attack—"

"Why not call an ambulance?"

"There's no time," she said, pulling one of the back doors open.

Between them, they heaved Masters' body onto the back seat of her Peugeot and Lisa ran around to the driver's side.

Please, don't die, she prayed. *Please, don't die.*

She stuck the keys in the ignition, rammed the car into gear, and pulled away from the kerb with a squeal of tyres.

CHAPTER 3

"You've not lost your touch, that's for sure." Ryan rubbed the side of his jaw, and tested it to make sure it wasn't broken.

"Aye, and there's plenty more where that came from," Phillips snapped. "What d' you think you're playin' at, anyway? I thought you were *dead*, you—you—*pillock!*"

Anger warred with sheer elation at the sight of his friend standing there, living and breathing, and he turned away to hide the tears that sprang to his eyes.

"I'm sorry, Frank," Ryan said quietly. "Let me explain what happened."

"Somebody better," came the muffled reply.

"In here," Ryan said, and held open the door to the service stairs. "I'm still supposed to be dead, so I'm trying to keep a low profile."

"Thinks he's Lord Lucan, now," Phillips muttered.

They sat on the stairs, side by side, and Ryan took a deep breath.

"You remember, somebody ordered my assassination," he said, as casually as one could, in the circumstances.

"I could hardly forget, since I was nearly blown to smithereens by a car bomb that was meant for *you*," Phillips said, dryly.

Ryan nodded, remembering that awful day. "Well, as you know, they tried again by coming for me at home," he said. "Except, it wasn't me they found there." He swallowed a painful lump in his throat. "I had no idea my father had travelled north, with Jack," he continued. "The gunman mistook him for me because we have—or *had*—the same height and bearing."

"I'm sorry, lad," Phillips said, softly.

Ryan looked down at his hands. "They shot him with a long-range rifle," he said. "Because of me."

Phillips thought of Charles Finley-Ryan. They'd only met a few times, but he was an honourable man who'd loved his son, dearly. His death wasn't the outcome any of them would have wanted but he knew that, if Charles had been given the choice, he'd have protected his son at all costs, even if that meant forfeiting his own life.

It's what any of them would do, for their children.

"I'd stayed at Morrison's place, the night before," Ryan continued, and Phillips made a mental note to ask him about her décor some other time. "We—that is, me, Sandra and Jack—decided it would be best if nobody knew I was alive, at least for a while. It would've been a pointless waste of resources trying to protect me, and I'd have spent every day living in a state of fear, thinking there'd be another gunman coming for me, at any time. This way, their guard will be down. They think I'm already gone, and their job is done."

"D' you mean to tell me, all this time, Jack and Sandra *knew* you were still alive? Of all the sneaky, no-good buggers—"

"Now, think of your blood pressure," Ryan warned him, and narrowly escaped another right hook.

"I'll give you *blood pressure*," Phillips growled, and pointed an accusatory finger at his chest. "If you *ever* keep me in the dark again, you won't have to worry about some faceless assassin, that's for bloody sure. It'll be me!"

Ryan smiled. "I've missed you, Frank."

"Aye, and don't think you can soften me up with any of that, either."

Ryan's smile grew wider. "I mean it."

Phillips gave him a sideways glance, and folded his arms across his chest. "You could've told me," he muttered. "Or did you think I couldn't be trusted?"

"Don't be daft," Ryan said. "I've wanted to call you every day, but I couldn't risk your recovery. I wanted to explain this to you, in person, when I could be sure the worst of the danger had passed."

Phillips had suffered a cardiac arrest following the car bombing, and had been hospitalised for several days. The doctors had since given him a clean bill of health, but Ryan would never forget seeing his greatest friend lying ashen on the tarmac, no longer breathing.

"I'm as fit as a fiddle," Phillips declared. "I don't need any babying from you, or anyone else."

Ryan nodded. "I know you don't," he said. "But I couldn't have lived with myself, if I'd been responsible for putting you in any more danger, especially when you were vulnerable." He paused, and tucked his tongue in his cheek. "Of course, I consider you fully expendable, now."

"Oh, that's charmin', that is."

They smiled at one another, and Phillips relented. "I missed you, too, lad," he said. "Don't think I'll be givin' you any more eulogies, mind. I wouldn't trust you not to come back from the dead a second time."

"I heard your eulogy was very moving."

"Of *course* it was," Phillips muttered. "You know fine well, I'm a brilliant orator."

"And so modest, with it."

Phillips' lips twitched. "So, what's the plan?" he said.

"When the time is right, I'm going to reappear," Ryan said. "For now, Morrison thinks it's safest for everyone that I monitor developments remotely, from Devon or here in London. Anna and Emma are still at Summersley, with my mother."

Although their home was in Northumberland, Ryan—together with his wife and daughter—had retreated to his family's home in Devonshire, a beautiful country estate that had passed through the generations. His father had always intended Summersley to pass to his only son, but Ryan had chosen to carve out a very different kind of life for himself as a murder detective, and the prospect of managing a large estate held no interest for him. If it weren't for the fact his sister and father were both interred in the grounds, and his mother wanted to remain near to them, he'd have suggested they sell the place and donate the proceeds to a worthy cause.

Phillips checked the time on his FitBit, and Ryan raised an eyebrow, thinking the man had clearly gone off the rails, since he'd been gone.

"I'd better be heading off to the briefing," he said. "Are you coming?"

Ryan shook his head. "Most of the people attending still think I'm six feet under," he said. "I'll catch up with the headlines, later."

They stood up, and Phillips held his arms out. "Howay," he said. "Bring it in, lad."

Ryan walked into his bear-like embrace, and it was like coming home.

CHAPTER 4

Lisa Cookson drove at breakneck speed through the quaint streets of Alnwick, then made a hairpin turn into the car park of a small community hospital on the edge of town. It had no A&E department, the infirmary being used to treat outpatients or those with minor injuries, but she didn't stop to worry about that. Casting a worried eye over the man collapsed on her back seat, she pulled into a disabled parking bay and leaned on the car's horn to attract attention from anyone within earshot.

One of the nurses popped her head out of the main doors, to see what all the commotion was about. "Everything okay?" she called out.

"No! I've got a man here, in critical condition!" Lisa shouted back, and yanked open the back door. "I need help!"

The nurse, who wasn't in the habit of running as a general rule, nonetheless shouted for help to her colleagues and then picked up her heels and rushed across the tarmac.

"I think he's having a heart attack," Lisa told her, breathlessly. "His airways seem to be clear, but he's struggling to breathe—"

The nurse took in the situation and, with the timely arrival of two of the other nurses, they managed to drag Masters' unresponsive body onto a trolley and rolled him towards one of the consultation rooms inside the main building. Lisa followed them inside, where a visiting consultant obstetrician abandoned a woman in her second trimester to attend to the unexpected crisis.

"What happened?" she asked, and checked Master's vitals with nimble hands.

"I honestly don't know," Lisa replied, from the doorway. "I was heading back to my car, and I saw him collapse against the wall. He was clutching a hand to his chest and seemed to be struggling to breathe, so I went over to see if I could help. He said his stomach was cramping…he also said something about feeling numb. I'm a first aider, so I would have performed CPR, but he was still managing on his own—just. I didn't think there was time to wait for an ambulance…I hope that was right."

The consultant nodded. "You made the right call," she assured her, and took the man's blood pressure, which was dangerously low. "Do you know who he is?"

Lisa shook her head. "No, I'm afraid—"

"Not to worry, we'll find out."

There was a short, tense silence, and then the consultant made a judgment call of her own. "Get the paddles ready," she instructed one of the nurses. "He's going into cardiac arrest."

They kept the equipment for emergency use but so far hadn't ever needed it, so the nurse looked at her in momentary confusion before scurrying across the room.

"He doesn't seem to be having a regular heart attack," the consultant said, mostly to herself. "He's wearing running gear, and looks generally fit and healthy. I don't think it's a stroke—"

She turned to Lisa. "It's best you leave the room," she told her, and Lisa nodded, eyes widening as she backed out of the doorway and almost collided with one of the nurses.

"Ambulance is on the way," the nurse said, and then spotted the defibrillator. "Is he—"

The consultant set the paddles on Masters' chest.

"*Clear!*"

They watched his body jerk upward, then waited to hear his heart rate sound on the monitor.

When it didn't, the consultant set the paddles on his skin again.

"One more time," she said, between gritted teeth. "Clear!"

His body rose and collapsed against the trolley, but there was still no comforting *beep*.

The consultant blew out a shaky breath, and tried several more times before admitting defeat.

"He's gone," she said and, bearing down against the unexpected grief, checked the time on the wall. "Patient pronounced dead at thirteen-thirty-seven."

In London, a collection of senior police officers gathered in a conference room at New Scotland Yard, where Frank Phillips joined them belatedly and slipped onto a chair next to Chief Constable Morrison.

"Find anything interesting, while you were gone?" she asked, in an undertone.

He gave her the side-eye. "Aye, you could say that," he replied, and shook the Kit Kat that Ryan had procured for him.

There was no time for further conversation before the Met's Chief Constable, a man by the name of Steven Porter, came to his feet and addressed the room. "Thank you all for coming, especially on a Sunday," he said. "I especially want to thank our colleagues who've travelled from further afield, including Northumbria, Devon and Cornwall and other constabularies."

He nodded to Morrison and Phillips, then to the others who'd been up at the crack of dawn to travel to London.

"In a moment, I'm going to hand over to DCI Hassan, who's our acting DCS in Major Crime Command, here in London, as well as having oversight of the Central Unit, which handles murder investigations within the city centre," Porter said. "We're joined by colleagues from the other units, and I want to assure you all that this task force will have the full operational support of my wider staff. The gravity and urgency of the situation can't be overstated, nor can the potential reach of this terrorist organisation—which is perhaps the best descriptor for their network—so I speak for all of us when I say we're committed to eliminating it, as swiftly and efficiently as possible."

There were nods around the room, and then Porter stood aside to make way for Hassan.

"Thank you, Chief Constable," he said. "And welcome to the first meeting of Operation Strangers. Before we get into the nuts and bolts, I'd like to invite our colleagues from the Northumbria Constabulary to bring us up to date with the facts, since they were the ones to uncover the threat in the first place, and have the most relevant knowledge to hand."

He nodded towards Phillips, and all heads turned in his direction.

"That's your cue," Morrison said. "Get up there, champ."

"I don't usually do the presentations," he hissed. "That's Ryan's job."

"Well, he's not here," she hissed back, with a gleam in her eye.

Unable to argue with that, at least not *publicly*, Phillips smoothed down his tie—a snazzy little red number with a pattern of embroidered yellow zigzags—and moved to the front of the room with all the enthusiasm of a man making his way to the guillotine.

"Er, thanks," he said. "I'm—ah, I'm DS Frank Phillips."

He shifted his feet, and wondered why he suffered no stage fright performing karaoke on a regular Friday night, but was as jittery as a teenager in front of a roomful of murder detectives.

Tough crowd, he thought.

"Aye, well, as you know, this is a massive operation," he said. "We became aware of this—this killing scheme, if you want to call it that, after a recent investigation in Dunstanburgh, where a photographer was found dead after an apparent accident on the rocks. Further investigation revealed it was murder, but there was no obvious motive or suspect in the case, and the only person who might've had a reason to want the bloke dead had a solid alibi."

He scratched his chin.

"Next thing you know, we were called out to another case, this time a woman killed in a hit and run," he said. "Again, the only person who might've wanted her bumped off had a cast-iron alibi. But, lo and behold, we found a connection between the two cases, even though the victims were completely unconnected."

He was getting into the swing of things, now, Phillips thought, and puffed out his chest a bit.

"Turns out, the bloke with a motive in the first case ended up being the hit and run murderer in the second, even though he didn't know the victim or the person with the motive, which was her husband," he told them. "We asked ourselves: why the heck would somebody kill a woman they didn't know, or help out a bloke they didn't know, and who didn't have any money to pay him to do it—or have any history of blackmail?"

He looked around the room, and knew he had them in the palm of his hand.

"Well, we found out that somebody was placing regular classified ads in *The Northern Fisherman* magazine, giving details of the next person due to be murdered and staged as an accident or suicide, even setting out the deadline it needed to be done by. It seems this scheme allows people to put in an order for someone to be killed, and it'll be fulfilled by someone else in the network. Murder in exchange for murder, by people who don't even know one another."

"Ingenious," Hassan remarked, from the sidelines. "It means the killer never has any connection to the victim or the true suspect, who can plan their alibi."

Phillips nodded. "We've got a big job on our hands," he said. "Our team's already found dozens of previous suspect cases, all listed in past classifieds in that magazine, but there's no telling how many more there are out there, in different magazines and in different parts of the country. That's where you lot come in."

There were more nods around the room.

"D' you think the pattern will be the same?" one of them asked.

Phillips nodded again. "It's worked well for them, so far. There's no reason why they'd change their MO," he replied. "I'd look for local magazines or newspapers with a small circulation in your area, and cross-check classifieds against past cases of accidental deaths, suicides or suspicious cold cases, and see what that throws up. They're only using magazines where payment isn't required to place a classified ad, which means we can't track them down using bank details. It'll take a lot of leg work to get the full picture."

LJ ROSS

"We've already found several red flags in Central Command," Hassan said. "I've got our intelligence analysts compiling a list of potentials, but there could be any number of them."

"As I say, it's a big job," Phillips replied. "It could go back years."

"Surely not," one of the other DCIs remarked, a bit nervously. "Whoever's behind all this couldn't have got away with that volume of suicides or accidentals without us ever noticing it."

"But that's exactly what's happened," Morrison said, and they turned to her. "Investigating officers have to make judgment calls in any given case. If something looks like an accident, and there's no other evidence to suggest it may be suspicious, it'll be treated as an accident and ruled accordingly. I can only imagine how many cases have slipped through the net because officers did their jobs exactly as they should have." She let that sink in. "The fact is, we have skin in the game, now, and we're onto them."

"Not forgetting the murder of your DCI Ryan," another voice said, and a rumble of condolences went around the room, which made Phillips feel decidedly guilty.

"Yes—a great loss to the department," Morrison said, smoothly. "He's one of ours, which makes this personal."

"Has there been any progress in finding his killer?" Porter asked.

"We're still investigating," Phillips said, and hoped he didn't sound too shifty. "There's reason to think the perp was also responsible for the bombing outside HMP Frankland."

He experienced a sudden flash memory of an explosion, followed by a phantom burning sensation in his leg, and then shoved it away. "*Anyway*," he said. "The key thing is to track down who's behind the scheme, and to figure out how it all began. We need to find the source."

"Thank you, DS Phillips," Hassan said, with an appreciative nod. "One other thing to mention is the press. I think we're all agreed that it's in the public interest to keep a lid on any news coverage, because the last thing we need is widespread panic. That being said, some of the details in the classified ads have already leaked, but I've got our legal team working to enforce a media blackout."

"I'll add whatever weight I can," Porter said, and made a mental note to call a few of the editors he knew personally.

Hassan proceeded to go through a checklist of action points, with each regional head agreeing to take steps to crack down on any network operating within their constabulary, but every man and woman in the room knew that their task was constrained by the size of their pockets. Time and resources were at a premium, and the public purse was already stretched to its limit without the addition of such a colossal task.

From his position in the meeting room next door, where he listened with the help of an open conference call, Ryan leaned back in his chair and thought of the kind of person who took it upon themselves to construct such a network, with the sole purpose of making murder cheap and easy.

Were they evil, or just ill? he wondered.

Either way, he'd put a stop to it.

CHAPTER 5

The Bigg Market, Newcastle upon Tyne
April 2007

Eddie Delaney snorted another line of coke off the cistern in one of the gents toilets, rubbed the excess powder from his nose, and then opened the cubicle door. Hard, thumping music shook the walls of the club, and he splashed some water on his face before wandering back out into the fray. He was a good-looking young man of twenty-three and he knew it; tall, with floppy brown hair that would probably recede but which, at least for now, fell across his forehead in an attractive, artless way that gave unsuspecting women the impression he was a 'sensitive type'.

Eddie smiled to himself, felt the drugs fuel his system, and swaggered into the crowd of pulsating bodies. His eyes tracked over the women he passed, until he spotted one he liked.

In fact, she was already looking at him.

Not surprising, really.

She was definitely his type, Eddie thought, being slim, leggy, and with curves in all the right places. She wore a black mini-dress and heels, and seemed tipsy enough to be up for anything, with the right encouragement.

Perfect.

He pasted a smile on his face, one he'd practised in the mirror numerous times, and moved through the crowd to join her.

"Hello," he said, leaning down to speak into her ear. "I'm Eddie! What's your name?"

"Hi," she replied, swaying to the music. "I'm Tanya!"

"I like your dress," he said. Really, he meant that he liked her *body*, but he knew it sounded classier if he complimented her outfit. "Are you here with anyone?"

She shook her head. "Just a couple of friends, but they're dancing," she said, and made a show of looking around. "D' you wanna get a drink?"

He gave her another winning smile. "Sure," he said, and estimated two, maybe three drinks and he'd have her naked in the nearest cheap hotel.

They weaved a pathway through people gyrating drunkenly to Usher and 50 Cent, and fought their way through to a bar queue that was three persons deep. Eddie set about elbowing his way to the front.

"What d' you want?" he asked her. He didn't mind forking out for a few cheap drinks; especially, as a means to an end.

"Whatever you're having!" she said, and gave him a flirtatious smile.

Eddie ordered a couple of vodka Red Bulls and helped himself to an eyeful of the barmaid's cleavage, while he was at it.

"Here you are," he said, and handed one of the plastic cups to Tanya. "D' you wanna find a quiet spot where we can, er, get to know each other?"

In answer, she took his hand and led him to a shadowy corner, where a number of other couples had paired off and were enjoying the relative privacy.

"Oops," Tanya said, and dropped her bag, spilling its contents all over the sticky floor.

Eddie wondered how much longer he'd have to play the gentleman. "I'll get it," he said, with forced cheer. "Hold my cup for a minute."

His back was turned for seconds only, but that was all the time she needed to drop a little sachet of powder into his drink and swill it around.

"Thanks," she said, when he straightened up and handed her the bag.

Eddie retrieved his cup, and held it up. "Here's to a great evening."

"I'll drink to that," she said, and touched her cup to his.

The woman who called herself 'Tanya' watched him take a long gulp of the amber liquid, and then excused herself to go to the ladies room, promising to be back soon. Instead, she left the club, and walked swiftly out into the night, a nameless woman who'd never be found.

Within five minutes, Edward Delaney collapsed, his body convulsing violently amongst the crowd of faceless strangers who stared at him with vacant eyes.

Within another five, he was dead.

———

"Kev…look at this!"

His wife called to him from the kitchen door, but Kevin didn't hear. He was sitting at the bottom of their small garden, staring despondently at the lawnmower rusting away amongst a patch of weeds. He'd intended to cut the grass, that morning, just as he'd resolved to do it every previous Saturday, without success.

"Kev!"

This time, he shook himself, and looked across at his wife. At first glance, with the sun shining down upon her hair, he might have thought it was Emily standing there waving to him. But then a cloud passed over the sun and he remembered she was gone.

"Yes?" he said, wearily. "What is it?"

Since he made no move to come to her, his wife hurried across the overgrown lawn, a copy of that morning's local paper held tightly in one hand. "Look at this," she repeated, and held out the front page for him to see. "There—look at the headline—"

Kevin struggled to read without his glasses, and had no idea where he'd left them, but he managed to make out the larger lettering and, in any case, it was accompanied by the picture of a man he'd have recognised anywhere.

MILLIONNAIRE'S SON DIES IN CITY CLUB

"It's Eddie—Eddie Delaney," his wife whispered, a bit unnerved by his silence. "The article says he died in some club in town, after a drug overdose."

Still, Kevin said nothing, but continued to stare at the picture.

"Kev? I thought you'd want to know. Was I wrong?"

His hands began to shake, and he handed the newspaper back to her. How could he tell his wife that thoughts of how he'd kill that young man were all that'd sustained him since Emily died? How could he tell her that he felt robbed... cheated, somehow, by Fate? It seemed unfair that he should die by his own foolish hand, in such a cowardly way, rather than suffering a proper punishment.

"I'm glad you told me," he said, to make her feel better. "At least he won't be able to harm any more women or girls, now."

"Exactly," she said. "It isn't how either of us would've wanted it, but at least he's gone."

It wouldn't bring Emily back, he thought.

"I'll mow the lawn, in a minute," he said, changing the subject.

She understood that he wanted to be alone again, and left him to his memories. Back inside the house, she looked at the newspaper headline again and smiled.

There was some justice in the world, after all.

CHAPTER 6

Elsdon, Northumberland
Sunday, Present Day

Detective Inspector Denise MacKenzie rested her arms on the wooden fence at the stables where her daughter's horse was liveried, and looked across the fields towards a beautiful house built at the top of the hill. The house belonged to their good friend, Anna Taylor-Ryan and her late husband, DCI Maxwell Finley-Ryan—known to all who knew and loved him simply as 'Ryan'. It had been over a month since he'd passed away, but that was no time at all, and the pain of his loss was still raw for all of them. Whenever she went into the office, she still expected to find him there, barking orders about a case or laughing about something or other.

He was sorely missed by all of his friends, herself included, but nobody missed him more than her husband, Frank Phillips. The two men had been inseparable for over a decade, despite being different in almost every respect, and

Ryan's death had hit him the hardest of all. It was a good thing, in her opinion, that the Chief Constable had taken him on a trip to London—if only to give him a change of scenery, for a few hours.

"Are you all right, Mum?"

MacKenzie turned to see her daughter crossing the paddock with her horse, Pegasus, walking beside her. With long red hair similar to her own, and an infectious smile, Samantha had been a gift in their lives since the moment they'd met. She and Frank hadn't been blessed with any biological children, but parenting Sam had taught them that genes weren't the be-all and end-all. In fact, Mother Nature couldn't have conjured up a child more physically or emotionally suited to the pair of them if she'd tried, and deciding to adopt had been the best decision they'd ever made.

"Ah, I'm right enough," she replied, in her soft Irish burr. "I was just thinkin' of Anna, you know, and of how she'll be coping. I'll give her a ring, when we get home."

Samantha rubbed the horse's neck and thought of their family friend. When she heard the news that Ryan had been killed, she'd cried enough tears to fill an ocean, but she was mature enough to understand that, whilst her teenage heart might have felt broken, it could *never* compare to the heartbreak his wife and daughter must be experiencing.

"Do you think Anna will ever come back here?" she asked, looking over at the house.

Having no family of her own, they knew Ryan's wife had taken their daughter to stay with his parents, in Devon.

"I don't know," MacKenzie said. "Anna has her job at the university in Durham, but she doesn't have any other family left in these parts. If I were her, I don't think I'd want to come back to the house where my husband was murdered, so, perhaps she'll decide to make a more permanent move to Devon, where Ryan's mum can help with Emma."

Samantha thought of the little girl she'd come to love, almost like a favourite cousin. "I miss them," she said.

Denise held out an arm, and drew her in for a hug. "I do, too," she said, and heaved a long sigh. "You know, before all of this happened, Ryan mentioned something to Frank about moving house. He and Anna wanted to move to Bamburgh, and they suggested we could try living in the countryside by moving into their old house."

Samantha looked at her in surprise. "They did?"

MacKenzie nodded. "In many ways, it would have been ideal," she said. "We've wanted to move out of the city for a while, and your horse is here, practically at the bottom of their garden. If we lived in their old house, you could walk to the stables every day before and after school, if you liked."

Samantha had come to them from a very different background to most children, as the only witness to her biological mother's murder, as part of a travelling community who toured their circus around Europe—and dealt drugs, at the same time. Her father had also been killed, which left her alone in the world but for the friendship of a horse named Pegasus, whom she'd cared for since he was a foal. When they'd looked after and then adopted their little girl, Frank and Denise hadn't even contemplated parting Samantha from her greatest friend, though they might have wished he'd been a cat or a goldfish, rather than an Arabian horse who seemed to live better than they did. Still, her natural affinity with horses and her gifted ability to ride them had catapulted her into the world of junior showjumping, where she was already a champion.

"Maybe we can go and visit Anna and Emma in Devon," Samantha said. "I've never been to Devon."

MacKenzie had already offered to drive down to visit and, come to think of it, Anna had been unusually taciturn and quick to put her off making the trip. At the time, she'd assumed it was because her friend needed more space to grieve in private, and so she hadn't pressed the matter. However, on reflection, it seemed out of character for Anna to be so antisocial, even in the circumstances.

"I'll ask her again," she said, thoughtfully. "She might be ready for visitors, now."

Samantha leaned on the fence beside her mother, and they watched Pegasus nibble happily at the grass. "It still doesn't feel *real*," she said, after a minute. "I thought Ryan was..." She trailed off, feeling embarrassed.

"Invincible?" MacKenzie suggested, and pulled her in for another hug. "So did I, Sam. He was always so strong, and such a natural leader...I think we were all guilty of thinking he would live forever."

They fell silent, and Samantha rested her head on MacKenzie's shoulder. "It makes me worry about you and Dad," she said. "What if something happens?"

Denise closed her eyes, enjoying the feel of the sun against her skin and the warmth of her daughter's love, which shone even more brightly.

"I can't promise you that either of us will live forever," she said. "Nobody ever does. But I *can* promise you that we'll love you and support you for as long as we can. We'll do all we can to stick around for as long as possible—for some of us, who shall remain nameless, that means eating half as many bacon stotties as we might have done, once upon a time."

Sam giggled. "What about Jammie Dodgers?"

"Those, too."

Phillips' eyes strayed to a packet of custard cream biscuits but, just as he was about to snaffle one, some otherworldly sixth sense stayed his hand. It was as though his wife's hawkeyed gaze watched him from afar, to make sure he was sticking to the diet plan they'd drawn up a while ago.

"—Frank?" Ryan's voice cut through his reverie, and he snapped to attention.

"Hm?"

"I was just saying, there are a few things still left outstanding," he repeated. "We could do with having the bomb squad's report from the car bombing at Frankland because it would be useful to know what device they used, for a start. Then, there's ballistics. Have they come back with any details around the provenance of the bullet used to kill my father?" Ryan took a hasty gulp of coffee, to distract himself from the mental image.

"I'll chase them up," Frank promised. "Faulkner said he'd come back to me with a full report on forensics, too. You never know, there might've been some LCN DNA left near the scene."

He referred to Tom Faulkner, the senior Scenes of Crimes officer attached to the constabulary. Although it was highly unlikely, there was always a chance that whichever assassin had taken the shot at Charles Ryan might have left something of himself—or *her*self—behind, in the form of Low Copy Number DNA, which was the smallest traceable forensic evidence admissible in court.

"Digital Forensics will be continuing with their cross-referencing of death certificates and classified ad data that's available online," DCI Hassan said, and then, much to Phillips' consternation, popped a biscuit in his mouth. "Ryan's agreed to oversee that aspect of the investigation, remotely."

"Just because you're 'dead', it doesn't mean you can take unapproved leave," Morrison chimed in, with a certain dark humour they all appreciated.

"Chance would be a fine thing." Ryan laughed, and then turned to Phillips. "There's one other thing I wonder if you'd help me with, Frank?"

His friend raised a bushy eyebrow. "Anythin'," he said. "Unless it involves wax, latex or Lycra. Those days are behind me."

Hassan laughed richly.

"I'll hold you to that," Ryan said, and barely held back a shudder. "It's about the window, at the house in Elsdon. I was hoping to have it replaced, before we return home, whenever that may be. I don't want Anna or Emma to see that."

He spoke of the large picture window overlooking their garden in Northumberland, which had been shattered by the bullet that killed his father.

"Consider it done," Phillips said, without hesitation. "We've already had the place cleaned up...it'll be good as new, by the time you come home."

Ryan gave him a smile that didn't quite reach his eyes. "I don't think I'll ever be able to look at the place in the same way again," he said. "But that's a problem for another day. In the meantime, there's the more pressing matter of dismantling a murder network before any more people wind up dead."

"Which reminds me," Morrison said. "Are you sure that you're safe at your parents' home in Devon?"

The Summersley estate included a sprawling house and acres of land which, to many people, was the stuff of heritage days out or the backdrop of period drama pieces of the *Pride and Prejudice* variety. For Ryan, it had been his childhood home. His late father might have been disappointed by the choice he'd made to become a police officer but, as a former military man and high-ranking diplomat, Charles Finley-Ryan had also understood how strong the call of public service could be and had been proud of the man his son had become.

"There's a security team living on-site," Ryan assured her. "They were hand-picked by my father, and some of them had been part of his personal security detachment, from the old days. They're the best there is, but still, the best protection is that whoever made an attempt on my life continues to believe I'm dead."

It was true, Morrison thought. So long as Ryan's would-be assassin thought they'd succeeded in killing him, he would be safe from harm. On the other hand, if word got out that he was alive, that might prompt them to try again—the police investigation hadn't yet uncovered the rules of the murder scheme, but it seemed fairly certain that, in order to procure a death, a person must be willing to commit a murder themselves. If they failed, they owed a debt and might even be in danger of elimination themselves, as a warning to others.

"In that case, we'll continue as before," Morrison said. "We'll continue investigating, and you must continue to exercise all possible caution, Ryan." Beneath the stern warning, there was genuine concern.

"I'll be careful," he said, and looked at each of his friends. "We all should."

CHAPTER 7

Despite having only recently qualified as a solicitor, Stacey Hitchens was already beginning to question her choice of profession. Everybody told her she was lucky to have secured a position at a brand new firm in her home town of Alnwick, but it was hard to feel especially grateful when she found herself at the office on a Sunday afternoon, rather than sipping a cocktail somewhere in the sunshine, or—better yet—topping up her affiliate earnings on social media by posting some spicy content of herself working out down at the gym.

Stacey flipped her long, ice-blonde hair over one shoulder and turned on the energy-saving lights in the office, which made barely a dent to the generally grey and depressing air of the small country solicitors' workspace, with its magnolia walls and carpet-tiled floors. She was hopeful of a bonus at the end of the year, and a good reference when she moved on to a bigger firm, and if that meant putting in a bit of overtime, she supposed it was worth her while.

Before settling down to a long afternoon of due diligence, she made herself a cup of tea in the little office kitchen and then rooted around her desk drawer for one of the protein bars she kept in there, selecting one with 'cacao', which, she told herself, was just as good as chocolate.

Five minutes later, she crumpled the wrapper and fired up her desktop computer. She inspected her nails while she waited for it to come alive, and blinked several times to clear the black spots which swam in front of her eyes.

She was more tired than she thought...

Stacey looked at the computer screen, which was dark around the edges. With a soft *tut*, she wiggled the monitor, but it wasn't the computer that was at fault, it was her entire field of vision. She blinked rapidly, and rubbed her eyes, but it didn't help.

"What's going on?" she asked the empty room, closing and re-opening her eyes.

Her face began to feel numb; a prickling, pins-and-needles sensation that spread from her temples over her cheeks and down her neck. Nausea followed swiftly, and her stomach cramped painfully.

Then, very suddenly, she found herself struggling to breathe.

Eyes wide with terror, Stacey fumbled for her smartphone and stabbed the '9' button three times. After endless seconds during which she felt as though she was breathing through a straw, her call was answered.

999...which emergency service do you require?

"Ambulance," she gasped.

Ambulance emergency, is the patient breathing?

"Can't breathe. Can't see...can't feel...can't feel my hands..."

Okay, what's the address of your emergency?

"Solicitors...Lovett and Heatherington...Alnwick—" Stacey broke off to drag air into her oxygen-starved lungs. "Please," she whispered. *"Please come—"*

An ambulance is on the way to you now, however there's an emergency doctor in the area, so he's likely to arrive before them. Is the door unlocked so he can get in?

"Yes..." Stacey managed, before she passed out.

"Voila! The last of the furniture is officially built!"

Jack gave a funny little bow, like a French courtier, and Charlie laughed at him.

"I think that deserves a glass of wine," she said. "Unless you've got other plans? You've given up so much of your day, already."

"Happy to help," he replied. "Besides, I'll never say 'no' to wine, especially after that last IKEA job. At one point, I thought we weren't going to make it."

Charlie chuckled as they made their way to the kitchen. "The power of teamwork," she said, loftily. "That, and brute force."

She procured a bottle of red and two plastic cups bearing a *Paw Patrol* logo. "Sorry," she said, with a rueful smile. "I've no idea where the wine glasses are, so these will have to do."

"At least it's not *Peppa Pig*," he said.

"Cheers to that," she muttered darkly.

They each took a healthy gulp, and Jack rolled his shoulders, easing out the kinks after several hours of bending and lifting. Charlie found herself watching the action, and wondering what those shoulder muscles might feel like beneath her hands. Embarrassed by the direction of her own thoughts, she took another hasty swig of wine, and averted her gaze. Clearly, it had been too long since she'd had any male company, and her hormone-addled brain was latching onto the first attractive bloke in her vicinity.

"Do I have something on my face?"

Charlie realised her eyes had strayed back to Jack again, and he was now looking at her with a quizzical expression. "What? No...no, I was just...staring into space."

"I know the feeling," he said. "It's been a long day, and a heavy couple of weeks."

"Grief can make you feel tired," she said, and then it was Jack's turn to look away, feeling all kinds of guilt at having to keep the truth about Ryan from his new workmate. There were good, solid reasons for it, but he was not a secretive person by nature, and he liked his new friend.

In fact, he liked her a lot.

The thought came to him, unbidden, and he felt doubly guilty. His former partner, Melanie, had left him to travel the world and work through the trauma of having survived a serial killer, but the status of their relationship was unclear. She'd told him not to wait for her, and her e-mails and other communications had been very sporadic over the past few months—but he still loved her.

Didn't he?

Yes, of course he did. Even if Mel didn't seem to be reciprocating that love, or even any kind of friendship, he remembered the good times they'd shared together and hoped to share again, in the future. Any further rumination on the subject was interrupted by the persistent ringing of his phone, which he'd tucked into the back pocket of his jeans.

"*Nine to Five?*" Charlie queried, recognising the ringtone as being one of her favourite Dolly Parton numbers. "You just went up in my estimation."

He smiled, and answered the call, which was from MacKenzie. "Hey, Mac. How's it going?"

"Sorry to bother you on your day off," she replied. "I've just taken a call from the Control Room to say they need someone from Major Crimes to attend the RVI."

She referred to one of the major hospitals in the North East.

"I'd go down there, myself, but I'm on my way back from the stables with Sam," she said. "Frank isn't back from London yet, and—"

"It's no trouble," Jack said, easily. "Charlie and I have finished moving her mountain of boxes, so I can head down there now. Do we have any further details about the case?"

"Apparently, it's a young woman by the name of Stacey Hitchens, resident of Alnwick," she said, rattling off the facts while she navigated her car out of Elsdon and back towards the motorway. "She's in a critical condition, but that's all I know. Control said the call came through from the hospital, rather than from one of our first responders or the general public, so they must have reason to think the circumstances of her admission are suspicious."

Charlie gesticulated at him, pointing towards her own chest and making a walking motion with her fingers to indicate she was happy to help out.

"Okay, I'll see what they have to say," he said. "Listen, I've got Charlie here with me, and she's offering to come along too."

"The more the merrier," MacKenzie said, and was pleased to think they'd become such fast friends.

Then, she found herself wondering if they could be *more* than friends...

No, she thought, dismissing the idea.

At least one heart would be broken.

CHAPTER 8

Twenty minutes later, Jack performed a questionable parallel parking manoeuvre in a side street near to the Royal Victoria Infirmary. The hospital occupied a prime spot in the centre of Newcastle beside a number of university buildings, so there was rarely any chance of finding a parking space. Luckily for them, it was a Sunday, and most right-minded people were at home relaxing with their families, or out enjoying the late afternoon sunshine with friends.

"How did Ryan always seem to find a space?" Charlie wondered aloud, as they walked towards the Accident and Emergency entrance.

Jack had never thought about it, before. "Now you come to mention it," he said. "How *does* he manage it?"

She glanced at him, noting his use of the present tense, which suggested he hadn't quite come to terms with Ryan's passing. Then again, it was always hard to lose a good friend, especially one who'd been more like a brother.

They walked through a set of automatic doors and into the bustle of the A & E department, which was teeming with people. They dodged a man who looked as though he'd imbibed a year's worth of alcohol and was swaying badly on his feet while hurling verbal abuse at staff and patients alike. Ordinarily, Ryan would handle volatile situations such as these, but Jack supposed he should step up to the plate and prevent a public nuisance—

"Come on, feller," Charlie said, taking the man firmly in hand. "Settle down, and behave yourself."

Jack watched as she marched him towards an empty chair and sat him down.

"Right, now, listen to me," she said, in the same tone she'd have used with her toddler. "There are lots of people here who are suffering more than you—"

"You—you don' know what I suffer!" the man howled.

"Tell me, then," she said.

"I—" He paused to burp, loudly. "I—I've had too much to drink." He said this as if conveying a state secret.

"I see," Charlie said, and looked at him properly, trying to locate the trauma that had brought him there. "Have you injured yourself?"

"Um," he said, and scratched his head, trying to remember.

Then, it came to him.

"Oh, yeah," he said. "I cut my finger."

He held out a thumb, and she saw a thin red line to indicate where he'd sustained a paper cut.

"There's nothing else?" Charlie asked, while Jack continued to look on with a degree of awe. "Nothing more serious? Did you fall over?"

The man shook his head, proudly. "Nope! But this really hurts," he said, and held out his grubby thumb once again. "I dropped a glass and cut it."

Charlie sighed, and sat down beside him.

"This isn't the place to come, when you're feeling lonely," she said gently. "I know of a crisis centre, not far from here, which helps men like you who are having a few issues with alcohol and other substances. They have counsellors there who'll talk it over with you and try to help, if they can. Shall I see if anyone's free to come and pick you up? You never know, you might meet a few friends."

His eyes filled, and, after some sort of internal battle, he nodded.

"Aye—alreet. Thanks, petal."

"Let me find a plaster for that finger," she said, and went off in search of one.

"Is she your lass?" the man asked Jack, once she'd left.

Lowerson shook his head, taken aback. "No—no, we're just work colleagues," he said.

"More fool you," the other man said, and burped again.

The interlude with Drunky McDrunkerson, as Jack had christened him, had taken up ten minutes of their time which, they hoped, had been time well spent. A member of the Men's

Crisis Centre had assured them somebody would be along to collect him within the hour and so, with a quiet word for the receptionist on duty, they left him in her custody and awaited the arrival of the consultant who'd called them in to assess Stacey Hitchens.

"Are you from the police?"

They turned to see a woman approaching them, dressed in scrubs.

"Yes," Jack replied, and produced his warrant card. "DC Jack Lowerson, and this is my colleague, DC Charlie Reed."

She inspected their identification. "I'm Amrita Kumar, one of the doctors in acute medicine here," she said. "Thanks for coming so quickly."

"We understand you have an admission you're concerned about?" Charlie said.

"Yes, if you'd like to follow me," she said, and led them towards the Intensive Care Unit and, from there, towards one of the private rooms where a young woman lay inert and surrounded by monitors.

Kumar paused outside the door. "The name of the patient is Stacey Hitchens," she said. "She was admitted not long ago, transferred to us from Cramlington. We've put her in a drug-induced coma, and stabilised her for now, but she was in a critical condition when she arrived. She was unconscious but displaying a range of severe symptoms, including chest constriction and breathing difficulties, and the paramedics say she'd already reported symptoms of nausea, numbness, stomach cramps and loss of vision."

Kumar tucked her hands in the pockets of her scrubs.

"We've ruled out a heart attack or stroke," she said. "I'd have been surprised if it was either of those things, considering she's young and healthy."

"I'm sorry, Doctor Kumar, but I'm not sure how we can help," Jack said. "Do you suspect foul play?"

The consultant nodded. "Yes," she said. "We're awaiting the results of a blood test, but I suspect Stacey might have come into contact with, or ingested, a poison. Of course, it could have been accidental, but this is the second patient to display symptoms of this kind today."

"The second?" Charlie queried. "Who was the first?"

"A man named George Masters," Kumar replied. "He experienced all of the same symptoms and was attended to at Alnwick Infirmary, which was the closest facility. Unfortunately, he was pronounced dead shortly afterwards, but his body was transferred down to us here for postmortem. The pathologist is a friend of mine and happened to mention the case earlier today, which is why the similarity between the two flagged as being suspicious to me—especially since they both hail from Alnwick."

Jack and Charlie exchanged a look.

"Would your pathologist friend happen to be Jeff Pinter?" he asked.

Her face lit up at the mention of his name. "Yes, of course, you must already know him," she said. "He's a brilliant clinician, so I'm sure he'll find anything there is to find."

They couldn't disagree with that.

"My priority is obviously Stacey," Kumar said. "If she's fallen foul of poison, she needs to be given an antidote, as soon as possible. However, we have no clue which poison she might have taken, and it could take days to find out—that's longer than she has to live. I won't sugar-coat the situation: every minute counts, because Stacey might only have a few hours left. Her family are on their way here now, and I'll have to tell them to prepare themselves for the worst."

"Can we see her?" Charlie asked. "There might be something on her person that might provide a clue."

"It doesn't seem to be anything contagious, so, yes, we can go in," Kumar said, and opened the door to Stacey's room. "The nurses have already checked her body for any sign of a needle or other wound, but there's nothing obvious."

They stepped inside, where the recurrent beep of a heart and SATS monitor echoed around the small room. In the centre lay a pretty girl in her mid-twenties, whose face and limbs were a sickly grey colour beneath a layer of fake tan. Her platinum blonde hair was tied back and lay limply against the pillow, while a leather handbag rested on the visitor's chair beside the bed.

"Does that belong to her?" Jack asked.

Kumar nodded. "There's nothing in it of any medical interest," she said, and turned to them with serious eyes. "What I really need to know is what she had to eat or drink before she came in and, ideally, it would be good to have some samples the lab can test. The paramedics say she was picked up from her workplace, but she'd only recently arrived there, so it's possible she could have had something at home beforehand, or picked something up on the way to the office. Her family say she's recently rented a small cottage in Alnwick—I made a note of the address."

They took down the details and, shortly after, Kumar was called away.

As soon as the door closed behind her, Jack pulled on a pair of nitrile gloves and snatched up Stacey's handbag. He produced a set of keys on a fluffy pink keyring, and held them up.

"These should help," he said.

"Don't we need a warrant before searching her office, or her house?" Charlie said.

Jack looked across at the woman lying on the bed, fighting for her life, and thought of what Ryan would do in the circumstances.

"She'll be dead before we can get it in front of a judge," he said. "It's worth the risk."

CHAPTER 9

It was almost seven o'clock by the time Ryan arrived back in Devon.

He'd chosen to drive from London using a rental car, which avoided any risk he might run into somebody he knew on a train, or of his image being captured on the CCTV cameras at Paddington. The size and scope of the network they hunted was still an unknown quantity, and there was no telling who was in its employ, so it paid to be cautious— besides, he'd given his word that he would be.

It was a tiring journey, but he didn't mind; especially once he left the motorway and made his way through verdant fields into the heart of Devon. It was slow going, but eventually he came upon the little signpost for Summersley, the village that shared the same name as his ancestral home. Once, its stone cottages had housed estate workers, but nowadays they were the province of holiday makers or local families who'd made the village their own and set up independent businesses in order to enjoy a quiet, rural life.

Passing through the village, he came to a large set of stone pillared gates, and slowed the car to key in an entry code on the security pad. Almost immediately, a disembodied voice spoke to him through the speaker, and asked him to look directly at a camera lens fitted beside the keypad. Only once Ryan's identity had been verified did the security guard open the iron gates and allow him to enter.

The driveway was long, and lined with ancient oak trees on either side. At the end of the driveway, a large house came into view, its façade painted in an aged white that reflected the last rays of the dying sun. A stable block and other outbuildings stood a short distance away, used as garages and general storage for junk, as Ryan's mother liked to say. Lawns spread out on either side of a turning circle to the front of the house and, at the back, formal gardens led down to a small, man-made lake, beyond which stood a beautiful marble crypt built in the style of a Capability Brown folly. More lawns and woodland surrounded the gardens, and a well-worn pathway led through the trees and down to the estuary which could be seen from the upper windows of the house. It was an idyllic setting, Ryan knew, but he'd have much rather seen it put to better use than for the privilege of a single family. Whilst his father was alive, that had been a difficult conversation, Charles Finley-Ryan having been indoctrinated from an early age as to the proper custodianship of the family seat. However, he had hopes that, in time, his mother might reconsider the position.

Ryan parked the car and waved to one of the security staff, who emerged from the side of the house. "Only me!" he called out, and received a cheerful wave in return.

Rather than using the front door, Ryan made his way around the side of the house to the kitchen door, which he was pleased to find safely locked. He was about to use his key, when he spotted a dark-haired woman with the face of an angel through the window, filling a glass of water at the sink. He smiled and wondered, as he often did, how he'd ever been lucky enough to find the other half of himself out of all the billions of people there were in the world.

He raised a hand and tapped the window.

Anna looked up sharply and, for a moment, he saw fear in her eyes. She masked it quickly and smiled at him, then unlocked the door. "What're you selling, this time?"

In answer, he scooped her up, lifting her off the floor to administer a thorough kiss. "You can have that one for free," he muttered against her lips. "Where's Emma?"

"In bed," Anna replied, and ran her fingers through his hair.

"Where's my mother?"

"In the library," she said.

Since they were unlikely to be interrupted, Ryan lifted her into his arms and pressed her body back against one of the kitchen walls.

"Did you miss me?" he said, and pressed his mouth to her neck.

"*Always*," she said, and her eyes closed as he found the sensitive spot behind her ear. "I thought you'd be tired, after your journey..."

Ryan looked up, and his eyes were molten silver. "I always keep a reserve of energy for emergencies."

"You're going to need it," she said, and tugged his face towards her.

Later, when Ryan had replenished his depleted reserve with a plate of food and a glass of wine, he and Anna made their way through to the library, where they found his mother reading a book of poetry beside a crackling fire. She looked up as they entered, and smiled at them both with eyes that were the same startling shade as her son's, albeit their colour dimmed by sadness.

"There you are," she said, and started to rise from the sofa, but Ryan waved her down again and crossed the room to plant a kiss on her cheek. "I was starting to worry."

Ryan threw another log on the fire, and gave it a stab with one of the iron pokers propped against the fireplace.

"Has there been any progress in the investigation?" Anna asked, curling up on the sofa opposite.

"It's still early days," he said. "I saw Frank, today."

"You did?" Anna said. "He must have been...*well*, I can only imagine how he must have been. Was he responsible for the bruise on your chin, by any chance?"

Ryan rubbed the side of his jaw, and shrugged. "I don't blame him," he said. "I'd probably do the same, if he led me to believe he was dead and then turned up like a spectre at a wake."

"Surely, he understands the circumstances," Eve said, and beckoned him forward so that she could inspect his bruise with a maternal eye. "Oh, you'll live."

Ryan smiled, and took a seat near the fire. "Frank understood," he said. "Once the shock had worn off." He thought of the relief he'd felt at seeing his friend looking so well again. The last time they'd seen one another, Frank had been in the throes of a cardiac arrest. "John Hassan knows, and Jack Lowerson and Sandra Morrison, of course," he said. "I'll bet Denise MacKenzie will find out before the end of the day, but that's it, for now. The smaller the circle of people who know I'm still alive, the smaller the risk." He gestured to a stack of old papers lying on the coffee table in front of his mother. "What's all this?"

"I started to go through your father's desk," Eve said, and her voice wobbled. "I found a file from his early days in the army, back in the seventies and eighties."

Ryan picked up an old picture of his father in military dress and felt his chest tighten, for it was as though he was looking in a mirror.

"I know," Eve said, watching the play of emotions on his face. "The similarity is striking, isn't it? No wonder—"

She stopped herself just in time, but Ryan already knew what she was going to say, because he was thinking the same thing, himself.

No wonder the gunman thought Charles was his son.

He set the photograph back down again. "They'll pay for what they did," he said.

"What leads a person to set up a network like that?" Eve wondered aloud. "They must be *evil*."

"Or insane," Anna said.

Eve looked down at the picture of her husband, then across at her son. "I've lost my daughter as well as the love of my life," she said, simply. "I want whoever pulled the trigger to be punished, but Anna is right. The person who started this network in the first place can't be normal."

"If Frank was here, he'd say they have to be a raging fruitcake," Ryan said, and managed to coax a smile from her lips. "Whatever the reason," he said, as the light of the fire danced across his eyes, "I won't rest until they're behind bars or in a strait jacket—either will do."

All Saints Cemetery
May 2007

Kevin looked down at his daughter's grave and thought of her lying there, beneath the earth. The grief counsellor they'd forced him to speak to had talked of a 'cycle of grief' and coming to a stage of acceptance that Emily was never coming back. He'd attended her office, each week, and gone through the motions of saying what he thought she wanted to hear, so that his wife would feel she'd been able to help him.

She meant well, he knew that.

The fact is, she couldn't fix a heart that had not only been broken but entirely, irreparably stolen from his chest, leaving only a bare cavity where it should have been. Emily had taken that with her, when she'd departed the world. Not when she'd decided to string a rope around her neck, but much earlier, when that…that *animal* had attacked her, and the system had abandoned her, resulting in a feeling of worthlessness her young mind wasn't able to overcome.

His wife thought he'd feel better after finding out Edward Delaney had died, but, in fact, the opposite was true. If Delaney was alive, he could imagine killing him, with his bare hands…choking the life out of his scrawny neck until his eyes bulged out of his arrogant head.

But he wasn't alive.

The brat had taken one too many pills and died on the squalid floor of a club in Newcastle which, he supposed, was better than him dying a hero's death. Edward Delaney had been anything but a *hero*.

Kevin laid a bunch of flowers on top of the small mound, and then put his hand on the cold marble headstone, closing his eyes as he said 'hello' to his daughter's memory, as he did every morning and evening. Sometimes, he thought he heard her reply; just a word here and there. His wife was worried he was losing the plot, but Kevin could see the world very clearly. Far more clearly than before, in fact.

He knew what he had to do.

It was the only way.

CHAPTER 10

Sunday, Present Day

While Ryan navigated his way through winding roads in Devonshire, Frank Phillips stepped through the front door of his home in Kingston Park, on the north-western edge of Newcastle upon Tyne. He hung up his coat, toed off his comfortable Hush Puppies, and hadn't made it past the hallway before he heard the thundering sound of footsteps clattering above his head and down the stairs.

"Dad!" Samantha launched herself at him, and was caught in his strong arms.

"There's my girl!" he said, with a laugh. "By gum, I'm sure you've grown another inch since I left, this mornin'."

She stood up straight. "Really?'

"Aye, I wouldn't be surprised," he said, and ruffled her hair. "Where's your mam?"

"Through here!" Denise called out from the kitchen, where she had her hands full removing a burnt chicken from the oven.

Frank followed the scent of smoke, while Sam skipped off to the lounge to watch some teenage vampire programme or another, and found his wife flapping a tea towel to clear the air.

"Evenin', Nigella!"

She gave him a withering look. "Watch it, Frank, or you'll be eating buckwheat salads for a week."

As a threat, it couldn't have been more effective. "Let me help you with that," he crooned, and took the tray from her hands. "Why don't you sit yourself down, and I'll make us both a nice cup of tea?"

She capitulated, and gave him a kiss on the way to the kitchen table. "Welcome back," she said. "How was London? Were there any interesting developments?"

"*Well*," he said, and considered how to impart the news about Ryan in the kindest, most sensitive way he could. "That bloody *git* of a friend of ours isn't dead, after all."

MacKenzie blinked. "*What*? Are you talking about *Ryan*?"

"Aye, who else?" Phillips demanded.

"I don't understand," she said, with deceptive calm. "You're telling me Ryan's still alive?"

He took a gulp of tea, felt it burn his throat, and nodded. "Aye, that's what I'm tryin' to tell you. He's been holed up at his parents' house in Devon, this whole time."

He proceeded to bring her up to speed with the situation.

"I'm sorry about his father," she said, first of all. "That must have been awful for Jack, too, since he travelled up from Devon with Charles and was a witness to the shooting. It also explains why he's seemed a bit distant, these past few weeks.

I put it down to grief over Ryan, but it seems we were mourning the wrong Ryan."

Phillips kept his voice low, in case any little ears should overhear their conversation. "It's all strictly 'need to know'," he said, sounding like an extra from a bad spy movie. "We agreed I could tell you because, let's face it, I can't so much as eat a Bounty bar without you sniffin' it out. There's nee chance I could hide a whopper like this, is there?"

"Certainly not," she agreed. "Which reminds me to ask you about the Mars bar you must've eaten on the train home."

"How d' you know about *that*?" he blustered.

"I always know," she said, ominously. "However, I'll let it slide, since you were probably not in your right mind after seeing Ryan's ghost."

"You're an understandin' woman," he said, and wondered if he could leverage it so far as a takeaway curry.

"Don't push it, Frank," she said, reading his mind.

"I was only thinkin' of a few poppadoms, maybe a lamb bhuna and a peshwari naan—"

MacKenzie thought of the conversation she'd had with Samantha, earlier that day. "We're going to stick to our 'once a month' rule," she said. "Not because I don't love a chicken korma, but because I love our daughter, more. Sam's been worrying about mortality, after Ryan's supposed death—and your stay in hospital."

That changed everything, and all thoughts of starchy food flew from Phillips' mind. "She has?" he said softly, and looked over his shoulder towards the living room, where they could hear the dim sound of the television. "I'll speak to her about it."

"I already have," Denise said, and took his hand. "But it wouldn't hurt to have some reassurance from you, too."

"Do you think she'll be all right, once she finds out Ryan isn't dead?"

"*He isn't?*" Samantha's high-pitched voice made them both jump, and curse the thin walls in their house.

"God Almighty," Denise muttered, and clasped a hand to her heart.

Sam skipped into the kitchen, her face a picture of delight. "Ryan's *alive?*" she said again.

"Aye, he is," Phillips said, and gave her a disapproving scowl. "But you shouldn't be eavesdroppin'."

"It's a bad habit," she said, and they had to admire her honesty. "But this is the *greatest* news!"

Phillips rolled his eyes, and wondered how he could possibly have forgotten the gigantic crush his daughter had developed on his best friend. It didn't matter that Ryan was old enough to be her father and, indeed, *was* a father. The bloke looked like Superman and spoke like Mr Darcy, so she didn't stand much of a chance, just like the rest of the female population.

"Now, listen," Denise said, becoming serious. "You have to keep this a secret."

Sam listened attentively, while her mother laid out some ground rules and explained the reasoning behind them.

"I won't tell anyone," she said. "I *promise*. But when are they going to be able to come home?"

Frank and Denise looked at one another.

"As soon as they can," he answered.

"I hope so," Samantha said.

They all did, Frank thought.

CHAPTER 11

Darkness had fallen by the time Jack and Charlie returned to Alnwick, where Messrs Lovett & Heatherington occupied one of a series of Victorian houses now converted into offices. Jack pulled his car up to the kerb outside, and they peered through the windshield into the surrounding gloom, relieved only by a series of streetlamps that shone an eerie yellow glow over the deserted street.

"This is probably a really nice place, in the daytime," Jack remarked. "Why is it that, after dark, it resembles something from *The Amityville Horror*?"

"Occupational hazard combined with an overactive imagination?" Charlie ventured. "We've seen far too much and met far too many weird people, in our line of work."

"You're not wrong, there." He reached across to open the glove compartment and retrieve a torch, but the action caused him to brush her knee, accidentally.

"Sorry," he said, and dropped the torch in the footwell.

"My fault," she muttered, and picked it up again. "Here."

"Thanks," he said.

There was a short, awkward silence.

"Should we—"

"We'd better—"

They both laughed nervously, then practically threw themselves from the car and into the surrounding night.

"Must be one of these," Jack said, and proceeded to try each of the keys on Stacey's fluffy keyring until one of them worked in the office door. "Aha—open sesame!"

They stepped inside but, rather than turning on the lights, Jack waggled his torch.

"No need to attract undue attention to ourselves," he said. "Let's get in and out of here as quickly and quietly as possible, then move on to Stacey's cottage."

Before Charlie could reply, a loud, chirping noise began to sound overhead, indicating the countdown to an impending alarm.

"*Uh-oh...*" Jack said.

"How did the paramedics set the alarm, after they took Stacey off to hospital?" Charlie demanded.

"Who knows?" Jack said, and looked around for the source of the offending noise. "Maybe somebody rang one of the partners from the hospital and they came afterwards to sort it out? Where the *hell* is the keypad?"

Just then, an ear-splitting alarm went off, and they both swore loudly.

"Quickly," Jack said, and chucked her a pair of gloves and a face mask. "Better put these on, just in case."

They made their way through the small office space at lightning speed. A quick recce revealed five rooms on the ground floor, comprising of a waiting room and reception area, two larger offices belonging to the eponymous Lovell and Heatherington, respectively, as well as a small staff kitchen and a disabled unisex toilet at the back. They had more luck finding Stacey's workspace on the first floor, which held two smaller, shared offices and a conference room. It wasn't immediately obvious which desk belonged to her, so they checked each methodically until they came to one bearing the milky remains of a cold cup of tea.

"This looks like the one!" Charlie yelled over the alarm, which continued to bleat around their heads.

While she emptied the remains of the cup into a sealed, plastic bottle, Jack rifled through the wastepaper basket. It contained only a crumpled protein bar wrapper, which he transferred into an evidence bag before moving on to search the desk drawers, which were unlocked.

"She liked her protein bars!" he shouted, pointing at a stash of them inside the bottom drawer.

He grabbed them up, and stuffed them inside another evidence bag, for comparison at the lab. There was a sizeable stash of make-up and a small canister of hair spray, all of which he also shovelled into evidence bags.

"Let's check the kitchen," Charlie suggested, and they hurried back downstairs to the staff kitchen, where they went through a couple of large bins—one for general waste, another for recycling—and found both of them empty.

"Must have been emptied by the cleaners on Friday evening," Jack said.

"There's only a few half-eaten sandwiches in the fridge and a carton of semi-skimmed milk," Charlie called back.

"Better take some samples, anyway," he replied.

"*What's that?*"

"I *said*, we'd better take them for testing!" he shouted, over the din.

Charlie nodded, and decanted everything.

"I'll take some of the coffee, tea and sugar, just in case," Jack added.

"Okay, I'll grab some of the kettle water—"

Suddenly, the kitchen door burst open.

"*FREEZE!*"

A bright light shone in their faces, and they raised their hands to shield their eyes from its glare.

"Don't move!" a voice shouted at them. "We've got you surrounded—and I've got a taser!"

Recognising the voice, Charlie lowered her hands again. "Come off it, Waddell. Nobody's ever gonna issue you with a taser!"

Police Constable Waddell might not have been the sharpest tool in the box, but his heart was in the right place. "*DC Reed?* Is that you?"

"Yes, it's me!" Charlie shouted back. "Stop shining that torch in my face and make yourself useful—figure out a way to turn off the alarm! There must be a phone number beside the keypad, or something!"

"Y-yes, ma'am," he said, and then, as if suddenly remembering why he was there, he turned his torchlight on the pile of evidence bags. "What are you doing in here, anyway?"

"Now isn't the time for a briefing!" she told him, and pointed an imperious finger towards the door as Jack looked on with renewed admiration for her people management skills.

First, Drunky McDrunkerson, now PC Plod...

Waddell scuttled off and, after making a final check of the kitchen, Jack and Charlie snatched up their bags and slipped past him to make a hasty getaway into the night.

Stacey Hitchens' cottage was located within a short walk of her office and, much to their relief, she hadn't set an alarm before leaving it, earlier in the day. Jack used the fluffy key ring again, and they let themselves into a narrow hallway, where their nostrils were assailed by a potent scent of lilies sitting on the console table.

"Lilies always make me think of funerals," Charlie said.

"I know what you mean," Jack replied.

They made their way through each room, which didn't take too long in the modest two-up, two-down cottage. They found nothing of interest in the living room, aside from a yoga mat and a ring light, but there were countless sources of possible toxicity in the kitchen, from the fridge to the pantry cupboard and the bin.

79

"I can't see any mouldy sandwiches or dodgy-looking oysters," Charlie said, from behind a face mask. "There's a fridge full of other food, though. Should we take a sample of everything?"

Jack thought of the possibilities upstairs, including toothpaste, mouthwash, face creams and make-up, and weighed it all up against the time they were losing by standing there, talking about it.

"I think we'll have to take a sample of anything that's open, or looks like a reasonable prospect," he said.

She nodded and, together, they worked their way from one cupboard to the next. There was a certain voyeurism in rifling through another person's home and possessions, but, as Jack would later remark, it was better to be doing it in the pursuit of saving a life, rather than in the aftermath of losing one.

An hour later, they let themselves out of the house again.

"That should do it," Jack said, pocketing the keyring. "We don't have any way of knowing whether Stacey stopped into a café or a shop on her way to the office without CCTV or witnesses, neither of which we'll find in the time we have. She could have thrown some packaging away in one of the public bins—"

"It doesn't seem likely," Charlie said, as they made their way back to the car. "I checked out her social media accounts on the way over here and, from her profile, it seems that Stacey spends a lot of time at the gym. Her parents say she goes on Saturday and Sunday mornings, and after work mid-week."

"She was wearing leggings and a gym top when the paramedics picked her up," Jack put in. "But there was no gym bag at the house or in the office."

Charlie had a sudden flash of inspiration. "Her car," she said, and snapped her fingers. "We passed that big, warehouse-sized gym on our way into town—remember? You could walk to it from here, at a push, but it'd save time to drive there. Maybe Stacey left some of her stuff in her car."

Jack looked at the cars lining the kerb on either side of the street. "Which one's hers?"

Charlie took the keyring from him, and pressed the button on Stacey's car key. Sure enough, the headlights on a white Nissan Micra flashed twice.

"Bingo," she said.

Inside, the car was immaculate, just as the cottage had been. As a personality, it seemed Stacey was fastidious, with labels for all manner of goods neatly printed on the side of her Tupperware and every surface in her home kept sparkling clean. The only exception to this was the green health drink she'd left half-finished in a shaker bottle within the car's central console, beside a gym bag bearing a 'HardBody' logo on the passenger seat beside it.

Jack leaned across and grabbed the bottle. "Come on," he said. "Let's get all this back to the lab, and see if they find anything in it."

"There are so many samples," Charlie said. "I don't know how forensics will be able to get through it, in time to help her."

"We can only do our best," he said. "Besides, Pinter's already at the hospital performing that autopsy on George Masters, and he's agreed to parachute a few of his lab staff in to help us out with the testing."

He was an irrepressible optimist, Charlie thought. Of course, she knew he must have his dark days, as everyone did; but, from all she'd seen of Jack Lowerson, he was a positive, generous person who tried his best. She wondered how Melanie Yates could have left such a kind man.

Charlie knew a bit about leaving men behind.

She knew that it took guts, sometimes, and a courage you didn't know you had, until you needed it. In the case of Jack Lowerson, she'd need to develop a different kind of courage altogether. She needed the courage to protect herself from the pain of unrequited feelings.

Had she ever had that kind of courage? Charlie wondered.

She'd find out, soon enough.

CHAPTER 12

Anna found Ryan in his father's study, a lone silhouette standing by the window looking out across the lake. It was a position his father had occupied many times, which was a sobering thought in light of recent events, and it prompted her to hurry across the room and tug him away.

"Don't stand so close to the window," she said.

Ryan pulled her into his arms. "I know you're frightened," he said. "I feel the same way. But we have to carry on behaving as normally as possible, or we'll go mad."

Anna closed her eyes and heard the thud of his heart beating strongly against the wall of his chest.

"I know," she whispered. "But I can't help it…I keep thinking someone's out there, hiding in the shadows."

"The security team are out there," he reminded her. "We've got two private security personnel manning the grounds, twenty-four hours a day, both of them with military backgrounds. They're the best there is."

The knowledge didn't make her feel any better.

"What are you doing in here, anyway?" she said. "I thought you were coming up to bed."

Ryan looked around the room that had been his father's domain for almost fifty years. "I don't know," he said, and lifted a shoulder. "I wanted to feel close to him, I suppose. I thought it might help to be around his possessions."

Anna's arms tightened around his waist. "And did it?"

"I don't know," he answered. "The more I find out about Charles Finley-Ryan, the more I realise how little I knew him. There are albums of photographs he never shared, letters from comrades in the army and diplomatic service, notes of thanks from other diplomats, presidents and prime ministers while he was an ambassador...my father lived an extraordinary life."

"But, to you, he was just 'Dad'?"

Ryan smiled, sadly. "Exactly," he said. "To me, he was an untouchable hero. Distant, sometimes, but fun-loving, when he wanted to be. He loved us all, very much...perhaps, more than I realised. I felt abandoned by him, growing up, whereas I understand now that sending his children to boarding school was his way of protecting us from the work he did, and the danger it might bring."

He understood that now, more than ever.

"He was the product of a strict upbringing," Ryan continued, and had a dim memory of his paternal grandparents, David and Isabella. He seemed to recall starchy dinners and oppressive weekend trips where, even as a very young child, he'd been obliged to wear formal clothing and display impeccable manners.

Manners maketh man, his grandfather would bark.

It was a far cry from the warm, playful grandfather Charles had become when Emma was born, and Ryan could only hope she remembered some of the good times they'd shared.

"I wish we'd taken more photographs," he said. "But my father hated having his photograph taken."

"You hate having your photograph taken, too," Anna said. "Although, according to Denise, the police photographer said you had a natural flair for modelling when you did that Christmas calendar, last year."

Ryan flushed. "That was for *charity*," he said.

"All I'm saying is, if anything ever happens to the day job, you can always try the catwalk."

He raised an eyebrow. "Look, Doctor Taylor-Ryan, if you're trying to objectify me...it's working."

She grinned. "I'm climbing the walls in this place," she said. "I'm trying to write, but all I can think about is the looming threat. It helps to have a distraction like you."

"Oh, I'm a *distraction* now, am I?"

"You've always been distracting," she said, tartly. "Spending so much time together, day to day, has only proven it."

He huffed out a laugh. "You're saying I'm difficult to live with, now?"

Anna shook her head. "*No,* I'm saying I enjoy having you around far too much," she told him. "Nothing much ever gets done."

He smiled, and wrapped his arms around her again. "There are worse things," he said. "Some spouses resort to murder-suicide after a few weeks of living together without office breaks. I wouldn't want to think of the state we'd find Frank in, after Denise had finished with him. The poor bloke would probably wind up beaten to death with a stale stottie cake."

Anna laughed. "Or strangled by his Lycra shorts?" she suggested.

"Don't mention the Lycra," he said, thinking of his friend's brief foray into cycling. "Those yellow shorts of his were traumatising."

She smiled, but knew that Ryan secretly admired his friend's quest to remain fit and healthy. "How did it feel to see Frank again?"

Ryan's face softened. "Long overdue," he said. "He isn't just my sergeant or my friend, as you know. He's part of the family…they all are."

Anna gave him a quick squeeze, then wandered over to a large captain's desk, where a collection of photographs had been laid out. She picked up one that had yellowed with age but clearly showed a much younger Charles Finley-Ryan dressed in a light, eighties-style linen suit that looked very striking against his dark hair. He stood beside a sea plane wearing aviator sunglasses to shield his eyes from the bright sunshine, suggesting he'd been on some far-flung, exotic island when the photograph was taken.

"The resemblance is uncanny," she said, looking between Ryan and the image of his father. "I only ever knew your dad with grey hair but, even then, there was no mistaking the relationship between you. Looking at this picture of him when he still had dark hair like yours, it's even more pronounced."

Ryan came to stand beside her. "Yes, I think that one was taken in the early eighties," he said.

"He was very dashing," Anna said, and felt profound sympathy for Eve. "I can't imagine what your mother is feeling. I don't know what I'd do, if I lost you."

"You won't," he assured her. "But, if you did, you'd survive because you're strong, like she is."

Anna put the photograph back in its album. "Let's not talk about it," she said. "Let's not even *think* about it."

Ryan wrapped his arms around her waist. "Do you need some more distraction?" he murmured.

Anna's head fell back against his chest. "I thought you'd used up your energy reserve?"

"Ah, well, I forgot to mention I have an auxiliary reserve," he said. "It may need some priming, but it's generally reliable."

"Generally? That doesn't sound too promising."

"Well, I must admit, it's sometimes prone to combustion."

She laughed. "It's lucky you're good-lookin'," she joked. "With this kind of bedroom patter, you'd struggle to get anywhere, otherwise."

"You love my corny banter."

"I love *you.*"

"Close enough."

CHAPTER 13

It was almost midnight by the time Jack pulled up outside Charlie's new flat. On reflection, it would have been easier if they'd taken their own cars, since they'd also made a detour via the RVI to drop off the samples they'd collected, and now he'd have to drive all the way home to the house he owned jointly with Melanie, in East Boldon. On the other hand, he'd enjoyed the company.

"Would you like anything to drink, for the road?" Charlie offered.

There was something else he needed with far greater urgency.

"D' you mind if I use your loo?"

She grinned, and shook her head. "Sure, come on in."

Jack made a bee-line for the cloakroom, while Charlie kicked off her shoes. Once he'd relieved himself, he reached for the bottle of hand soap which was, he noticed, in the shape of a duck.

Cute, he thought.

There was also a small set of plastic steps, presumably so that her son could reach the sink, as well as a couple of framed pictures featuring Charlie and Ben that she'd unpacked but not yet had time to fix to the wall. Although a few of his cousins had young children, the job didn't always allow for lots of quality time to be spent with any of them and, looking at the pictures of Charlie and Ben, he told himself it was high time that changed.

Jack towelled his hands and thought that Charlie's son looked a lot like her, but his nose was a little rounder, suggesting he might have inherited the shape from his father.

She still hadn't breathed a word about Ben's father, and he was too courteous to ask.

But he wondered.

Jack straightened up the hand towel, and made his way through to the kitchen, intending to say goodbye. When he got there, he found a mug of steaming hot chocolate waiting for him on the counter, and decided it would be churlish not to drink it.

"I'm not sure if you like chocolate…" Charlie began.

He was incredulous. "What kind of person doesn't like *chocolate*?" he said.

"I don't know…some people?"

"Psychopaths," he said.

Charlie burst out laughing. "Hang on, does vegan chocolate count? Because I'm pretty sure that's what you normally order from The Pie Van."

"It counts," he said. "It just doesn't taste as good."

"Vegans say it does," she argued.

"Vegans lie just as well as carnivores, vegetarians and pescatarians do. I should know, because I'm trying to be one, and I know damn well that so-called 'vegan chocolate' doesn't taste as good as Cadbury's Dairy Milk."

"Careful," she said. "Your clean-living reputation will be shot to pieces, if I let these secrets get around the office."

"I don't have a clean reputation," he replied, becoming serious as they looked at one another across the kitchen. "You must have heard a few things about me, by now? The staff canteen is a cesspit of gossip and depravity—and that's just Frank."

Charlie chuckled. "I might have heard a few birdies wittering," she admitted, and thought of the tales she'd heard about Jack having found himself in hot water over the death of a former superintendent, Jennifer Lucas, whom he'd had a relationship with and who had, by all accounts, treated him miserably. It happened a few years ago, but Charlie knew that it took time for memories to fade and scars to heal.

"I'm sure the 'birdies' were *singing*," Jack said. "Well, I guess I don't have anything to hide. I was young, and exercised poor judgment in romantic and professional terms, which almost cost me everything. It tore up my family, because my mother…" He swallowed, caught off-guard by emotion. "My mother is serving twenty years to life."

Charlie had heard that part of the story, too. "I'm sorry," she said, and he toasted the mug of hot chocolate, putting a brave face on it as he always did.

"Yeah, well. Life moves on."

Charlie shook her head. "It does, but some things have a nasty habit of lingering, in here," she said, and tapped her chest. "You should be proud of how you've bounced back."

Jack smiled at her. "Thanks," he said quietly. "I couldn't have done it without my friends."

He polished off the last of his drink, and moved over to the sink to wash out the mug. Charlie opened her mouth to tell him he needn't bother, that she'd do it later, but ended up saying nothing and instead enjoyed the simple, unexpected feeling of having someone in her life who thought about the little things.

"I should head off, or I'll be like the walking dead tomorrow," Jack said.

"It's Jeff Pinter I feel sorry for," she said, thinking of the pathologist. "He's pulling an all-nighter, to help us out."

He made a sound like a raspberry. "Jeff already looks like the Grim Reaper," he said, without malice. "He can catch up on his beauty sleep when we find the source of the poison."

They walked towards the front door, and she held it open for him.

"I was thinking," Charlie said.

"Uh-oh."

She gave him a playful shove, and he grinned.

"I was *thinking*," she began again. "Why would anybody want to poison George Masters, or Stacey Hitchens, anyway?"

"That's the mystery," Jack said, and wriggled his eyebrows.

"Oh, that's the spot…aye…" Phillips made a low, rumbling sound of pleasure while Gladys Knight sang about midnight trains to Georgia from the small radio beside the bed.

MacKenzie gave him a long, sideways glance. "Will you keep it down, for heaven's sake? I'm trying to finish my book."

Phillips turned off the hand-held back massager he'd been gifted for his last birthday. "That's the problem, when you've got an elite athlete's body," he said, and flexed his biceps. "These muscles are like a finely-tuned engine…they need lookin' after."

"Mm hm," she said, not looking up from her Kindle.

"O' course, there are *other* ways to work out the aches and pains," he mused, and chanced a glance in her direction, only to find her nose firmly in the fictional world of historical heroes in kilts.

Drastic measures, he thought, and popped open the top button of his striped pyjama top.

When, unbelievably, that seemed to have no impact whatsoever, he rolled onto his side and propped his head on his hand.

"What's your book about?" he asked, innocently.

"It's an Anglo-Scottish romance, set in the sixteenth century," she said.

"Sounds good," he replied. "Y' nah, some of my ancestors were Scottish."

She grunted.

"I probably have a kilt lyin' around here, somewhere."

She grunted again.

"I can do the Gay Gordons like nobody's business."

"I've seen it," she muttered.

"Och aye, well there's a few things you haven't seen yet, lassie," he said, in a broad Glaswegian twang, and whisked the e-reader from her hands.

"Wha—?" She started to laugh, as he ripped open his pyjama shirt with a flourish and came for her with a glint in his eye.

Much later, she laid a hand on his furry chest and smiled. "You were right," she said.

"What about?"

"There *were* a few things I hadn't seen yet."

"Aye, well, don't get used to it," he said, primly. "I can't be rippin' shirts, every day of the week, y' nah."

She laughed, and reached across to turn out the light. "Never change, Frank."

"No chance," he said, and gave a jaw-cracking yawn. "'Night, love."

CHAPTER 14

Monday

"Mummy? When's Grandad coming back?"

Anna looked at her daughter, then across the table at Ryan, who set down his cup of coffee and stroked a gentle hand over Emma's hair.

"He's not coming back, sweetheart," he said. "Remember, we talked about it? Grandad died—"

Emma's lip shook, and she pushed away her plate. "I don't *want* him to die!"

Ryan felt a knot of pain settle in his stomach, but he continued to speak in soothing tones. "None of us wanted him to die," he said.

"Grandma says he's gone to Heaven," Emma said. "Do you think that's where he is?"

It was difficult to have an in-depth theological conversation with a toddler, but Ryan would never lie to her.

"I don't believe in Heaven or Hell," he said. "But, if I did, I'm sure your grandad would be in Heaven."

Emma seemed to understand. "Why don't you believe, Daddy?"

Ryan had always been proud of how inquisitive his daughter was but, just then, he found himself wishing she was a little *less* so. "Well," he said. "That's a big question." He thought of the problem of 'evil' in the world; the inconsistencies across different religions and deities…

They could wait until another time.

"Let me put it this way," he said, leaning forward so their dark heads were close together. "If I don't believe in anything after we die, that means I'm even more excited to be alive. Every day feels fresh and new, and I make the most of it. I love to see you, and Mummy, and Grandma, and—"

"And Rascal!"

Ryan grinned, and thought of the Labrador puppy who'd become his daughter's faithful shadow. His father had picked him up just before he died, intending to train him and keep him there at Summersley, but even the village idiot could see that the dog would be coming home with *them*, whenever the time came, and that he'd be the one doing the early morning and late evening walks.

"And Rascal," he said.

Right on time, they heard the yapping of a dog at the back door, and Eve Ryan let them both inside the warm kitchen with a breathless laugh.

"Gosh, this dog has some energy!" she said. "Morning, all."

"Morning," Ryan said. "Would you like some tea?"

"Love some," Eve replied, and turned to her granddaughter. "I think this puppy needs rubbing down, and then some water."

"I'll do it!" Emma said, eagerly.

Anna took the dog's lead from her mother-in-law, and led the two youngest members of the family towards the boot room, where there was a stack of old towels and a mountain of doggie snacks in the cupboard. Eve smiled as she watched them go, and then joined her son at the breakfast table.

"Here you are," he said, and handed her a cup of Earl Grey, which he knew was her favourite morning tipple.

She took a sip, and then leaned back to warm herself by the large Aga cooker which pumped hot air into the room.

"What are your plans for today?" he asked her.

"I'm going to keep going through some of your father's things," she said, and tried to keep the melancholy from her voice.

"There's no rush," Ryan said. "I can help, if you like?"

Eve shook her head. "Thank you, darling, but no." She reached across and patted his hand. "What are you going to do?"

"Actually, I have a friend coming to visit," he said.

Eve frowned. "A friend? Is that safe?"

"He's extremely trustworthy," Ryan assured her. "You might remember me mentioning Doctor Alex Gregory? We met on a case, a few years ago, and kept in touch. He's based in London, but he's making the trip out here, to keep things simple. I'm hoping he can give me a few pointers on the kind of person, or people, behind the murder scheme."

"Is he a psychologist?"

Ryan nodded. "And a qualified psychiatrist, actually," he replied. "He worked at Southmoor for years, but he spends a lot of his time profiling serious criminals for the police."

Eve had heard of Southmoor Hospital; it was one of a handful of 'special' hospitals, built exclusively to house the most dangerous, mentally unwell criminals in the country.

"He must have a strong constitution," she said.

Ryan agreed. "He has a very steady pair of hands."

"Like you," Eve remarked. "Which is probably why you're friends. That, and the fact you both apparently have a flair for working with criminal minds."

"Speaking of which, an idea came to me during the night," he said. "I'm going to speak to the Digital Forensics team about it, to see if they think it'll work."

She raised a finely arched eyebrow. "I'm all ears."

While Ryan spoke to his mother about strategies to entrap a killer, an erstwhile non-violent man was feeling positively murderous. Doctor Jeffrey Pinter was Northumbria Police Constabulary's most experienced pathologist, having worked for them in a freelance capacity for over twenty years. That being the case, he was no stranger to the occasional 'out of hours' emergency request, but his efforts the previous evening topped them all. He and three of his staff had worked through the night to complete the postmortem examination of George Masters, as well as analysing the majority of the samples Lowerson and Reed had procured, in order to determine which poison had been used to kill Masters and which might yet kill Stacey Hitchens. She was holding on by a thread in the Intensive Care Unit several floors above the mortuary, where he greeted Jack and Charlie with all the friendliness of a reptile.

"Thanks for doing this, Jeff—"

He frowned heavily at the pair of them. "I had *plans*, last night," he said, drawing out the word so they would understand that those plans had—somewhat optimistically—included the prospect of nudity with his most recent girlfriend.

"Once again—" Charlie began.

"I don't think the pair of you understand how difficult it is to get a date, when you work in a mortuary," he said.

Jack opened his mouth to argue that, actually, they could easily imagine how hard it would be to persuade any eligible individual to date a man who spent most of his days handling cadavers, but, catching Charlie's eye, he decided to keep schtum.

"That must be very frustrating," Charlie said.

"It is," Pinter snapped. "As for the lab results, I can only hope they're accurate, given the rush job we've been forced to do—"

"With your professional eye overseeing things, I'm sure they will be," she said, falling back on a bit of flattery.

Pinter opened his mouth to say something else, then changed direction. "I don't think we've met before, have we?" he said.

Charlie hoped he wasn't about to unleash a charm offensive.

"This is DC Charlie Reed," Lowerson said, with a mischievous smile. "She joined us recently from the Alnwick office."

Pinter adjusted his glasses, and held out a gloved hand. "Oops," he said, and began peeling off the glove, which bore some questionable stains. "Delighted to meet you. Anytime you'd like a personal tour of the mortuary, just let me know."

"No need," she said, quickly. "Er, maybe you could walk us through your findings from last night?"

"Oh," Pinter said. "Yes, of course. Well, I suppose the most important thing to tell you is that we now know which poison was used."

He paused, for dramatic effect, and Jack ground his teeth. "Well?" he prompted. "What was it?"

"Actually, it was *two* poisons," Pinter said, with no small degree of smugness. "Ricin and aconite. We found traces of both in the residue of Stacey's health drink—the one that looked like green sludge."

"I'd better let her doctor know," Charlie said, and started to turn away.

"Already done," he said.

There was something undeniably irritating about Jeffrey Pinter, but he was also the best in the business, and his fast work might have saved Stacey's life.

"We're grateful to you," Charlie said. "How easy is it to get hold of ricin, or aconite?"

"Well, technically speaking, it isn't ricin that we detected but ricinine, which is an alkaloidal component of the castor bean plant, and ricin is found naturally in castor beans," he said. "Ricin can be made by processing castor beans and purifying the waste material to form a powder, which is poisonous. It's actually quite a complicated process, but it can be done easily enough with a bit of help from YouTube, I imagine."

"What about castor beans?" Jack said.

"You could order them online within five minutes," Pinter said. "But they can also be grown by anyone with a mind to."

Which didn't narrow things down very much, Charlie thought. "And the aconite?" she said. "How easy is that to procure?"

"Again, it's very easy to buy the dried plant extract online," Pinter said. "That's because it's widely used in Traditional Chinese Medicine—in small doses, of course. It was still used in Western medicine until the mid-twentieth century... if memory serves, a woman was convicted of murder for poisoning her husband with a spicy aconite curry, back in 2010."

"In other words, both toxins are widely available," Jack muttered, and ran a tired hand over his face.

"Unless you know where to find a ready supply on your doorstep," Charlie said, and they both turned to her. "The Poison Garden."

"Of course," Pinter said, and tapped his forehead as if to reprimand himself for not suggesting it.

"I don't understand," Jack said. "What poison garden?"

"It's in Alnwick," Charlie said, remembering that Jack was a city boy who obviously hadn't discovered some of the county's unique attractions. "It's the brainchild of the Duchess of Northumberland, and forms part of the Alnwick Garden, which is a complex of formal gardens adjacent to the castle in the centre of town. The poison garden is a small, separate part of the main gardens which people can visit and take a tour around, if they want to—they're not kidding about the 'poison' part, though; it contains more than a hundred toxic plants, and people aren't allowed to touch, sniff or eat any of them, for obvious reasons."

"The question is, do they have *Ricinus communis* or *aconitine*—better known as monkshood?" Pinter wondered aloud.

"Even if they do, surely they have strict protocols that would prevent anyone stealing it?" Jack said. "I presume the place is staffed by professionals, if they're allowing the general public to visit?"

Charlie nodded. "There's a team of expert gardeners who look after the Poison Garden and keep an eye on things," she said. "That being said, people find ways and means, don't they?"

"If they're determined to kill, they do," Pinter said, and looked down at the silent figure in the room. "It seems too much of a coincidence for both victims of poisoning to have come from the same town where there's a famous poison garden, that's for sure."

"Perhaps it provided the inspiration," Charlie said. "If not the actual poison."

They ruminated on that, while the air conditioning whirred loudly overhead.

"What about timescales?" Jack said. "How long would it take to kill someone like Masters, with either ricin or aconite?"

Pinter blew out a gusty breath, and pretended to think about it. "If it was just ricin alone, I'd expect death to occur within thirty-six to forty-eight hours, depending on dosage," he said. "However, factoring in the aconite, you've essentially got a double strength toxin at work. The concentration levels were pretty high in the sample you brought from Stacey's drink, which doesn't help, either. So, on the face of it, death could be expedited to within a twelve-hour period, or even less, depending on how much was ingested."

They looked across at the shrouded figure of George Masters, who lay on a stainless-steel gurney.

"We plan to search his home and workplace today," Jack said. "We'll be on the lookout for something similar to that green juice."

Pinter nodded. "It's very possible he died because he drank more of a solution than Stacey did," he said. "If she manages to hold on for the next twenty-four hours, she has a decent chance of survival."

They nodded.

"Let's hope so," Charlie said. "Is there anything else you think we should know?"

Pinter shook his head. "Masters was a fit, healthy man," he said. "His liver and other major organs were in excellent condition, prior to this unhappy ending, and he had a minimal body fat percentage. My guess is that he unwittingly took a fatal dose that would have been strong enough to kill a horse, never mind the average man—although, I'll be able to confirm that once the final toxicology report comes through. If I'm right, it suggests a fair degree of premeditation."

This time, Charlie held out her hand. "Thank you," #she said.

Pinter's ears turned pink. "My pleasure," he said.

As they made their way back through the basement corridors of the RVI towards the lifts, Jack turned to Charlie.

"I think you've pulled, Reed."

"Shut it, Lowerson."

CHAPTER 15

It was with a considerable spring in his step, a twinkle in his eye, and a general air of insufferable wellbeing that DS Phillips swung his car into the staff car park at the Northumbria Police Constabulary Headquarters, in the east end of Newcastle upon Tyne. The skies were an ominous grey, but his mood was sunny enough to counterbalance the impending rainfall, and it was grating on MacKenzie's last nerve.

"You needn't look so *pleased* with yourself," she told her husband. "Jesus, Mary and Joseph…you might as well sky-write the fact you managed to get lucky, last night."

"And this mornin'," he reminded her, wickedly. "Don't forget this mornin'."

She gave a long-suffering sigh, which ended on a smile. "Aye, well, there's no need to broadcast our private life, is there?"

After some painstaking manoeuvres, he brought the car to a standstill. "Who's broadcastin' anythin'?" he said. "I've just been drivin' along in me automobile, mindin' me own business…if you ask me, it's *you* who's got rumpy-pumpy on the brain."

Outrage robbed her of speech.

"It's those saucy books you've been readin', that's what's to blame," he continued. "There's probably a load of husbands out there, fightin' for their lives, all thanks to the exploits of *Laird* Whatshisface of *Loch* Lomond."

Mackenzie started to deny it, then gave a negligent shrug. "If you want to blame anything, blame *Outlander*," she said. "And, before you start on at me about *that*, don't think I haven't noticed you paying close attention whenever a film with Helen Mirren happens to be on the box."

"*Excalibur*," he said, and stared off into the middle distance. "I'll never forget when I first saw that film…at the Tyneside Cinema, it was—"

"Never mind all that," she said, and gave him a none-too-gentle jab in the ribs. "Let's agree that, if Liam Neeson ever turns up dressed like Rob Roy, or Helen Mirren waltzes through the front door dressed as Morgan le Fay, we're allowed to have a wild night with each of them. Until such time, there's murders to be solved."

"You know," he said, thoughtfully. "If I picked up a kilt, and you picked up some floaty whatnot, we could play dress up—"

"*Out!*" she snapped. "The last thing you need is any more encouragement."

He gave a bawdy laugh. "Howay and give us a kiss… *sassenach*."

She checked that none of the other staff were around to see, and then grasped his face in her hands. "What'll I do with you?" she murmured, and kissed him before he could utter a reply.

Ten minutes later, Phillips and MacKenzie convened in the Chief Constable's office, having been admitted by her new Personal Assistant who was, if possible, even more terrifying than the last.

"Frank, Denise," Morrison said. "Come in and take a seat."

They settled themselves on the uncomfortable visitors' chairs arranged in front of her desk.

"I should also say, 'welcome to the club'," Morrison added, drily. "I presume Frank's told you all about our mutual friend?"

MacKenzie nodded. "I've never felt more relieved to have been lied to—which is something I never thought I'd say."

"I know what you mean," Morrison replied, and moved across to her personal coffee machine, the use of which tended to be an indicator of whether or not one happened to be in her good books. "Would you like a coffee?"

They both smiled broadly, and she set the machine to percolate.

"So, now you're au fait with what's been going on, I suppose you also know that we've got an enormous task on our hands."

MacKenzie nodded again. "I understand the Met are employing a lot of their digital resources to compare classified ads with accidental deaths, or those ruled as suicide."

"Yes, they are," Morrison said, and handed them each a cup. "We need to know how far back this network extends, and how wide."

She checked her watch. "I've got Faulkner coming in, along with one of our firearms and explosives experts, to go over some of their findings from the scene at Ryan's house," she said. "They should be here any minute. As a reminder, neither of them is aware of Ryan's true status."

They nodded.

"How did—" Phillips began, and then hesitated.

Morrison cocked her head. 'What's that?"

"I was only going to ask, how was Ryan's father's body removed without Faulkner's help?" Phillips asked.

"Charles Finley-Ryan was a retired senior diplomat, so we were able to call upon the services of a military team from Catterick army barracks," Morrison said. "We felt it was safer not to risk having a paper trail within our jurisdiction, in case our files have been compromised. The threat to Ryan's life, and that of his family, warranted the subterfuge, but I can't imagine Faulkner was pleased about it—"

There was a knock at the door.

"Speak of the Devil," Phillips murmured.

"Come in!" Morrison called out, and they turned to face the new arrivals.

Tom Faulkner was their most senior forensics expert, and had worked with them for many years, though it was always strange to see him in ordinary clothing, without a polypropylene suit covering his body from head-to-toe.

Neil Jones was another familiar face around the constabulary, being their go-to person in all matters pertaining to explosives and firearms.

"Faulkner, Jones, thanks for joining us," Morrison said. "Come in and pull up a chair, if you can find one."

"Jonesy!" Phillips exclaimed, after nodding a welcome to Faulkner. "It's been a while since we've seen you down at the karaoke, lad. How've you been keepin'?"

They exchanged a warm handshake.

"Busy, as always," he said. "Good to see you again, Frank—and Denise."

He treated MacKenzie to a couple of air kisses.

"I was sorry to hear about Ryan," he said, taking a seat beside Faulkner. "He was a good man."

The others in the room fell silent.

"He was," Morrison said, stepping into the breach. "Which is why we're all here, trying to make sense of what happened. I'm hoping the pair of you can shine some light on things—let's start with the scene at Ryan's house in Elsdon. What can you tell us, Tom?"

Faulkner took off his glasses to rub them against his jeans. "Before we get started, I just wanted to say, I'll do whatever it takes to crack this one, because Ryan was a very good friend to me," he said, and thought of the times Ryan had helped him out of some very sticky financial spots. "That being said, I wish I had more good news to share. In terms of the scene up at Elsdon, the fact is, we found no trace of LCN DNA in the woodland where the shot was likely to have been fired, and we scoured a significant area looking for it." He spread his hands. "Given that Ryan's body was removed before we could assess it *in situ*, we weren't left with much to work from there," he said, with a touch of irritation.

Morrison offered no explanation or apology, so he continued.

"Anyway," he said. "It was also difficult to identify the shooter's position in the woods overlooking Ryan's home, because the bullet's trajectory would have been affected when it went through the window."

Jones nodded his agreement. "From the ballistics side, the bullet was a very common calibre used in long-range rifles," he said. "Easy to come by. Of course, we'll do our best to try and trace it, but I wouldn't advise anyone to hold their breath."

It was disappointing news, but not unexpected.

"What about prints?" MacKenzie asked.

"We examined likely spots where the shooter might have been positioned, and took a few impressions and photographs of possible footprints," Faulkner said. "None of them were distinct enough to be of any use." He let out frustrated breath. "As for the scene inside Ryan's home, apart from the bullet we found no evidence of any suspect DNA," he said. "We found plenty belonging to Ryan, Anna, Emma, and separate samples we've identified as belonging to you, Frank, and you, Denise, which must have been deposited at some time during a previous social visit. We found a surprising quantity of DNA belonging to Ryan's father, but nothing belonging to his mother. We assume there was an accident, perhaps some sort of prior injury, during his father's last visit, but it's impossible to say for certain because the team performed an extremely thorough clean-up after removing Ryan's body."

Morrison took a gulp of cold coffee. "Mm, well, it's clear you've done your best with what was available, Tom—"

"I'd like to request your permission to go over everything again," he interrupted her, with a stubbornness he rarely exhibited. "Ryan was my friend, and I want to be sure I've done all I can to find whoever was responsible."

Morrison glanced at Phillips, then MacKenzie. "I'm sure you've done a *stellar* job," she said. "I have no doubt you've left no stone unturned."

"Please, ma'am," Faulkner said. "It would mean a lot to me, and I'm happy to do it off the clock, on my own time."

Morrison couldn't find an adequate reason to refuse him, without mentioning the small matter of Ryan still being *alive*, so she acceded to the request. "Er, yes, all right then."

"Thank you," he said.

"What about the bombing outside Frankland Prison?" she said, moving the conversation on. "What were your findings there?"

"The car was completely incinerated," Faulkner replied. "Even after a painstaking search through the wreckage, there was absolutely nothing to find. I'm hoping it's a different story from your side, Neil?"

Jones made a bobbing motion with his head. "Well, the first thing to say is that it's likely to have been military-grade explosives that were used," he said. "I'm still waiting to receive confirmation from the Ministry of Defence; they've had a few other things on their plate lately, so there's been a delay, but I'm hopeful of receiving their report sooner rather than later."

"What makes you think it was a military-grade explosive that was used?" MacKenzie asked.

"Because I deal with 'ordinary' explosives every day, and provide certificates for the kind of devices in general circulation," he said. "The radial impact alone suggests a more sophisticated level of device."

"Seems like we're dealin' with someone who fancies themselves as Rambo," Phillips said. "Somebody with military training, or experience, but we've got no clue about his identity or why they're doin' what they're doin', and they could strike again, any time, any place."

"If the objective was to kill Ryan with that car bomb, then, sadly, that objective has been met," Faulkner pointed out.

"There was only one figure captured on the CCTV footage of the car park," Morrison said. "They were obviously well aware of the position of the cameras, given their body language and clothing, which is why we haven't been able to make an identification. Thankfully, it was enough to alert the prison guards to try to warn Ryan— they were too late to stop you from being injured," she said, turning to Phillips. "But, despite their efforts, you're still with us."

"I'd have been a big miss," Phillips agreed, without any false modesty.

The other two men laughed, while MacKenzie merely shook her head. "There's still time for someone to place an ad," she said, and wiped the smile off his face.

"Have there been any developments in the case of Marcus Atherton?" Morrison asked them, before full-scale war could break out.

Atherton was a former journalist who was found dead in an apparent accident, having been asphyxiated during a carbon monoxide leak from the gas fire in his home. It might never have been deemed suspicious, were it not for the fact Atherton had been the first person to make the connection between an unusually high number of accidents and suicides in the region, alongside the name of each victim being published in a series of classified adverts in *The Northern Fisherman.* Equally, the correlation might never have been discovered were it not for the magazine choosing to transfer their content into a digital format, which allowed Atherton to begin searching for the names of the deceased online. When those names flagged in a series of classified ads in the same magazine, Atherton smelled a rat—or, rather, a *fish*. In the circumstances, the team suspected he'd been murdered, to prevent him from revealing his concerns to the police.

"Only confirmation of what we already knew," MacKenzie said. "Namely, that Atherton had performed the internet search that, ultimately, got him killed. I've asked the team to go back over historic searches, to see if he'd stumbled across anything else that may be of interest to us."

"His phone provider also confirmed the call Atherton put through to that victim up in Dunstanburgh," Phillips said, referencing one of the network's past victims. "Atherton obviously tried to warn him, but didn't manage to get through or leave a message. Still, he made the call, and considerin' there was no connection between them other than Atherton having found the vic's name in one of those adverts in *The Northern Fisherman*, it seems pretty clear the bloke was onto somethin'."

"A lot of the surfaces at Atherton's home were suspiciously clean," Faulkner reminded them. "Even for the most fastidious household, that's very unusual, so we could certainly hypothesise that whoever clubbed him, turned on the gas and staged his body to make it look as though he'd fallen and hit his head, was also responsible for doing a thorough wipe-down afterwards."

"Aye, and not forgettin' that Atherton's home computer was wiped clean of its search history," Phillips put in. "Pity for them that he used the work computer to look a few things up, n'all."

"Unfortunately, still not quite enough to convict anyone," Jones said, and it was true. "What about the suspects we've charged for that murder up at Dunstanburgh, and the other one—the hit and run, out near Hadrian's Wall?"

"Neither of them is talking at the moment," MacKenzie said. "They're probably too frightened of the consequences, if they do. But we're still working on them, and the reality of a life term in prison should start kicking in pretty soon."

Morrison came to her feet, and moved across to the window, where a pigeon she'd named 'Priscilla' had come to sit on the window ledge and nibble at the bird feeder she'd fitted to the wall outside. It probably wasn't regulation, but the job had to have *some* perks and, if first class travel wasn't one of them, she'd decided feeding the birds damn well would be.

She watched the bird peck at the seeds, its beak darting back and forth in fast, precise movements, and smiled to herself.

Just like police work.

"There's no quick fix," she said, turning back to the people in the room. "It's a question of going through every step with a careful eye, so we don't miss anything. We could come across something out of the blue, like Atherton did, but it's more likely we'll have to go through the steps until we find what we're looking for. Everything starts small, so we just have to follow this snowball back to the first snowflake and figure out who started the ball rolling."

On which note, they were dismissed.

CHAPTER 16

Newcastle upon Tyne
Football transfer season, 2007

Kyle Rodgers wasn't too happy about the prospect of moving to Bournemouth.

There was nothing particularly wrong with that part of the world, but he was a Geordie lad, born and bred, and he liked his home city. He had friends there, family—who he never saw, but *could* see, if he wanted to—and the priceless popularity that came from being the poor local kid who'd done well for himself, thanks to his own raw talent. Ever since he'd been a toddler, Kyle had possessed the kind of hand-eye coordination others could only dream of. It'd been almost too easy to sail through the football academy, and then take up his rightful place with The Magpies, where he was welcomed with open arms by executives, teammates and fans alike. Nowadays, he couldn't go into a shop without somebody stopping him for an autograph, nor step inside a pub or a club without having over-tanned women in low-cut dresses fling themselves at him, in the hope of becoming the next Footballer's Wife to grace a quadruple-page spread in *Hello!* magazine.

Sadly, for them, he was more interested in men.

If he was really honest, he was more interested in *boys*.

Barely legal.

The younger the better.

So, what? he thought, defensively. *If those skinny, dewy-faced lads had reached the age of consent, they could make their own decisions.*

In the years that would follow, various high-profile sex scandals would come to light and society would talk more openly about imbalance of power, or the coercive nature of a relationship where one party was famous, with powerful friends and boundless wealth, while the other was young, inexperienced and without access to any of those privileges. As it was, Kyle lived in a halcyon time for predators such as himself, and he took full advantage.

Which was another reason to lament the transfer from Newcastle to Bournemouth, he thought. While he was sure he could find some young blood on the south coast, there was plenty on tap in Newcastle and he knew exactly where to find it. Some of them cried about it, the next morning, but that was their lookout.

It was his word against theirs, anyway.

Kyle smiled at his reflection in the giant mirror above his bathroom sink, and flexed his pectoral muscles. As a professional footballer, it was part of his job to remain fit, but he'd have done it anyway because he liked to be strong in comparison with the young men he took to bed. If *GQ* wanted to name him Number Five in their 'Sexiest Men of the Year', that didn't hurt, either.

It all helped with the public image.

Occasionally, he threw a few quid at the food banks, or at some local sports academy, and the news lapped it up. They'd write a sycophantic article about how he'd never forgotten his 'council house roots'—which always made him laugh because, let's face it, he'd done everything he could to forget the hellhole where he'd grown up.

Kyle looked around the bathroom, at its marble walls and theatre-style lights illuminating the mirror, and was upset all over again. He didn't want to move, and he especially didn't want to leave his home, which he'd tailored to his exact needs over the years—including a series of tiny, unseen cameras fitted in guest bathrooms and bedrooms throughout the house, for when he was feeling voyeuristic. It was probably illegal to film people without their consent, and to keep the intimate footage, but, since they'd never know about it—

The doorbell sounded downstairs.

Kyle had forgotten there was a visitor expected at the house that day, and tugged on a pair of lounge pants before jogging downstairs to open the door.

"Mr Rodgers? I'm Janet, from *Prestige Home Cleans*," she said, and produced a little ID card for his inspection, although she was also wearing a pale blue polo shirt embroidered with the company logo. "I think you were expecting me?"

"Aye—yeah, come in," he said.

"I understand that you're looking for a deep clean, after you move out?"

"Yeah," he said, already bored by the conversation. "I have a regular housekeeper, but she's—er—she had a bereavement, so I need someone to fill in and do a thorough job after the movers empty the place."

"I completely understand," she said. "I only need ten minutes to look around the house, to get an idea of how long it will take, and allocate the staff accordingly."

"Fine, help yourself," he said. "I'll be in the kitchen."

"Are you sure you don't mind me wandering around—"

"It's fine," he muttered. *Anything incriminating was locked away.* "Just take your shoes off."

He sauntered across the hall towards a set of glass doors, beyond which she could see an enormous, gaudy-looking kitchen that must've cost him an arm and a leg. Janet waited until he disappeared from sight, and then slipped out of her loafers and headed towards the staircase, a small handbag slung over her shoulder. She hurried upstairs and, after a quick peep behind the various doors, found the master suite. It was an oppressive room decorated in black and white, but she wasn't there to admire the interior design, so she made directly for the ensuite bathroom, taking care to keep her head down.

Janet paused, listening for any movement in the corridor outside, and then picked up a circular canister of powdered toothpaste from the countertop. It was marketed for smokers, who tended to have stained teeth, but it looked a lot like the powdered version of various class-A drugs—such as the one she had in a small plastic bag in her pocket.

She took it out and, with another glance over her shoulder, tapped the powder into the toothpaste and mixed it together so that the two were indistinguishable.

Are you nearly finished? Kyle called up the stairs.

"Yes," she called back.

And so are you.

———

Two days later

Kevin sat in the stuffy meeting room and stared listlessly at the linoleum floor.

He heard the voices of the people around him, droning like flies on a summer day, and it gave him a headache.

He didn't want to be there.

He didn't want to be in a drab, miserable room, surrounded by drab, miserable people, just like himself. His wife thought it was a good idea to share their grief with other people who'd lost loved ones—and she seemed to enjoy hearing about all the different ways in which violent, unexpected death had broken the hearts and minds of the strangers who gathered for a weekly support group at the community centre—but it was something he could do without.

"—Kev?"

He realised the group leader had asked him a question. "Sorry?"

"I asked if there was anything you'd like to share with us, today?"

He felt his wife's eyes boring into the side of his head, and tried to think of something to say. "Um…" he said.

There was a long pause, while the group waited expectantly.

"I—" Kev's eyes raked over the people sitting in the circle around him, and he felt whatever was left of his soul fly from his body. "No," he said. "I don't have anything to say."

He didn't need to look at his wife, nor at the group's leader, to know they would be disappointed. He'd been coming for ten weeks now, far longer than was usual, and hadn't uttered a single syllable that could be described as an expression of his feelings after the death of his daughter, or her attacker.

Her murderer, he amended.

Eddie Delaney hadn't wound the electrical cord around her neck, but he might as well have.

"—heard about that footballer?"

Kevin tuned in again and caught the tail end of someone talking about the death of a footballer whose name he recognised immediately.

Kyle Rodgers.

"They say he had a heart attack and passed away instantly," the group leader was saying. "Now, Kyle was obviously a young man in the prime of his life, just like your son was, Maureen. I mention it to illustrate that, sometimes, there's no rhyme or reason to these things. He may have had a congenital heart defect, just like your Sam did."

Maureen cried softly, and nodded. "His poor family," she said. "You never expect these things to happen…"

Kevin glanced at his wife, saw her nodding in sympathy, then looked back down at the linoleum.

———

Half an hour later, there followed the obligatory tea, coffee and biscuits, for those who had nothing better to do with themselves. The first time they'd come, Kev had tried to make banal conversation about the weather. Now, he simply left his wife to it, and waited for her in the car.

"How's Kev doing?" One of the other group members, a young woman called Marie, offered his wife a cup of tea, which she took.

"Not so good, to tell you the truth," she replied. "He spends most days in a kind of trance."

"It gets you like that, sometimes," Marie said.

The two women stood in comfortable silence, each lost in their own thoughts.

"What do we do, now?" Marie asked.

"Keep going," came the reply. "Just keep going."

CHAPTER 17

The real estate business had been kind to the late George Masters, who'd lived in a large stone villa on one of the nicest streets in Alnwick. Jack and Charlie thought this, as they approached the front door and prepared to speak to his grieving widow, and mother to their one-year-old baby.

"Ready?" Charlie whispered.

"I hate this bit," Jack muttered. "But it comes with the territory."

She squared her shoulders and pressed the doorbell, which was answered by a woman who reminded them strongly of Colleen Nolan.

"Look, this isn't a good time," she said, straight off the bat. "My daughter's lost her husband, and she doesn't need people coming to flog cleaning products or whatever—"

Charlie held out her warrant card. "DC Charlie Reed and DC Jack Lowerson," she said. "From Northumbria CID."

"Oh—"

"We're hoping to speak to your daughter about her husband."

"Mandy's very upset," she said. "We all are."

"It's important, Mrs—?"

"Dixon," she said. "Mrs Joanna Dixon." There came the sound of a baby crying upstairs. "You'd better come in," she said, and ushered them inside. "Mandy's in the living room. You go straight in, and I'll go and get Lily."

She bustled upstairs to see to her baby granddaughter.

"Mum?" Amanda Masters opened the living room door, and they saw a very attractive woman in her mid-thirties, dressed in Christmas pyjamas and a stained woollen jumper. Her face was pale and streaked with tears, while her oat-blonde hair had been scraped into a messy bun on top of her head. In short, she looked exactly as they would expect to find someone who'd just lost her husband, and father of her child.

"Mrs Dixon has gone to get your daughter," Charlie said, before the woman could panic at finding two strangers in her hallway. "We're DCs Reed and Lowerson, from Northumbria CID. Are you Mrs Masters?"

Mandy nodded. "Yes," she said, in a voice that was barely audible. "I've already spoken to the family liaison officer."

"I'm glad you're being looked after," Jack said. "But we're not from the local team, Mrs Masters. We're from the Criminal Investigation Department and, as part of our work, we investigate deaths we've deemed to be 'suspicious'."

She frowned, and raised a shaking hand to her head. "I'm sorry—I—I don't understand. Are you saying George's heart attack was *suspicious*?"

"Perhaps it would be easier if we took a seat in the living room, and talked about it there?" Charlie suggested. "We understand you're under a lot of emotional strain at the moment, and we want to offer you our most sincere condolences at this difficult time."

The words sounded horribly trite, but they were well-intentioned.

"Thanks," Mandy mumbled. "Yes—okay, come through." She shuffled back into the living room, which looked as though it had recently been hit by a hurricane. Baby toys, clothes and used bottles jockeyed for position with mountains of used tissues and other paraphernalia which, it seemed, nobody had mustered the strength or motivation to tidy away. Disorder was a common feature of grief, they knew; in some, it could manifest as almost manic levels of activity and cleanliness, whereas, in others, their lives slowed down to the point of becoming dysfunctional.

Hopefully, that stage would pass quickly for Amanda Masters.

"Take a seat," she said, clearing a bunch of baby books from one of the sofas. "Would you—er—do you want anything?"

"No, thank you, Mrs Masters," Jack said.

She slumped into an armchair made of soft, buttery leather, and rubbed the heels of her hands over her eyes. "You—you said you thought George's death was—suspicious?" She looked between them with haunted eyes.

"Yes, I'm afraid so," Charlie replied. "An emergency postmortem was performed on your husband's body last night, and a toxic green health drink was found in his stomach."

She avoided using the word 'poison', and watched closely for any reaction, but Mandy continued to stare at her in a state of muted shock.

"Do you know whether your husband drank anything matching that description?"

Mandy raised a hand to her lips, and nodded. "Yes," she whispered. "Yes, he does. It's a green powder, which he shakes into water with a special bottle."

"Do you have it?" Jack asked.

"There should be some in the cupboard," Mandy said. "I'll show you."

They made their way through to a large, well-equipped kitchen at the back of the house, which overlooked a generous, manicured garden. Mandy opened one of the cupboards, and stepped aside so they could see its contents.

"He had an online subscription," she said quietly, as they surveyed a collection of sachets and the shaker bottles she'd told them about, all branded 'GREEN POWER'.

"How often are the sachets delivered?"

"Monthly, I think."

"Do you drink it, too?" Charlie asked, as she picked up one of the sachets with a gloved hand.

Mandy shook her head. "I had a sip, when he first started, but I can't stand the flavour, the smell...anything about it, really. George was the only one who—who—" She dissolved into tears, and rested her elbows on the countertop so she could hold her head in her hands. "Sorry," she gasped.

"There's no need to apologise, Mrs Masters," Charlie said, and thanked Jack when he procured a box of tissues.

"It's just—I don't know what to do, now. What about Lily?" she said, and looked at the ceiling, where they heard her mother singing to the little girl in her bedroom above. "We never got around to arranging any life insurance...we meant to, but George was always so healthy."

"I'm sorry to hear that, Mrs Masters," Jack said, and forced himself to continue asking the difficult questions.

Clarity and compassion, Ryan would say.

"Do you know how long Mr Masters had his subscription for Green Power?" Jack asked.

"I don't know...a year, maybe?" Mandy was starting to fade away, and they knew it wouldn't be long before she checked out of the conversation completely. "I think his obsession with healthy living began not long after I found out I was pregnant with Lily," she said. "She came as a bit of a surprise and, to be honest, George lost any interest in me...physically, that is. He spent all his free time either at work or at the gym, drinking his health drinks—"

"Which gym did he attend?"

"Oh, it's called HardBody," she said. "It's on the edge of town, almost straight off the motorway."

They knew it, and so did Stacey Hitchens.

"Do you mind if we take these sachets for testing?" Jack said.

Mandy shook her head. "You really think something in there killed him?" she said, and her hand strayed to her throat.

They had no time to formulate a reply, before she hurried over to the fridge.

"I should empty everything out of here—just in case."

She scrambled for a bin bag underneath the sink, and then proceeded to dump the contents of the fridge inside it.

"Mrs Masters—" Charlie said.

Mandy looked across with eyes that weren't quite focused.

"It's only the green juice we're interested in, at the moment," Jack said. "There's no need to throw everything out."

"I can't take any chances," Mandy said, and carried on throwing away unopened packets of ham and cheese.

"Er, why don't you let us deal with this, Mrs Masters?" Charlie said, taking the bin bag from her hand.

Mandy looked down at the bag, then at the fridge, and nodded.

"Okay," she muttered. "Okay…yes."

Charlie looked over at Jack, who nodded his agreement to her unspoken question.

"Thank you for your time, Mrs Masters," he said. "Once again, we're very sorry for your loss."

"Mama."

They turned to find Joanna Dixon in the doorway, holding a cherubic baby girl in her arms. Lily Masters had her father's eyes and her mother's blonde curls, but a smile that was all her own.

"Mama!" she said again, and held out her arms.

Mandy took her daughter in her arms, feeling the warm weight of her like a comfort blanket.

"We'll see ourselves out," Jack said, and waved to the little girl, who looked at him with big brown eyes and gave him a gummy smile.

Once the door shut behind them, Jack and Charlie took a deep, cleansing breath.

"That was intense," he said. "Fancy a quick walk, to blow off the cobwebs?"

She agreed, and after depositing the powder samples in the boot of the car, they began wandering towards the centre of town, their footsteps keeping pace over the old paving stones.

"What did you make of her?" Jack asked, after a couple of minutes passed.

Charlie thought of the woman they'd just seen, who'd appeared a shell of the person she'd once been, according to the family photographs on the walls of their home.

"I thought Masters' wife seemed genuinely shocked by his death," she said. "There wasn't any attempt to hide the green powder, or to prevent us from taking it away. I had the impression she wasn't all there, which is probably down to the shock."

Jack looked up at the sky, which was a bold blue peppered with fluffy white clouds, then at the classic architecture pervading the pretty little market town, and wondered, as he often did, how it was possible that bad deeds could happen in so beautiful a landscape.

"It seems that Stacey and George have more than a taste for green vitamin powder in common," he said. "Both are members of HardBody Gym…or, rather, George Masters *was* a member."

Charlie looked across at his placid profile. "You thinkin' what I'm thinkin'?"

"That Mr Masters might have strayed from home?" he said. "Yeah, I'm wondering about that. Then again, just because the physical side between them had dwindled—"

"According to her," Charlie put in.

"According to her," he agreed. "Even if that was the case, it doesn't mean he was off having an affair. Plenty of marriages have dry spells, so I hear."

Charlie thought about how her own dry spell had lasted so long, it felt more like an *age*.

Even a *millennium*.

"What do you think?"

"What?" she said, sharply. "*Nothing.* I wasn't thinking anything about anything."

Jack stepped aside to allow a woman on a mobility scooter to pass.

"I mean, I'm not thinking anything concrete…at least not until we've had a chance to speak to George's friends, the people at the gym…that kind of thing," she amended quickly.

He gave her an odd look. "Fair enough," he said. "Mandy says there was no life insurance, so that's another thing to bear in mind. We can double check, of course, but, if she's right, that doesn't give her much of a financial incentive to see her husband off, does it?"

"Not on the face of it."

They were approaching the old gatehouse to the town, which had been built over a stone archway known as 'Bondgate Arch'. Passing through the arch would take them to the centre of the town, with its many shops and restaurants, but, instead, Charlie veered to the right.

"Where are we going?" Jack asked, as a large car park came into view.

"This is the closest entrance to the Alnwick Garden," she said. "And, more importantly, the Poison Garden. I thought we could take a look and see if anything jumps out at us."

"Not literally, I hope."

"This isn't *The Day of the Triffids*."

"Still…"

"Not scared, are you?" She raised an eyebrow, and he lifted his chin.

"Not at all," he replied. "I was more concerned in case *you* might be, that's all."

Charlie laughed. "Jack, let me tell you something. When you've seen some of the gunk and goo that a baby can produce, and you've survived every virus known to mankind because the little carrier monkey brings a new one home from nursery every week, the thought of a poisonous weed just doesn't scare you that much."

It was only later that he realised the prospect of dealing with all that gunk, goo and viral infection didn't scare him that much, either.

It was something to think about.

CHAPTER 18

Doctor Alexander Gregory stepped off the train at Totnes alongside a handful of other travellers who'd made the journey from London to Devon, and began making his way towards the exit turnstiles. Although he enjoyed living and working in the city, life there had been very heavy, lately, and a brief sojourn to the country had come as a welcome relief.

Passing through the turnstiles, he paused to scan the car park, where he spotted a dark green, old-style Land Rover. Its headlights flashed and he headed over, slinging his overnight bag onto his shoulder as he crossed the forecourt with long-legged strides. The driver leaned across to open the passenger door as he approached, there being nothing so modern as electric locks in the battered old vehicle.

Gregory hopped inside, and turned to his friend. "You look remarkably well, for a dead man."

Ryan grinned. "It's the caffeine," he said. "Thanks for coming, Alex."

"I'd never pass up the opportunity of seeing Summersley for myself. According to Frank, it's second only to Buckingham Palace."

Ryan started the engine, and smiled. "Frank is prone to exaggeration," he said. "But it is a lovely place, if you like that sort of thing."

"You don't?"

"It'll always hold happy memories for me," Ryan said. "But it's not home."

As they navigated the sleepy streets of Totnes, Alex wondered what it might feel like to call somewhere his home. Sadly, that was something he'd never truly experienced; not since he was a very young child and, even then, 'home' had only been an illusion.

"So," he said. "Tell me, how can I help with your current predicament?"

Ryan's hands were competent on the wheel as they swerved around a rogue tractor and headed for the undulating hills that would take them towards Dartmouth Estuary.

"I need your insight," he said. "You're an expert on criminal minds—"

"I could say the same of you," Alex replied, and it was no idle flattery. In their own ways, each man had learned to appreciate the other's perspective, and the role of both forensic psychology and good, solid policework in bringing justice to the dead.

"I'm too close to the project," Ryan said. "If I'm not worrying about some madman hiding in the bushes, I'm thinking of how I'll make them pay for murdering my father. I'm too angry to see things clearly."

Alex knew all about anger, and how it could play tricks on the mind. He knew about revenge, and how the dreadful need for it could fester, spreading like a fungus until your entire being was consumed by it. "You've been down this road before," he said. "When your sister was murdered, you told me you almost killed her killer."

Ryan thought of Keir Edwards, and gave a brief nod. "I didn't," he said, but wondered if the outcome would've been the same without Phillips' intervention. "That was a long time ago."

"Not so long ago," Alex said, pressing his foot against an invisible brake as they rounded another hairpin bend. "Time is a very nebulous thing, when it comes to loss. It can feel like forever has passed, or the reverse."

Ryan had to admit, he was right. "It's different, this time," he argued. "I'm older, for a start, and this isn't my first rodeo. I won't let a need for revenge overpower good sense."

Alex had to be content with that. "You said you've got a security team in place?"

"We're as safe as I can make us," Ryan replied, and slowed the car to make the turn towards Summersley village. "But I know we can't hide forever. I need to stay ahead of the network, and find its leader, before they uncover the fact that I'm alive and send somebody to rectify that." Ryan's heart gave a solid thump against his chest, just thinking of it. "I thought of sending my mother, Anna and Emma away, to our place in Florence," he said.

"Would they be safer there than with you?"

"I don't know," came the honest reply.

They fell silent, and Alex admired the pretty village they passed through as he considered what he would do in the same situation.

Ask for Ryan's help, he realised. Just as Ryan had asked for his.

"Tell me about the network," he said. "I need to know about how it operates, to understand the kind of mind that could have set it up."

Ryan proceeded to talk about the murders they'd uncovered, as well as the way the network seemed to work.

"Quid pro quo," Alex surmised. "It's deadly, because it seems a participant isn't required to have money or status in order to have somebody killed; all they have to do is be willing to perform a murder for somebody else. Is that right?"

"Yes. If it wasn't so deranged, I'd admire the simplicity of the concept," Ryan said, and brought the car to a stop outside a tall set of gates. Alex was suitably impressed when the electronic entry system crackled into life and they were asked to confirm their identities, while being scrutinised through the lens of a camera trained directly on them. Only then were they allowed to pass through, following which a man emerged from a stone gatehouse to perform a manual check. He was around their age, and was dressed in comfortable outdoor clothing, but it was the rifle resting in the crook of his arm that brought the most comfort—and discomfort.

They continued along a beautiful tree-lined driveway, and Alex made a hasty reassessment of Ryan's upbringing. He'd known it was privileged, but then, his own start in life had been privileged, at least at the beginning. However, there were *degrees* in all things, and his comfortable middle-class home near Richmond Park paled in comparison to the acres of prime land and the picture-perfect house that suddenly came into view. It was the stuff of Austen and Bronte, and of a bygone era and lifestyle that very few people would ever know.

Alex looked across at his friend. "I think I understand why you changed your name," he said. "Maxwell Finley-Ryan grew up here, but 'Ryan' left, didn't he?"

"Yes," Ryan said. "And I can't turn back."

Alex turned to look again at the view, and thought of the person who'd begun the network that had been responsible for dozens, if not hundreds, of murders.

They couldn't turn back either.

Newcastle upon Tyne
January 2008

Kevin sat in the community centre for what, he knew, would be the very last time.

He'd tried, he really had, but there was no turning back from the course he'd set, just as there was no bringing Emily back from the dead.

Life simply had no meaning, anymore.

He thought that love for his wife would sustain him and that, once the worst of the grief passed, their shared memories and mutual support would guide him through, with the help of the group therapy sessions he'd come to hate, almost as much as he hated life itself.

"Right, let's see how many of you managed to do something active, this week," the group leader said, looking around the motley collection of grieving people. "Who went for a walk, a swim, or some other form of active physical exercise?"

There was a pause, then a few people raised their hands.

"Marie? Let's hear about what you did."

The young woman whom his wife had befriended gave a self-conscious shrug of her slim shoulders. "I went for a walk on the beach," she said. "I took my mother's dog with me, and drove to Druridge Bay."

"Well done," the leader said, warmly. "How did you feel afterwards?"

"Good," Marie admitted. "It felt good to have the wind on my face, and feel alive again."

Alive again, Kevin thought. *What he wouldn't give for a taste of that feeling.*

"Druridge Bay was my brother's favourite place," Marie continued. "We used to go all the time, when we were kids."

"And how did you feel, remembering that?" the leader asked, as gently as she could.

"It felt okay," Marie replied. "I spoke to him, as if he was beside me, and told him about—" She broke off, and looked at her hands.

"Many people talk to their loved ones who've passed," the leader said. "There's no need to be embarrassed. I'm sure lots of us here have done the same."

There were nods around the group.

"You were telling us about how you'd spoken to your brother?"

Marie nodded. "I was only going to say that I told him about my life, and what's happened since he died."

Kevin thought of the private chats he'd held with his daughter, while he was sitting in the garden or alone in the house. He knew she wasn't really there; of course, he did.

He wasn't completely insane.

Was he?

He began to laugh, and the group turned in surprise, discomfited by the wild, maniacal sound.

"Kevin?" his wife said, putting a hand on his arm. "What's the matter, Kev?"

That only made him laugh harder, until tears rolled down his face and his stomach ached.

What's the matter, Kev?

Everything, he could have said.

Nothing would ever be right again.

CHAPTER 19

Summersley House,
Present Day

"Uncle Alex!"

Gregory turned to see Ryan's daughter bounding across the flagstone terrace, with a handsome Labrador puppy lolloping beside her. The sun had broken through the remaining clouds to shine brightly down upon their small gathering and, were it not for the unfortunate circumstances, it would have been a perfect scene.

"Emma!" he said, rising from the chair to catch her up in his arms. "You've grown taller since the last time I saw you."

"Will I be as tall as Daddy?"

Alex glanced over at his friend, who stood well over six feet. "You never know," he said. "And who's this?"

Emma wriggled out of his arms to crouch down beside her puppy. "This is Rascal," she said, proudly, while the dog began gnawing on the edge of his jeans.

"No!" Ryan said, in a firm voice.

The dog's bottom hit the floor with an audible *slap*.

"Good boy," Ryan said, and produced a treat from his pocket. "Emma? Why don't you fetch a toy for Rascal to chew?"

The little girl raced through the French doors into the kitchen, and was back in less than thirty seconds with a rubber toy in the shape of a turkey that had seen better days.

"Here, Rascal!" she said, in her singsong voice. "Eat this, instead of Uncle Alex's trousers."

While the dog entertained himself, Emma climbed up onto one of the free chairs and, a moment later, they were joined by Anna and Eve.

The men came to their feet in almost perfect unison.

"Alex," Anna said, and opened her arms to embrace him. "It's lovely to see you again."

"Well, I thought I'd slum it for the day," he joked, and then turned to the lady of the house who hovered quietly beside her daughter-in-law. "Lady Finley-Ryan? It's a pleasure to meet you."

Ryan had his mother's eyes, Alex thought. They were a striking blue-grey colour that changed with the light, and with their mood. In this case, Eve's were a deep, stormy grey, which reflected the sadness she harboured.

"Doctor Gregory," she said.

"Alex," he replied.

"And please call me Eve," she said. "Welcome to Summersley. Thank you for coming all the way from London to see us; Ryan's told me so much about you."

"All bad, I hope."

Eve smiled, and decided she liked Ryan's friend, with his sharp green eyes and his gentle humility. "Quite the contrary, I assure you," she said, and indicated that he should have a seat.

"Grandma?"

She turned to Emma, who reminded her so much of her own little girl, and who now rested in the marble tomb across the lake from where they now stood. "Yes, darling?"

"Can I go and play on the swings?"

"I'll take you," Anna offered.

"I'll come, too," Eve decided, and turned to her son. "It'll give you two an opportunity to talk shop, without needing to worry about little ears."

"We won't be long," Ryan said.

"Take as long as you need. Alex? Don't let him keep you from enjoying that sponge cake, will you?"

"No chance of that," he replied.

She smiled and rose elegantly from her chair. "Come on, Rascal!"

The puppy yelped and ran over Gregory's feet to chase after them.

"Sorry," Ryan said, with a grin. "This is probably a bit different to your usual consulting room, isn't it?"

"Don't be sorry," Alex said, and spread a hand over the vista. "To have the love of three fabulous women, and to have grown up in such a spectacular place...you're a lucky man, Ryan."

"I know," he said, quietly. "I don't deserve it."

"Life isn't about who's deserving and who isn't," Alex said, without rancour. "But, if it was, you'd have just as much claim as anyone, and more than most. You perform a public service, and have put your life at risk many times in the interests of protecting the most vulnerable. You're a good father, a good husband and, as far as I can tell without speaking to your mother about the difficult teenage years, you've been a good son, too."

"Debateable," Ryan said, with a smile.

"I know Frank and the others at Northumbria CID would agree with me when I say, you're a good friend and a good leader," Alex continued. "So, don't fall into the trap of thinking that you don't deserve to be loved, or to have blessings in life. You reap what you sow, and you've never trampled over anyone to be where you are today."

"Thank you for that," Ryan said, and looked over at the three women crossing the lawn towards the play area, which was hidden behind a cluster of trees. He wasn't ready to leave them and, he suspected, never would be.

And yet, nobody was immortal.

"I'm frightened," he admitted, and turned back to Alex with eyes that blazed. "I don't mind telling you that, because it's true. When it was my sister's killer, I knew his face, I knew his name...I knew the kind of animal I was hunting. It's the same in other cases, where the motivation is clear to me. I *understand* the beast, even without knowing them, and it helps to keep fear at bay. But now?" He shook his head. "I'm searching in the dark."

"Not quite," Alex said, crossing one leg over the other. "Let's think about motivation. You say you don't know what's driving the motivation behind this scheme, but I think you do. At its heart, the motive for killing is the same in every case you've ever handled, isn't it?"

Ryan was about to contradict him, then paused to reconsider.

Money, jealousy, sex, revenge...

"It all comes down to power and control," he said.

Alex nodded. "I've worked with some of the most disturbed minds in the country, but they're actually quite rare to find in the wild. You know better than I do, not every murderer is a Ted Bundy or a Dennis Nilsen. They're just Joe Bloggs, who needed his wife's life insurance money, or Jane Smith, who'd suffered years of systematic abuse before finally suffocating her husband in his sleep. They aren't always criminal masterminds, they're ordinary people who've either snapped or premediated something for a mundane, albeit immoral, reason."

Ryan thought of some of the people he'd put behind bars. "You're right," he said. "It's always a question of base motivation. It follows that, whoever started this network, did so to gain power or control of a situation they felt was outside of their control while a person was alive."

A shaft of sunlight broke through a thin layer of cloud, and Alex closed his eyes for a moment, enjoying the warmth against his skin. "Of course, there'll also be a secondary motivation," he said, opening his eyes again. "It could be a misguided belief in moral superiority, religion or some kind of cult, along the lines you've dealt with before—"

"Before he died, the journalist, Marcus Atherton, believed The Circle might have reformed," Ryan said. "The circumstances don't feel the same, but I won't rule it out because there's certainly a cult-like quality to the way this network operates. It's more like…" He considered the best analogy, and clicked his fingers. *"Fight Club,"* he said. "That's what it reminds me of. Nobody talks about it and, once they're involved, they're committed."

"There'll be an element of thrill-seeking for some of its members, too," Alex said. "As with all large-scale organisations, it becomes hard to manage every member within its fold. However, if we focus our minds on the original founder—"

"Or founders," Ryan said.

"Actually, that's far more likely," Alex agreed. "To build a quid-pro-quo model of killing, you need at least two people, don't you?"

Ryan watched a bee flit amongst the flowers in one of the many large pots decorating his mother's terrace. "The power and control could come from acquiring money, eliminating a rival or even a loved one, to assuage jealousy," he said. "But, if we're right, and there's been a quid-pro-quo relationship between at least two people from the very beginning, that also suggests a degree of rebellion against the ordinary rules of society. Clearly, they thought the law didn't apply to them, and went ahead to kill their intended victim or victims, and furthermore to provide a means for other people to kill with impunity. It suggests serious resentment for society, or its boundaries."

"And towards the criminal justice system?"

Ryan frowned, his black brows drawing together. "Yes," he said. "That's a distinct possibility. Most people, even those who've lost loved ones in the very worst circumstances, defer to the Rule of Law and trial by jury; they don't decide to administer their own capital punishment. The question is, did these 'founders' of the network have a bad experience of the justice system, or did they already have a taste for death, and a need to dish it out?"

Alex took a thoughtful sip of tea. "Desperate people commit desperate acts," he said. "There might have been a degree of madness—for want of a better 'catch all' term—when they started out. Grief isn't so very far from insanity, for some people going through it."

Ryan thought again of his sister's murder, and of how close he'd come to losing himself. "No," he said. "Sometimes, it isn't very much of a leap, at all."

"You're in a different place now," Alex assured him. "The circumstances are different."

Ryan wanted to agree with him, and to say that, no matter what the provocation, he'd never find his own soul, his own morals, compromised in the search for revenge.

But that would be a lie.

CHAPTER 20

Four hundred miles away in Alnwick, detective constables Reed and Lowerson stood on the threshold of a pair of tall, black iron gates bearing a stark, painted message:

THESE PLANTS CAN KILL

"Look at that," Jack said, with more than a dollop of panic. "There's a *skull and crossbones* painted beside it, as well. Even if you were *illiterate*, you'd know to stay out, so what kind of numpty goes inside, of their own volition?"

"You and me, for a start," Charlie replied, with a degree of cheerfulness he found wildly inappropriate, in the circumstances.

"I really don't see why we have to go *inside* the garden," he said. "Surely, we could just, you know, make an appointment and speak to the Head Gardener? Or call him, first thing tomorrow morning, and ask him all about whether someone could have nicked off with a few castor bean plants—"

"Actually, I just spoke to the Head Gardener," she said. "Lovely guy he was, too. He's arranged for one of the guides to give us a private tour of the garden after the next public tour finishes. That should be any minute now."

"Yippee," Jack said.

Charlie laughed, and gave him an elbow. "Oh, crack a smile," she said. "Nobody's going to force hemlock down your throat."

"What if I breathe something in?" he said. "One of the spores from those flowers could find its way into my lungs, and, the next thing you know, I'll be a goner."

"Can't be any worse than the fumes you breathe in the office," she replied. "The methane circulating around Frank's desk alone is a killer."

He couldn't help but laugh. "At least he hasn't been on that cabbage diet, lately. The smell's enough to put hairs on your chest."

"I'll look forward to that," Charlie said. "Strangely, Ryan didn't mention it as a selling point, when he offered me the job at HQ." Her smile slipped a little, when she remembered he was no longer with them.

Out of the blue, Jack's thoughts turned to Melanie, and of how she was growing further and further away from him. He'd sent another e-mail to her the previous evening, when he'd been unable to sleep. Not knowing exactly where she was in the world made it difficult to predict the time zone she was living in, or how easily she could access the internet, but he hoped she'd receive it sometime soon. Perhaps she'd even think about sending him a reply.

Just then, the gates opened, and a group of visitors piled out. Jack watched them chatter happily amongst themselves, as if they hadn't just survived a near brush with death.

Nutters, he thought.

A man of around fifty approached them, wearing an all-black get up which, Jack noted, included an embroidered skull and crossbones on the breast of his polo shirt.

You know, just in case any of them should forget.

"I'm Dean, one of the tour guides here at the Poison Garden. Are you DC Reed?"

"Yes, that's right," Charlie said, and the pair of them smiled like old friends. "This nervy-looking feller is my colleague, DC Lowerson."

He smiled at Jack. "Everyone's a bit nervous, the first time they visit," he said. "But really, there's nothing to be afraid of, so long as you abide by the rules."

"What—er—what rules are they?" Jack asked.

Was it his imagination or were they edging closer to the gates?

"Well, I have to give you the standard safety briefing," Dean said. "All of the plants in this garden have the ability to kill you, so you're not allowed to eat, touch, smell or stand too close to any of them. Hopefully, that's good common sense."

Jack nodded his head vigorously. "Yes, just...good common sense. No touching, no smelling, no eating..."

"Or, standing too close," Charlie finished for him.

"Right."

"Give me a minute to update the chalk board, and we'll get started with the tour."

"The chalk board?" Charlie enquired. "What's that?"

Dean moved across to a small board hanging from a nearby wall, which he held up for them to see.

"Number of faintings so far, this year," he said, and gave a wicked chuckle as he rubbed out the existing number and added two more. "Looks like it's going to be a bumper season."

"*Faintings*?" Jack repeated.

"Yeah, some people get caught out if they inhale too deeply downwind of some of the plants, and others keel over because their imagination runs wild," he said, and hung the chalk board back on its peg. "But I'm sure that won't happen to either of you!"

"Exactly," Charlie said, with a confidence Jack couldn't quite match. "We see much worse down at the mortuary, don't we?"

"Mfhh," Jack said.

"Actually, I'm pretty excited to be here, even if it is on official business," Charlie continued. "I lived in Alnwick for a while, but I never found time to visit. I've always meant to, though."

"Well, you're in for a treat," Dean said, and gestured them both through the gates.

"You okay, Jack?" Charlie whispered. "If you'd rather wait outside, I can catch you up with everything later?"

"No, no," he said, in his manliest tone. "It's fine. I'm fine. It's completely fine."

"Fine," she said. "I'm glad we cleared that up."

―――――――

Less than two minutes later

"We've got a fainter!"

When he opened his eyes, Jack saw two heads looking down at him with matching expressions of amusement and pity.

"My colleague is on the way with a wheelchair and the First Aid kit," Dean said, slipping a radio back into his pocket. "How're you doing?"

Jack was mortified, but he wasn't about to tell them that. "Much better," he said, and ignored the dark spots dancing in front of his eyes to force himself up. "See?"

"Whoa there, easy does it," Dean said, and took his arm. "Come and have a seat on the bench over here...that's right. Oh, be careful of that potted plant, it can—"

"Kill?" Jack interjected.

Charlie took his other arm. "Now, there's no need to be embarrassed," she said. "Dean says it's very common for people to faint within the first minute of entering the garden."

The first minute? Jack thought, and was mortified all over again.

"I do think that was some sort of record," Dean put in. "I'd barely mentioned the daffodils, when you hit the deck."

"I don't remember anything about daffodils," Jack muttered, and sat on the bench with extreme caution, half expecting some trailing ivy to wind its way around his neck.

"They can—"

"Kill me?" Jack said.

"He's obviously feeling better," Dean said to Charlie, who nodded.

A woman wearing the same uniform let herself through the gates with a wheelchair and a First Aid kit in hand.

"Is this the gentleman?" she said, casting her eye over Jack. "He looks a bit peaky, if you ask me—"

"I'm fine," he said, through gritted teeth. "I *don't* need a wheelchair."

"Did you hurt yourself, when you fell?"

Jack wasn't sure but, now she came to mention it, he didn't seem to have any bumps or bruises after fainting on the pathway, which was unusual.

"DC Reed broke his fall," Dean said. "Might've had a bit of a shiner, otherwise."

Jack looked at Charlie, who shrugged. "I've never had a man swoon in my arms before," she said.

"Oh, my God," he said, and slapped a hand to his face. "I can't believe this."

"At least you didn't fall into a patch of deadly nightshade," Dean put in. "That could—"

"Kill you," his colleague said, with a smile.

"Right," Jack said.

CHAPTER 21

"DCI Hassan."

"John? It's Ryan."

He was calling from a burner mobile, one of several he'd purchased in order to maintain a secure line with the few people who knew he was still alive.

"Just a minute," the other man said, and Ryan waited while his old friend from the Met found a quiet corner in which it was safe to speak freely. "Okay, shoot."

"How are things going with Digital Forensics?"

"I heard from Chiyo," Hassan said, referring to the head of that team. "They've already matched up a bunch of old death certificates with classified ads placed in a London-based magazine called, *The Weekly Wanderer*. It only has a small circulation, just like *The Northern Fisherman*, but it's managed to stay afloat for more than twenty years—God knows how."

"What's the demographic?" Ryan asked. "Amblers?"

"Yeah, specifically religious walks," Hassan said. "Very niche, and the audience may be small but it's loyal."

"So, the pattern's the same," Ryan said, and switched the phone to his other ear so he could make a quick note of the magazine. "How many names has Chiyo's team found?"

"Forty-eight," Hassan replied. "That's just in that publication, but they're cross-checking loads of others, nationally."

The line fell silent, while both men digested that information.

"Spanning what timeframe?" Ryan said.

"Six years," Hassan replied. "The most recent was ten days ago, which means the network hasn't stopped, ceased trading or whatever you wanna call it, despite the police interest. The arrogance is mind-boggling."

"Arrogance, or maybe they just don't give a damn," Ryan said. "They've checked out of ordinary society, so its norms don't matter anymore."

Hassan rubbed an ache at the back of his neck, and lowered his voice. "Look, mate, I don't mind tellin' you… I'm out of my depth with this. Every hour, the number of suspect deaths is rackin' up, but we're no closer to findin' the centre of it all."

Ryan heard fear in his friend's voice, and it echoed his own. "I had an idea about that," he said.

"Tell me."

"I need you to contact Greg Pulteney," Ryan said. "He's the editor and owner of *The Northern Fisherman,* and he's been cooperative, so far. If he grants us access to his website, we can replace the link that's normally used to post classified ads.

I want Chiyo to design something that looks identical to the user, but can track their location. Can he do that?"

"Are you kidding? Chiyo's a computer genius," Hassan muttered. "But we already tried tracing the IP address used to place all the ads, so far, and even GCHQ haven't found the originating source—they said the person placing the ads might be using a virtual private network to protect their identity. The next step would be to take down the site, not keep it active."

"If we keep it active, there's a chance the person or people behind this could trip up. At the moment, there's just a basic web form users fill in," Ryan said. "If Chiyo can produce something more sophisticated that can trace the source, we could get lucky."

"Anything's worth a try," Hassan said, and made a note to speak to Chiyo at the first opportunity. "How are you holding up, anyway?"

Ryan watched his friend kick a ball around with Emma, while dodging the clumsy paws of the dog, who ran between his legs. Standing a discreet distance away, on the far side of the garden, was a man wearing khaki combat trousers and a t-shirt, in deference to the unseasonably good weather. A rifle rested in the crook of his arm, and a mic was fitted to his right ear, into which he and his team exchanged regular updates. It wasn't what Ryan would have wanted for himself, or his family, but it was far better to be safe than sorry.

"So far, so good," he replied. "We can do this, John. We dealt with plenty of tough situations, in the old days."

Hassan smiled, thinking of when they'd been younger men. "Yeah, I guess we met a few interesting characters," he said. "Remember that case on Tower Bridge?"

"How could I forget?"

"Still," Hassan said, after they'd reminisced for a moment or two. "Watch your back, mate. You never know who's standin' behind you."

After the call ended and he was alone once again in his father's study, Ryan felt the hairs on the back of his neck prickle.

You never know who's standing behind you.

Ghosts, he thought.

They were everywhere.

"Are you feeling up to continuing the tour?"

Since fainting unceremoniously, Jack had given himself a stern talking to and was certain it would not happen again.

As certain as he could be, anyway.

All right; he was nowhere *near* certain that he wouldn't drop like a tonne of bricks, but his ego demanded that he at least try to make it past the daffodils, this time.

"I'm ready," he declared.

"That's the spirit," Dean said, and gave him a clap on the back. "Now, let me tell you about the laburnum tree."

He pointed to an attractive tree growing near one of the tall stone walls that enclosed the poison garden.

"It has a beautiful yellow blossom in late spring or early summer," he said. "But it's the second most poisonous tree in the UK."

"What's the first?" Charlie asked.

"The yew tree," Dean replied. "You wouldn't think it, to look at them, would you? But, like many of the plants in here, they're beautiful but deadly."

"Aren't they quite common?" Jack said, thinking that he was fairly sure he had a small yew tree growing in his garden, back home.

Dean nodded. "Yes, most of the plants in here grow naturally in the wild, and are quite easy to cultivate," he said. "Take the rhododendrons. Most people think of them as beautiful border plants, with bright flowers, but they're poisonous. For example, if you were to eat honey made by bees using nectar exclusively from rhododendrons, you'd find it had a red tinge to it, and it'd make you pretty sick."

"Noted," Jack said, and resolved to check the provenance of his honey purchases, from now on.

"I heard laurel bushes are quite dangerous," Charlie said, spotting one as they continued meandering through the garden.

"That's because they produce cyanide," Dean told her. "The leaves contain two chemical compounds which, when mixed together, emit cyanide gas. That's why you have to be careful around laurel cuttings or trimmings, where the leaves have been broken, especially in unventilated spaces."

As they continued along the pathway, they encountered a series of mounted gravestones into which the details of famous poisoners had been carved.

"Pinter was right," Charlie said, pointing to one entitled, 'The Curry Killer'. "He told us somebody had murdered their husband using aconite, and so they did."

"Ah, yes," Dean said. "Lakvir Singh used *aconitum ferox*, sometimes known as monkshood. It contains a highly toxic alkaloid called pseudaconitine."

"Do you have some in the garden, here?" Charlie asked.

Dean nodded, and gestured towards an innocuous-looking plant a short distance away. "Monkshood and wolfsbane are both types of aconitum," he explained. "Every part of the plant is toxic, and, when dried out and mixed in with something like curry, it can be deadly."

"It would be quite easy to produce in dried form, then?" Jack said.

"Very," Dean replied. "You don't need a license to own it, and you can buy it online, as far as I know."

"How long would it take to grow?"

"No time at all," he replied. "It's like a common weed, in that respect."

"What about ricin?" Charlie said. "Is that easy to access, as well?"

"It's less accessible than aconitum," Dean replied. "To the extent that it requires a bit more processing and extraction. But, it's still pretty easy, because it comes from the castor bean plant. We've got some, here."

157

They approached another cluster of plants which looked like they could have belonged in any garden in the land.

"Ricin is the deadliest poison known to man," Dean told them, conversationally. "Which is remarkable, considering you can buy castor beans across the counter. Thankfully, most people wouldn't know what to do with them."

Jack swallowed, hard. "Um, so, have you experienced any break-ins, here at the garden?"

"You do get the occasional person try to jump the wall," Dean said. "But we have very stringent security, as you can see. It would have to be a very foolish person who'd want to run the risk of tampering with the plants, here. Everyone who works here is an expert in handling them."

"What about maintenance?" Charlie said. "I take it you wear gloves?"

"And a hazmat suit," Dean said. "We don't take any chances."

"It wouldn't be easy, then, for a person to steal a cutting of any of the plants in here?"

"Not unless they had a death wish," he replied.

Or worked there, Jack thought.

Half an hour later, Jack watched their guide rub out the chalk board and chuckle to himself once again as he updated the number of faintings by one.

"Why does it *always* happen to me?"

"Aww," Charlie said, and they began to make their way back through the centre of town towards their car. "You were enjoying yourself, by the end."

"Whenever I forgot about the imminent threat of death, I did." Saying the words aloud made him think of Ryan, and the stress he must be under, living day-to-day with such a threat.

"A funny look crossed your face, just then," Charlie said. "What were you thinking about?"

"Oh—nothing, really," he lied. "I hadn't realised the garden was part of the local drugs education programme, that's all."

Charlie didn't buy it, but she let it slide because everyone was entitled to their secrets. "Yeah, well, the north of England has the highest rate of drug-related deaths in England and Wales," she said. "Anything that can help to stamp it out for the next generation has to be a good thing."

Jack nodded, thinking of the small crop of cannabis they'd spotted during the tour. The plants were strictly regulated by the Home Office, who'd granted a licence to the Alnwick Garden to grow a certain number, but the Head Gardener was responsible for filing paperwork every season, detailing the exact number of seeds they'd planted, how many plants had grown and been dug up, then destroyed at the end. Although they weren't required to by law, the gardeners also kept a record of the number of castor bean plants growing in the Poison Garden, though it was possible a cutting could be taken without their knowledge.

"What I can't figure out is why someone would choose to kill with a poison like ricin or aconite," Jack said. "I mean,

I know they're both deadly, but it must've taken some effort and preparation. Why not just stab them to death?"

"Poison is traditionally a woman's weapon," Charlie replied. "It might take some planning, but it avoids any messy blood spatter. It also ensures a slower, more painful demise."

"You sound like a woman who was taking notes, back there."

Charlie laughed. "No, but somebody obviously did," she said. "Because, in all probability, whoever killed George Masters and poisoned Stacey Hitchens is also from Alnwick, and they're likely to have been one of the thousands of people who tour the poison garden every year. As we've just learned, it only takes one seed for the idea to grow."

They walked for a few minutes, studying the faces of the people they passed, thinking that it could have been any one of them.

"I just had a thought," Jack said. "What if George and Stacey weren't selected?"

"What d' you mean?"

"I mean, what if a batch of that green health drink was contaminated?" he said. "They might have been accidental victims of chance, rather than deliberate targets."

"It's possible," Charlie said, and felt her stomach flutter with fear. "If that's the case, we could be dealing with more victims, very soon."

"We already know that Stacey's sample contained ricin and aconite," Jack said. "Let's see whether they find any in George Masters' stomach. In the meantime, we have the samples we took from his house, which we can pass on to Pinter's team, later today."

"There's one other place we need to check—the HardBody Gym."

"I was afraid you were going to say that."

"You're afraid of daffodils *and* the gym?"

"No, I'm afraid of daffodils and personal trainers."

Charlie treated herself to a sneaky peek at his rear end.

Not bad, she thought.

"Well, if one of them tries to accost you with a bunch of daffs, I'll protect you."

"Thanks," he laughed, and held open the passenger door to his car, without needing to think about it. "I'd do the same for you, if I knew what you were afraid of."

Charlie's smile slipped slightly, and she was glad of a moment to herself as he walked around to the driver's side—because how could she tell Jack that the one thing she was afraid of was the one thing he couldn't help her with?

CHAPTER 22

Alex Gregory found Ryan in the first place he should have looked, which was inside his family's beautiful mausoleum on the far side of the lake. After Natalie's death, they'd planted a Wisteria tree, which now grew over the columns and bloomed in season, its purple flowers softening the white marble exterior. Alex paused to appreciate its twisted branches, then made his way inside and moved carefully around the floor, reading inscriptions as he passed by each piece of sculpted marble.

David Arthur Finley-Ryan, 6th Bt. of Summersley, VAdm., V.C., O.B.E., b.1901 d.1974. Husband to Isabella, father to Charles and Helen.

The Hon. Isabella Finley-Ryan, née Pierrepont, daughter of Henry Pierrepoint, Duke of Neverton, b. 1918 d. 1993. Devoted wife to David, mother to Charles and Helen.

Natalie Marie Finley-Ryan, daughter of Charles and Eve, b. 1983 d. 2014. Taken too soon and forever missed.

Charles Samuel Finley-Ryan, 7th Bt. of Summersley, Her Britannic Majesty's Ambassador to France, G.B.E., G.C., b. 1944 d. 2024. Beloved husband to Eve, devoted father to Maxwell and Natalie.

"Peaceful in here, isn't it?"

Alex had become so immersed in reading, he'd forgotten he was not alone. Ryan was seated on one of the stone benches lining the mausoleum's circular interior, his long legs stretched out in front of him and crossed at the ankles.

"Yes, it is," he agreed. "It's cool, but doesn't feel *cold*."

"I think these places reflect the people who visit them, as well as those who are laid to rest here," Ryan said.

Alex wandered over to sit beside his friend. "Can I ask you something?"

"Sure, so long as it doesn't involve quantum mechanics or anything to do with artificial intelligence."

Alex smiled, and shook his head. "It's about the peerage," he said.

"You'd be better off asking my mother about that—I never pay attention to any of it."

"Point taken," Alex said. "I was only wondering why your grandmother, Isabella, has 'Hon.' in front of her name but your sister doesn't?"

"Ah, that one I *do* know," Ryan said, with a whisper of sarcasm. "My grandmother was the daughter of a duke—don't you know—whereas Natalie's the daughter of a lowly baronet. Apparently, someone, sometime, decided that you can only be referred to as 'Honourable' if you're the daughter of an earl or higher."

Alex tried to think of something polite to say that wouldn't involve inadvertently giving offence to generations of Ryan's family members.

"Bollocks, isn't it?" Ryan said, taking the wind out of his sails. "The whole antiquated system is cringeworthy. Who the hell ever thought it was a good idea to set up a social ranking system, anyway? It's embarrassing."

"People are just people, in the end," Alex agreed. "We're each a product of our upbringing, to some degree, although you seem to have bucked the trend a bit."

"True," Ryan said. "Tradition meant a lot to my father, probably because it meant a lot to *his* father, and so on and so forth. I couldn't care less about becoming 'Maxwell Charles Finley-Ryan, 8th Baronet of Summersley'."

"Technically speaking...now that your father is dead, doesn't that mean you actually *are* the eighth baronet?"

Ryan looked pained. "I—" He lifted an impotent hand. "Yes, I suppose so."

Alex nodded slowly. "You know, Phillips will never let you live this down," he said, into the quiet space.

"I know."

"If you thought faking your own death was bad, I'm here to tell you that this is much, much worse. In fact, you may wish to consider faking it again, just to avoid the aggravation that awaits you back at Police HQ."

"Believe me, I've considered it," Ryan said. "But I don't think my jaw could take another hit, if Frank found out."

A bruise still bloomed on his chin, to remind him.

"I'm your mother's emissary, by the way," Alex said, before he forgot. "I'm supposed to tell you dinner will be ready in"— he paused to check his watch—"ten minutes."

Ryan nodded.

"You're sure you don't mind me staying overnight?" Alex said. "I can easily catch a train back to London."

"We're happy to have you," Ryan replied. "It's nice to be reminded of the outside world, and to talk things over with someone who isn't immediately involved."

"I'm always here to talk, whenever you need to," his friend said.

Ryan understood the invitation for what it was: a clinical psychiatrist's offer to listen, without judgment. "Is this the part where I tell you about my dreams?"

"If you like, although I have a suspicion you rarely dream."

Ryan looked across at him, in surprise. "How would you know that?"

"Because you run on constant adrenaline, during your waking hours," Alex replied. "Physiologically, your body and mind will often be too exhausted to dream. It's likely you go out like a light and then wake up without the usual fog some people experience."

Ryan nodded. "That's about right," he said. "I have the occasional nightmare, if I'm dealing with a particularly bad case, but usually I don't dream of anything—I haven't for a long time, anyway."

"How about sleep, in general?"

Ryan uncrossed and re-crossed his legs. "Patchy," he admitted. "I'm getting a few hours a night, if I'm lucky."

"Some is better than none," Alex said. "You're under extreme stress at the moment, which you're managing well, so the fact you're not getting as much sleep as normal is to be expected. You won't be able to see a doctor, just now—would you like me to put my professional hat on and prescribe some sleeping tablets for the short term?"

"No thanks," Ryan decided. "I appreciate the offer, and the thought of a full night's rest is tempting, but I need to be in command of my faculties at any time, day or night. I can catch up on sleep when this is all over."

Alex nodded and hoped that would be soon.

"It's the *guilt* that haunts me," Ryan said, and his voice rang around the marble walls. "Knowing that if my father hadn't travelled north, he would never have been killed—and he only travelled because of the threat to my life. My choice of profession is what brought us here, and it's my fault he's lying across from us, now."

Alex listened, and wished he could wave a magic wand to take away the pain, but all he had was kind words and compassion. "You know, the inscription over there tells me that your father won one of the highest honours for gallantry," he said. "It also tells me he was one of the most senior diplomats in the country, having been an ambassador to France. He was honoured for his public service, and that's aside from anything he might have done in his role as head of the household here—as a father, a husband or anything else."

Ryan felt tears burn the back of his eyes, and he looked up at the domed ceiling, blinking them away. "He was all of those things," he replied softly.

"If he was, doesn't it seem likely he'd have wanted to die in the line of what he considered his duty—protecting the people most precious to him?"

Ryan thought of the man his father had been, and of how he'd demonised him for so many years, before he'd been old enough to understand the burden he carried each day. "He always wanted his death to mean something," he said, remembering a conversation he'd once had with Charles Ryan, over a dram or two of a very fine malt whiskey. "He said he never wanted to die without his faculties or with dementia, simply to be able to say he'd lived to a hundred and ten. He never wanted to go gentle into that good night."

Alex had seen how Alzheimer's and dementia could ravage people, and rob them of happy memories. He was hopeful of new treatments being approved in the next few years but, for those who'd already passed the point of no return, it was small comfort.

"Anger is the other overriding emotion I feel," Ryan admitted, since he was on a roll. "I don't want to be stuck here, Alex. I left home to make something of myself, and to be of service in my own way. This place has been a haven for us, but it's also a gilded cage. A big, beautiful, ostentatious cage."

"It sounds to me like your anger is derived from a loss of control," Alex remarked. "So much is out of your hands, at the moment, and so much has been *taken*."

Ryan stood up and began to pace around, no longer able to sit still. "I feel trapped," he said. "I know it's the safest thing, but I want to be out there, on the ground, hunting the bastard down."

"There's more than one way to snare a tiger," Alex said. "As for feeling trapped, that's a question of perspective. You could use this time at your childhood home to do what you've always said you didn't quite manage to do, while your father was alive."

"What's that?" Ryan asked.

"Get to know him."

CHAPTER 23

The HardBody Gym was exactly what Jack and Charlie imagined it would be. That is to say, industrial in an affectatious, deliberate sort of way, and filled with what people might once have called 'yuppies' and Phillips had always called 'dingbats'—with all the gear and no idea. This was no place for those wishing to lose weight, or to better themselves in a quiet, ordinary way; it was a place to be seen, and to sculpt bodies that were far above the norm.

The two detectives stood in the foyer, with its black-painted walls and garish, warehouse-style strip lights, and found themselves stricken by sensory overload.

"I don't know where to look first," Charlie said.

Every available wall was plastered with posters featuring motivational quotes, taken mostly from the *Rocky* franchise, while loud 'power' music leaked out of the main gym area, through a set of steel doors on the other side of an electronic gate positioned beside the reception desk. People in tight clothing seemed to be everywhere: milling around the foyer chatting and drinking water or some other protein-based drink; on television screens that streamed live classes that were running in one of the studios; and not to mention on the wall of framed 'Member of the Month' pictures, each featuring someone who'd pumped their muscles or lost more of their BMI than any other member in the past four-week period, and therefore had every right to look as jammy as they did.

"At least I know where to come when the midlife crisis hits," Jack said. "I wonder what the ratio of divorcees per square metre is, in here—"

Charlie was about to rebuke him for making uncharitable assumptions about the demographic, but then caught the tail end of a conversation being held by three men standing nearby, in which one of them declared he'd found, 'a second Jenny, but younger and fitter' while another warned him about younger second wives wanting more children, which should be avoided at all costs.

"Now, I remember why I didn't join this gym," she muttered. "Come on, let's see if we can find someone who knows George Masters or Stacey Hitchens."

"That shouldn't be too hard," Jack said, and pointed at the 'Member of the Month' display, where both George and Stacey's smiling faces had been mounted on the wall over the previous months.

They made their way over to the reception desk, which was staffed by a woman of around nineteen or twenty alongside a male colleague several years older. Both were dressed in branded 'HardBody' clothing which, to Charlie's eye, had been cut deliberately low in the bust area for the female staff, and deliberately tight in the torso area for male staff. There didn't appear to be any middle ground.

"Hi!" the woman said, and gave them a blinding smile. "Can I help you?"

"Yes," Charlie said, and showed her warrant card. "Can we speak with the manager?"

The woman, who turned out to be called Kayla, widened her eyes and then nodded.

"Yes, of course," she said, and called over to her colleague, who'd just finished dealing with a membership enquiry.

"Everything all right, Kayla?"

"Yeah, thanks Steve, have you got a minute? This is, er—sorry, what did you say your names were?"

"DC Reed, and DC Lowerson, from Northumbria CID," Jack said.

"DC Reed and DC Lowerson, from Northumbria CID," she parroted. "They want to speak to the manager."

"Well, you've found him," Steve said. "I'll take it from here."

He gave Kayla's spandex-covered arse a pat, as she moved away. "Why don't we go into my office?" he suggested, keeping a friendly smile on his face for the benefit of some of the gym's nosier members, who were craning their necks to try to eavesdrop.

He stepped out of the reception area, and they followed Steve's musclebound form to a door across the foyer, also painted in black but with the word 'MANAGER' on the front, in bold, graffiti-style lettering.

"How can I help you both?" he said, once the door was firmly shut.

Jack opened his mouth to reply, but was forestalled.

"Where are my manners?" Steve said, moving across to a small fridge and coffee station. "Would either of you like a drink? Maybe a smoothie?"

"Do you have any Green Power?" Charlie asked him.

"I do, indeed," he said, without pause. "We're all big fans of it, around here."

Steve didn't bother to mention that, as an approved supplier, they got a nice little affiliate income from the manufacturer if they pushed it to their members.

He began to reach for a sachet, but Charlie stopped him.

"Actually Steve—what was your second name?"

"Purdie," he replied.

She made a note. "Actually, Steve, we're both fine for a drink," Charlie continued. "We're here because we're investigating the death of one of your members—George Masters. Did you know him?"

"George? Yeah, of course," Steve said, and took a seat behind his desk, spreading his legs as wide as they could possibly go. "We were all really shocked when we heard the news—" He broke off, and gave Charlie a smile. "Wait a minute, don't I recognise you from somewhere?"

"I don't think so," she said, in a clipped tone.

"No, I definitely recognise you...did you used to be a member here?"

"*No*," she said, with barely concealed impatience. "I used to live in Alnwick, so it's possible you saw me around town."

"That's it," he said, and clicked his fingers. "You used to wear a uniform, then. Nice to see you out of it, now." He gave her a ludicrous wink. "You know, if you're interested in joining up, we've got ten per cent off this month for public sector workers. I could, ah, bump that up to twenty per cent, since I'm the manager—"

"As DC Reed has already informed you, she's no longer based in the area," Jack said. "Even if she were, we aren't allowed to accept freebies or discounts in the course of performing our public duty."

Charlie frowned at Jack, wondering where he'd ever got the impression that she was a woman who couldn't speak for herself.

"Sorry," the other man said. "I wouldn't want you to think I was trying to, er, you know—"

"Don't worry about it," Charlie said, briskly. "Now, turning back to the matter in hand. You were telling me you knew George Masters?"

"Yeah." Steve nodded. "Right, yeah. He started at the gym a few years ago, then we didn't see him for a while because he got married and all that. But then, about a year ago, he started up his membership again and we saw him around four, five times a week."

"How well did you know him?" Jack said.

"Just in passing," Steve replied. "He came along to a few of our social nights, and he was one of our regulars, as I've said."

"Do you happen to know if he was a fan of those green drinks?" Charlie said, and nodded towards his stash of Green Power.

"I don't know," Steve replied. "Every time I saw him, George was drinking water, because he complained a few times about the water cooler being empty. It's changed by an outside company, who can be a bit unreliable."

"What did you think of him, in general?" Jack asked.

Steve shrugged his Atlas-like shoulders. "Seemed a decent bloke," he said. "I know he ran an estate agency business, and quite a few of our members used it to buy or sell houses around here, without any complaints. He was popular—"

"With anybody in particular?"

For the first time, Steve became a bit cagey. "He was friendly with *everyone*," he replied. "George is married with a baby at home, you know."

"We *do* know, which is how we also know Mr Masters spent so much time here, rather than at home changing nappies," Charlie replied. "Any idea why that might have been?"

Steve shook his head. "Must've wanted to get into shape or let off steam," he said. "Those first few months of parenting can be rough, can't they? Like I say, I didn't really know him very well, although I could ask Fiona to come in and talk to you after she's finished with her private client. She was his personal trainer, for a while, so she might be in a better position to tell you more about him."

"That would be very helpful, thank you," Charlie said. "In the meantime, can you tell us anything about another one of your members, Stacey Hitchens?"

"What does she have to do with George's death?"

"We're trying to find the answer to that question, Mr Purdie," Jack said. "Did you ever see the two of them together?"

"Well, I'm sure I've seen them talking once or twice," Steve said. "But then, all our members chat amongst themselves and make friends that way. We're a very friendly club."

"I'm sure," Jack said. "Did you ever happen to see Stacey drinking Green Power?"

Steve thought about it, and nodded. "Yeah, I've seen her necking it, once or twice," he said, and began to worry. "Look, has something happened to her? Why do you keep asking me about the Green Power drinks?"

"Ms Hitchens is very ill but still alive—just," Charlie added. "We believe she may have ingested the same poison as Mr Masters."

"*Poison*? And...you think it was something in the Green Power?" Steve said, and his knees begin to shake beneath the desk as he imagined his business going up in a puff of green smoke.

"Yes, we're exploring that theory," Charlie told him. "Could you tell us when Mr Masters and Ms Hitchens last visited the gym here?"

Steve pulled himself together, and nodded. "Yes, um...yes, I can do that," he said, logging onto his computer. "Give me a minute to check the database for their membership numbers, then I'll cross-check to see when they last scanned in."

They waited while he located the information, feeling uncomfortable in the stuffy office with its ripe scent of stale sweat and the half-eaten tuna sandwich wafting from a bin beside his desk.

"Looking at the system, I can see the last time George came to the gym was Friday morning at nine-fifteen, and Stacey was last here on Sunday morning, first thing when we opened, at seven o'clock."

"Are you able to see when they were both at the gym at the same time?" Charlie asked, and Jack smiled across at her, having had the same thought himself.

Steve ran a hand over his head, which was closely cropped to hide a badly receding hairline and slicked with sweat, which shone beneath the glare of the strip lights. "Yes…give me another minute."

He performed some nifty searches.

"Should I—I mean, am I allowed to give you this information?" he asked, and peered at them above his laptop. "Do I need a lawyer?"

"I don't know, Mr Purdie, do *you* think you need a lawyer?" Jack replied. "Do you have some incriminating information you feel you should tell us?"

"*What*? No—I—no! I was just wondering whether you're supposed to have a warrant for this information or…something?"

It was a common thing for civilians to have absolutely no idea how the legal system worked—or indeed how the police actually policed—and, most of the time, it didn't matter. However, when a sudden interest in police procedure threatened to derail an active investigation that was already time-sensitive, they had to admit, it was hard to keep a sense of humour about it all.

"No," Charlie said, barely keeping the irritation from her voice. "We don't need a warrant for this information, because we're seeking to prevent the loss of further life. I'm sure you want to help us with that goal, Mr Purdie, rather than being in any way responsible for delaying a police investigation that could, in turn, cause further deaths?"

"No, no," he assured them, waving his hands in a kind of flapping motion that was entirely at odds with his persona. "I can tell you that George and Stacey happened to be here at the gym, at the same time, quite a lot over the past few weeks. They happened to come in at the same time, just after seven on Tuesday mornings and around six-thirty in the evening on Thursdays."

"Is it common for people to coordinate their gym schedules like that?"

"I suppose, when people make friends, they might start coming to the gym together," Steve said. "People sometimes spot each other, if they're lifting weights."

"Or if they're having an affair?" Charlie suggested.

Steve shifted uncomfortably in his chair. "It's possible," he admitted. "Look, I'm not going to pretend some of our members don't have relationships outside of the gym. Most of the people who come here have a lot in common, so it's a solid foundation."

Just then, there came a knock at the door, and an attractive young woman stuck her head inside. "Steve, have you—oh! Sorry, I didn't realise you were in a meeting. I'll catch you later."

"Just a sec, Fiona! I was going to come and look for you."

She stepped inside, and they were treated to another HardBody advert for beach-ready physique.

"These two visitors are from Northumbria CID," Steve said. "DC Lowerson and DC Reed, meet one of our best personal trainers, Fiona Duncan."

Jack told himself he wouldn't have been a heterosexual man if he hadn't noticed her long, tanned legs showcased by a pair of teeny, tiny hotpants, or the fact she had...well, an impressive set of lungs, as his dad might have said. Conscious that drooling was unbecoming, he looked away—straight into Charlie's knowing eyes.

She raised an eyebrow, and he felt a flush creep over his neck.

"A bit hot under the collar?" she asked.

"It *is* warm in here," Steve said, having missed her undertone. "Let me crack open the window."

"Did you say, 'CID'?" Fiona asked, while he grappled with the latch on an old window.

"Unfortunately, we're currently investigating Mr Masters' death as a possible murder," Charlie replied, and Fiona raised a hand to her mouth.

"Oh, my God," she said, and looked across at Steve. "Who'd want to murder George? He was just an ordinary guy...a family man."

"Anything you can tell us about him would be useful," Jack said, keeping his eyes firmly on his notebook. "We're trying to build up a picture."

She nodded. "Sure, I'm happy to help, if I can. I don't know what to tell you, though. He was a nice guy, always on time for our PT sessions, and he worked hard to improve himself," she said. "He occasionally slipped off the wagon and had a kebab, but—"

"We were thinking more of his character," Charlie said. "People often confide in their personal trainers, their hairdressers and that sort of thing, so it's possible he might have told you a bit about his life. For instance, do you know if anything was worrying him?"

Fiona thought about it, and then shook her head. "Not really," she replied. "I mean, he was sometimes tired, what with having a young baby in the house...and occasionally, he'd talk about a difficult client or something like that. In general, though, he seemed pretty happy."

"How about his home life?" Charlie said. "Did you get the impression he was a happily married man?"

"He seemed that way."

She didn't elaborate, so they moved to the next line of questioning.

"Do you know a member called Stacey Hitchens?" Jack asked.

"Stacey? Sure, I had a couple of sessions with her, a few months back. Why?"

"We believe Ms Hitchens might have been poisoned, along with Mr Masters," Jack replied. "We're trying to figure out if there's a connection between them. It's a sensitive question, but, to your knowledge, was there anything going on between George and Stacey?"

"You mean—like, an affair?"

"Yes, like an affair."

She shook her head, and the ponytail swished at her back. "No, as I say, George was a family man." She looked as if she was about to say something more, then thought better of it.

"Fiona? Is there something you feel we should know?" Charlie pressed her.

"Well…okay, look, I don't want to seem bitchy, but…it wouldn't surprise me, if Stacey had tried it on with George," she said, in a rush of words. "Some women aren't put off by a wedding ring, and there are quite a few prowling around, on the lookout, in here."

Charlie noticed that Steve began to play with his own wedding ring. "On the lookout?" she queried.

"You know, for a successful older guy," Fiona said, with a shrug. "There are plenty of them looking for a younger woman, too."

"You don't think George was one of them?"

She shook her head. "No, but you never know. Stacey might've been persuasive."

They asked a few more questions, before Jack closed his notebook.

"Thank you, you've both been very helpful."

"Listen, about the Green Power," Steve said. "Do you really think there was something off about it?"

"We know there was," Jack replied. "At this stage, we can't be certain that the poison didn't come from a contaminated batch, which George and Stacey might both have stumbled across. That being the case, we'd like to take some samples from whatever is made publicly available to members here, and we'd advise that you stop selling it, immediately."

Steve nodded, and made a mental note to put his lawyer on notice of any forthcoming claims.

"I drank some, this morning," Fiona said. "Should I go to the hospital and have myself checked out?"

"I did, too," Steve said, feeling queasy at the thought. "Maybe we should—"

"The symptoms are very obvious," Charlie told them. "George and Stacey both experienced severe breathing difficulties, abdominal cramps and blurred vision, among other things. If you'd ingested any of the same toxins, you'd most likely be suffering the effects of it by now."

Or you'd be dead.

CHAPTER 24

"Sing along if you know it!"

Denise MacKenzie leaned back in her chair and watched her husband belt out the chorus and jiggle his hips in time to an old Diana Ross tune, which only he could hear.

"You know, Frank, it's a mystery to me why nobody from *Britain's Got Talent* has come knockin' on the door."

"You and me both, pet," came the reply. "With pipes like these, I should've been packin' out arenas."

She grinned, and took the cup of tea he offered. "I'll have to head off to collect Samantha from school in about half an hour, but I was hoping to catch Jack and Mel—I mean—" She clapped a hand over her mouth. "I meant to say, Charlie—oh, *God*! I hope I don't put my foot in it while either of them is here. I don't usually mix people's names up, like that, but this Godforsaken perimenopause has got me all over the place."

Wisely, Phillips kept his trap shut.

"They don't look anything alike," she continued, as she and Frank made their way back to their open plan office, from the break room. "I suppose I'm just used to seeing Mel around the place."

"Aye, it's easily done," he said, taking a slurp of his own tea, and managing to spill some down the front of his chin. "Bugger."

"He still hasn't heard from her."

"Who?"

MacKenzie let out a frustrated breath. "*Mel*," she said. "Who d' you think I'm talking about? The Virgin Mary?"

He slurped more of his tea. "It's hard on the lad," he said. "Y'nah, Mel told him to move on, when she left to go travellin'. It's Jack that's holdin' the candle for her."

"He loves her," MacKenzie murmured.

"Mel's a lovely lass, and what happened to her was awful," he said. "But, if she doesn't want to come back, or carry on a relationship…" Frank made a sweeping gesture with his mug. "He's got a life to live, that's all I'm sayin'. There's plenty o' fish in the sea, and some o' them might be swimmin' right under his nose."

She gave him a pointed look. "I seem to recall, it took you long enough to see *this* fish swimmin' in circles around you, Frank Phillips."

"I was deaf, dumb and blind," he said. "Blame it on the peri-*man*-o-pause."

"You're still dumb," she muttered.

"Lucky for me, you love big, dumb animals. Speakin' o' which, here comes another one."

They turned to see Jack Lowerson entering the room, with Charlie not far behind him.

"Afternoon!" Phillips said, and raised his cup to the pair of them. "Where've you two been gallivantin' off to, then?"

"Alnwick," Charlie said, pulling out her chair. "We had a look around the Poison Garden, and managed to check out the gym where both poison victims were members. I think we came away with some useful information."

"Interestin' place, the Poison Garden," Phillips said, innocently. "Apparently, you get some numpties who go arse over tit, before they've even made it past the daffodils—"

Jack turned to Charlie. "You told them!"

"The first thing I did was ring Frank," she admitted, with a cackle. "Some gossip is just too good to keep to yourself."

Jack couldn't argue with that, considering he'd have done the same thing himself. "This means *war*," he said, with as much menace as he could muster at three o'clock on a Monday afternoon.

MacKenzie watched their playful rapport, and caught Frank's eye. "So," she said, turning the conversation back to business. "How's the investigation coming along?"

"Well, we know that both George Masters and Stacey Hitchens ingested the same poisons," Jack said. "Stacey's still holding on, which is good, but we can't count any chickens yet. We've just come from the hospital, where we dropped off some more samples we took from the gym in Alnwick, and Pinter told us the results of the toxicology analysis on the contents of Masters' stomach. The lab found high levels of ricin and aconite, which tallies with the ricin and aconite they found in Stacey's green health drink."

"Have you been able to find the source?" MacKenzie asked.

"We're fairly certain both victims ingested the poison while drinking a health drink called 'Green Power'," Charlie said. "As Jack says, we've already found the shaker cup Stacey drank from, containing the poisons, but unfortunately we think whichever vessel George used was washed up at home before we had a chance to find it."

"In terms of how the poison found its way into whichever vessel was used, that's another question," Jack said, and ran a tired hand over the hair that was growing too long over his forehead.

Charlie's eyes followed the action, until she dragged them away. "Um, yeah, that's right," she said, distractedly. "We've confiscated all the sachets of Green Power we could find, at both of their houses, and any that were plausibly at risk of having been contaminated at the gym, too. The lab guys are analysing them all, now, but it'll take days to get through it all."

"Was there any link between Stacey and George?" MacKenzie asked.

"Not really—aside from the fact they attended the same gym," Charlie said. "We've explored the possibility of a relationship between them, but there's no hard evidence to support that theory at the moment; only the circumstantial evidence of them both having accessed the facilities at around the same time, on the same days of the week, which could be coincidence or platonic friendship."

"Which means, you could have two completely unconnected victims who happened to ingest poison from the same contaminated batch of Green Power," MacKenzie said. "Most likely, obtained via the gym they both frequented."

"We can't rule out that possibility," Jack agreed.

"In which case, you know what you've got to do," Phillips said. "You've got to pick up the phone and speak to Environmental Health, and the Food Standards Agency. There's no evidence of widespread contamination yet, but you can't take risks with public health, not when there's even a remote possibility of a whole batch havin' been contaminated. For all we know, someone else is drinkin' from the same bad powder, and we'll be gettin' another call from the hospital."

"Frank's right," MacKenzie said. "Another thing I'd suggest you do, right now, is get in touch with the supplier and let them know there's a potential problem. They sometimes send out their sachets direct to people's homes, don't they?"

Jack nodded. "Masters had a home subscription and, judging by the number of sachets at Stacey's house and in her desk drawer, she also had a subscription. That being said, the gym push the brand as an affiliate, and sell individual sachets over the counter. We've already taken any open ones from the members' break room, and the manager has put a stop to all sales, and removed any sachets from public reach."

"Good thinking," MacKenzie said. "It begs the question how both Stacey and George happened to ingest a poisoned batch, if their Green Power supply came through the post, but perhaps their delivery came from the same bad batch?"

"There are still a lot of unanswered questions," Charlie agreed. "But, I think you're right, we need to contact the supplier and put them on notice. They should stop sending out any further deliveries until everything has been cleared up."

"They won't like it," Phillips said. "They'll lose a bit o' business, but that's the way the cookie crumbles. They'll lose a lot more, if the press get hold o' this."

Charlie made a small sound of dismay, and stood up in a hurry. "Sorry," she said. "I need to go and pick Ben up from nursery and, if I don't head off now, I'll be late." She turned to Jack. "Do you mind making those calls? I can log on this evening and catch up with the reports—"

Jack shooed her away. "Bugger off," he said, good-naturedly. "And don't worry about logging on, later. I've got this one."

Her whole body relaxed. "Thanks," she said, and gave him a smile before turning to the other two. "See you tomorrow!"

Jack watched her go, then turned back to his friends.

"I'll say 'goodbye', as well," MacKenzie said, and slipped on a worn black leather blazer that was one of Frank's personal favourites. "I promised Sam I'd take her for a pizza, tonight."

Before she left, she bestowed a kiss on her husband's upturned face, blew another for Jack, and then grabbed her bag.

"Say 'hello' to the walking dead, from me," she said.

"We will," Phillips promised, and calculated there was enough time for a second cuppa before their conference call with Ryan.

CHAPTER 25

Fifteen minutes later, Ryan shut the door to his father's study, settled himself at the old desk, and took out another burner mobile. He keyed in a number he knew by rote, and waited for it to be answered by a voice he knew as well as his own.

"Is that the underworld callin'?"

Ryan grinned. "Yeah, and I've got a message for you, from the Devil. He says you owe him at least seven lives," he drawled. "He's wondering when you're planning on paying up?"

"Tell him he'll have to wait," Phillips replied. "I've got a lot o' livin' to do, yet, and that includes goin' to Glastonbury next year."

"I didn't know you were a festival goer?" Jack remarked, since they'd put the call on speaker in one of the meeting rooms. "I can't see you in a tent, Frank."

"I'll have you know, I'm a whizz at puttin' tents up."

"How about putting them back down again?" Ryan asked.

"That's entirely beside the point," Phillips said. "Anyway, never mind all that. How's the wind blowin' down in Devon?"

"Fair, for now," Ryan replied, and it was true both literally and metaphorically, although he had the oddest sensation they were only experiencing the calm before a storm. "Alex Gregory is visiting us, for a night or two."

"Oh, aye? What does he make of it all?" Phillips asked, having met the criminal profiler several times and admired his talent for reading the darkest of minds.

"He thinks we're looking for someone who's lost faith in the criminal justice system," Ryan said. "A person who was wronged, somehow, but received no justice—or, at least, not the kind of justice they hoped for. The network they've created encourages anarchy and a disregard for basic societal norms, which also suggests they're unlikely to feel any remorse, or be susceptible to any of the usual appeals to better nature."

"D' you think it could be someone who was wrongfully imprisoned?" Jack asked.

"Possibly," Ryan said. "Or, more likely, someone who was the victim of a violent crime, and whose attacker walked free, or was given a lesser punishment than they feel he or she deserved? The possibilities are almost endless and, sadly, the number of potential examples of these cases is exponential. It would take our full team of staff several months to trawl through a list of all those wronged families or victims, interview each of them and investigate them individually."

"In other words, we need some other way to narrow it down," Phillips said. "It doesn't help that the list of potential victims is gettin' longer by the day, as well. I've been gettin' leads through from other divisions across the country, all of them with historic cases that look as though they connect to this murder network."

"DCI Hassan tells me there's at least forty-eight cases over the past six years which fit the bill," Ryan added. "This thing is big, and getting bigger all the time, but if we can trace things back to the beginning, we can start looking for any cases of perceived injustice, or wrongful arrest around that timescale. It might be the link that changes everything."

"Aye, well the team here's found ten more cases in the North East, and counting," Phillips said. "Historic cases are bad enough, but we could do with makin' sure there aren't any more new ones."

"I've asked Hassan to speak to Digital Forensics at the Met, to see if they can come up with a new link to embed on the *Northern Fisherman* website," Ryan said. "The one advantage we have is that whoever is behind this network doesn't know how much *we* know. The fact they're still posting classified ads on the site suggests they think they've flown beneath our radar. We can use that to our advantage."

"Are they stupid or just cocky?" Jack wondered aloud.

"Both," Ryan said. "Or, they don't care whether we find them, which is an even more interesting possibility. Sometimes, when a killer's escalated to the point of being unable to stop themselves, they start making deliberate mistakes so that we'll be more likely to catch them and forcibly stop them from killing again."

"Findin' the ones who started this whole shebang is one thing," Phillips said. "Doin' the dogsbody work for every single murder investigation is another. I don't think we'll finish investigatin' every one of these historic murders before I've retired."

"Look on the bright side," Ryan said. "The government keep putting the retirement age back, so you'll probably still be on active duty when you're ninety. That should give us plenty of time to see this through."

"Oh, aye, I feel much better about it, now."

Ryan smiled to himself, and watched dust motes dance on the air in his father's old room. "What about the—" He stopped, and swallowed the hard lump in his throat. "What about the shooting? Have there been any developments, there?"

"Not so far, lad," Phillips was sorry to report. "Mind you, Faulkner's like a dog with a bone. He's determined to find somethin' that'll help the case, and he says it's because you were such a good friend to him. He doesn't want to let you down."

Ryan sighed. "I hate having to lie to old friends," he said.

"Aye, well, you can make it up to him once you're back in the land of the livin'," Phillips said. "We've got to be sure you make it there, first."

"I know," Ryan said, and he turned to look outside the window, across the gardens to where his security team patrolled the perimeter. "Something has to give, Frank, and I have a feeling we won't have to wait too long for that to happen."

Lowerson and Phillips heard the fear Ryan was unwilling to speak aloud, and wished there was more they could do.

"Like Toto said, just hold the line," Phillips said, being of the firm view that most of life's best advice could be found in songs from the eighties.

"I'm holding on, Frank. There isn't anything else I can do."

While Eve offered to bathe her granddaughter before bed and Gregory took a call from his friend and colleague in criminal profiling, Professor Douglas, Anna took herself off to one of the smaller rooms in the house and settled herself at an elegant antique writing table with her laptop. Every day, she tried to write a little more of her second novel, while her first completed manuscript was being edited and proofread ahead of its grand publication—whenever that may be. Writing had become a welcome distraction, of late, providing her with a much-needed escape from the omnipresent worry that, one of these days, her husband would suffer the same fate as his father.

Anna propped her chin on her hands as she looked out of an enormous window facing the driveway outside. The sun had dipped behind the branches of the old oak trees, casting a dappled light through the leaves in one last hurrah before nightfall. She watched the changing skies before anxiety spoiled the moment, and she began to imagine every long shadow and every movement in the undergrowth was a person waiting to rip apart everything she held dear.

"Knock, knock," a voice said, from behind her.

Anna turned to find Ryan standing there, his tall body resting against the panelled doorframe. She experienced a frisson, deep in her belly, at the very sight of him. Ten years together and the excitement hadn't diminished; if anything, her love for him only grew stronger with the passage of time.

"Come in," she said.

"Am I disturbing you again?" he said, coming to wrap his arms around her.

"I wasn't making much progress on this book, anyway."

He kissed her neck, then took a seat on one of the occasional chairs nearby. "Want to talk about it?"

"Oh, it's nothing important," she said.

"Your work is always important," he said quietly. "I know that mine often intrudes into our lives, but that shouldn't diminish anything that you do, or that you want to achieve. I'll do everything I can to help."

And that, she thought, *was exactly why her love for him continued to grow.*

"I'm just finding it hard to concentrate, at the moment."

"I know," he said, and ran an agitated hand through his mop of black hair. "It's hard to think about anything else. But let's try. Have you thought any more about publishing your first book?"

Anna shook her head. "Now that it's written, I don't know that I'm ready for anyone to read it," she said, and gave a self-deprecating laugh. "I know, that sounds ridiculous."

"It's a great story," Ryan told her. "You know I'd never lie to you."

"I know, but these things are subjective," Anna said. "You're biased in my favour."

"Not about some things," he said. "I might think you're the most wonderful person in the world, but I know how much this new career means to you, so I would never be less than honest with you about your work, just as I know you would be scrupulously honest with me about mine."

Anna nodded, feeling a little better about things. "Well, if I decide to try publishing independently, rather than traditionally, then the next stage would be to think about a design for the cover of my book. I'm not sure what would work best."

"Why don't we have a look online, and compare other books in the same genre, to see what kind of thing is popular?"

"Oh, that's a good idea," she said, and turned back to her laptop to perform a search. "Mine is a bit of a supernatural murder mystery, based around Lindisfarne, as you know..."

Her voice trailed off, as her eye scanned the thumbnail images of a number of books in that genre, and fell upon one in particular.

"Ryan."

He caught a note in her voice, and came to his feet. "What's wrong?"

"Would you—would you come and look at this, please? Tell me if I'm being a bit paranoid."

He came to lean over her shoulder, and saw that she'd found a book entitled *Island Mystery,* written by Lin Oldman.

"Isn't that the author who ran that creative writing session you went to?"

Anna nodded. "Read the description," she whispered.

His eye dropped to a description of the book, and his eyes turned an angry shade of grey. "What the *hell*?" he said, and fiddled with the touchpad to select the option to read an excerpt of the book before purchasing.

Together, they read the first few pages, until they could stomach no more.

"I don't believe this," Ryan growled. "It's your book—almost word for word!"

"She's changed a few words, here and there, and fiddled with the sentence structure," Anna said quietly. "But, yes, I think that's my story."

Her voice broke, and Ryan took her in his arms. "They can't possibly get away with this," he said. "It's so flagrant."

"They'll say it's a coincidence," Anna said. "Oldman is known in the industry, whereas I'm not. Nobody would ever believe she'd do this."

Ryan muttered a few choice words. "They'll believe it, when I tell them," he said. "That's no coincidence. How did she get her hands on your manuscript?"

"The creative writing session," Anna said, dully. "I left a hard copy of the manuscript, and only realised after I'd left. When I rang the library to ask about it, they said they couldn't find anything lying around, so I assumed I'd made a mistake, or somebody had binned it. I never imagined anyone could be so underhand as to steal it."

"That's because you're a good person," Ryan said. "Your mind doesn't automatically think of ways to screw people over."

"I guess that's it, then—"

Ryan took her shoulders in his hands, and looked deeply into her eyes.

"No, it *isn't*," he said. "As soon as this is all over, I'm going to call the best intellectual property lawyer I can find, and we'll have this knock-off taken down faster than you can say, 'Thieving Bastard'."

Anna wanted to believe him, but she knew that the world wasn't always a fair place.

Some battles, you just didn't win.

CHAPTER 26

Jack Lowerson was the last person to leave the office, barring the cleaning team who were on their way in to begin an evening shift wiping away the worst of the day's grime. The streets were quiet at that time of night, with most of the working population having already made their way home, leaving only stragglers like himself to drive through the Tyne Tunnel and on towards the village of East Boldon.

It was a pretty place with a proud history, and had experienced a resurgence of gentrification in recent times. He and Melanie had purchased their house just as the area was 'on the up' and, after giving it a bit of TLC, he thought they'd made a lovely home together.

But that was before.

It was hard to forget Mel standing beside the living room window, watching the street outside with nervous eyes, or the nights when she'd stayed awake on the sofa, trawling over old articles and case summaries as her body and mind wasted away to stress and disorder. It had been hard, but he'd never blamed her; the loss of a loved one to murder was bad enough, but almost losing your own life to the very same murderer was more than many people could bear. It was no wonder she'd suffered post-traumatic stress disorder, and his only wish had been to help her recover.

The painful truth was that it was outside his control.

Coming home had been a lonely experience, during the months since Mel's departure. She'd taken most of her things and put them into storage, leaving only a few leftover items to remind him that he'd once had a partner in life, someone to come home to and confide in; someone to love and to care for.

Now, there was only the cat, Sir Pawsalot.

"Hello," he said, as the feline curled itself around his legs. "Sorry, I'm back a bit late. Are you hungry, hm?"

Jack had invested in an automatic feeder, which meant that the cat never went hungry in the event he was held up at work, but, from the look in its eye, you'd have been forgiven for thinking the animal had been on Phillips' cabbage diet.

Jack looked inside the fridge and selected a microwave meal. There was a time, not so long ago, when he'd enjoyed cooking, setting a table and eating a leisurely meal, but he hadn't felt the urge to make that kind of effort for himself.

It didn't seem worth the trouble.

The microwave pinged, and he emptied the contents of a vegetable curry onto a plate before sitting down at the little circular table in the dining area. Immediately, the quiet of the house surrounded him, and he decided to try the living room instead, where the television could provide some company while he ate, if only for a while.

He selected an old episode of *Friends* and wondered how his own circle was faring.

Then, he thought of Mel, and wondered whether she thought of him at all.

"Can't sleep?"

Charlie turned to find her mother standing in the kitchen doorway, dressed in the long towelling robe she'd given her the previous Christmas.

"Sorry, did I wake you?"

"No, love, I was already awake," she replied, and leaned on her walking stick as she made her way towards the table and chairs Jack had helped to set up.

"Here, let me give you a hand," Charlie said, and hurried over to take her arm. "Can I get you anything?"

"Only if you're making something for yourself," her mother replied.

"Are you feeling unwell?" Charlie asked, and reached for a small pan to warm some milk for cocoa.

"No, but these tablets are giving me a touch of insomnia," her mother replied. "I've tried everything, including reading football autobiographies, but nothing sends me to sleep."

"I could read from the Police and Criminal Evidence Guidelines, if you like."

Her mother smiled. "That won't be necessary," she said. "But I'm interested to hear about your day, if you have the energy."

Charlie began to stir cocoa into the milk, and turned the heat down on the hob. "We're investigating a suspected poisoning," she said. "Jack had to contact the supplier of a big brand of health drink, this evening, to ask them to stop distributing while our investigation is ongoing."

"Seems sensible," her mother replied.

"They weren't best pleased," Charlie said, and poured the chocolatey liquid into two cups. "Jack says—"

"You mention him quite a bit."

"Do I?"

"Mm hm," her mother said, and thanked her for the drink. "He must be special."

"He—" Charlie thought of her friend, of all the help he'd given her and the easy laughter they shared. "Yes, he is. I think you'd like him a lot."

"Perhaps you'll introduce us, one of these days?"

"It isn't like that, Mum. He is—or was—engaged, I think."

"Engaged isn't the same as being married."

"*Mum!*"

"I'm kidding," her mother said, and sighed inwardly. "So, he's just a friend, then?"

"A colleague and…yes, I suppose, a friend."

"A *good* friend, considering he helped to move everything in here and put up the furniture."

"Our relationship is strictly professional."

If she said it often enough, she might even convince herself.

"I just don't want to see you hurt, all over again," her mother said, and reached out a hand. "You deserve to find someone who can love you fully—and love Ben, like he was their own."

Charlie thought of her son, whose young life rested in her hands. "I wouldn't risk bringing anyone into his life who wasn't worthy," she said. "He's had enough disappointment."

"So have you."

Charlie said nothing, but gave her mother's hand a squeeze. "Come on," she said. "Let's try to get some sleep."

CHAPTER 27

Tuesday

"*Mum! Dad!* Wake up—we're going to be late!"

Frank and Denise sat bolt upright in the bed they shared, hair like haystacks and eyes clouded with sleep.

"What?" Denise mumbled. "What time is it?"

"Thought somebody was bein' murdered," Frank muttered, and fell back against the pillows.

"*Frank!*" Denise said, checking the time on the bedside clock. "Sam's right, we've slept in!"

"Couldn't've," he said, with his eyes closed. "I set an alarm, same as always."

"Well, there must've been a blip in the space-time continuum, because it's eight o'clock and we've got half an hour to get ready and get Sam to school!"

Frank opened a single eyelid. "Humph?"

"You heard me!" Denise said, and threw back the covers.

Galvanised, they raced into the bathroom, Denise to hurl herself beneath the shower spray while Frank watched in admiration—only to be sprayed himself, when she spotted him.

"Frank!"

"Alreet, alreet," he said, and began to brush his teeth—slowly—while continuing to enjoy the view reflected in the mirror above the sink. *Well*, he thought, it had to be an unspoken privilege of the marital union and, besides, he was sure he'd spotted her getting an eyeful while he was lathering up the Timotei.

And who could blame her?

"Swap!" Denise said, hopping out of the shower after a brief three-minute ritual. "You've got five minutes, max!"

Frank gave her what he considered to be his most alluring smile, took his time unbuttoning his tartan pyjamas—which he'd worn after their discussion about *Outlander*—and, upon stepping into the shower cubicle, applied a liberal amount of shower gel. He worked up an impressive lather, putting on a full show for his wife's enjoyment, only to turn around and find she'd already vacated the bathroom and was blasting her hair with the hairdryer, next door.

"I'm wasted around here," he said, and rinsed it all off.

Exactly five minutes later, he knotted a tie around his shirt collar, this time featuring a pattern of Northumbrian flags in shades of yellow and red. He found Denise racing around the kitchen, half a slice of toast clamped between her teeth as she poured coffee into two takeaway flasks for the road.

"Tfst," she said, and pointed towards another slice she'd buttered for him.

Frank thanked her and took a bite, wishing it had come with a dollop of marmalade.

"Okay, let's hit the road," Denise said. "Sam! Get your shoes on!"

They heard sniggering coming from the direction of the living room, and followed the sound. They found their daughter lying with her legs outstretched on the sofa, dressed in her uniform but appearing to be in no great rush whatsoever as she watched one of her favourite morning shows.

"*Oi*," Frank said. "What d'you think you're on—your granny's yacht?"

"Come on, we've got to hustle," Denise said, and started to turn back into the hallway until her eye caught the little clock in the bottom right corner of the television screen.

Seven-fifteen.

"Frank. Look at the time."

"I know, pet—"

"*Look at the time.*" Denise folded her arms, and jutted her chin towards the clock on the screen.

"Aye, it's seven fi—*eh*?" Frank took a few steps closer, to be sure he hadn't imagined it. "Are our clocks wrong?" he asked, and Denise cast her eyes heavenward.

"I think I know the source of the discrepancy," she said, and gave Sam the beady eye. "Very funny, young lady."

Frank looked at her. "You little monkey!" he said, and started to laugh.

"You should have *seen* the pair of you," Sam said. "I've never seen you move so fast!"

"Aye, well you'd better move fast, before I get my hands on you!"

With that, Frank wriggled his fingers to indicate a tickle fight was on the cards and, with a shriek, Samantha leapt off the sofa and ran from the room, laughing uproariously. Frank gave chase, and Denise smiled to herself as she took a seat on the sofa and switched the channel to the news while she enjoyed the rest of her coffee in peace.

An hour later, after the MacKenzie-Phillips clan had enjoyed a raucous morning of play-fighting and scrambled eggs, leisurely coffee and conversation, they waved Samantha off at the school gates and prepared to leave behind the joys of family time to face a harsher side to life altogether.

They parked in the staff car park and made their way towards the Pie Van for another medicinal coffee, spotting Charlie Reed heading for the main entrance and waving her across.

"Fancy a coffee?" Phillips asked.

Charlie smiled and thought, again, what a lovely team she'd wound up in. "Oh, thanks, Frank. I'll just have a breakfast tea."

"Go on and have a muffin, as well," he urged her. "Or an almond croissant?" His mouth watered at the prospect, but his will remained strong.

"No, I've already had breakfast," Charlie said.

"So?" Phillips argued. "You've gotta keep your strength up, y'know. It's hungry work, savin' lives and solvin' crimes."

"He's become a feeder, now that he's calorie counting," MacKenzie explained.

Charlie smiled. "I'm sure you've lost weight," she said, and it was true. He *had* slimmed down, quite a bit. "All that cabbage is paying off."

"Oh, aye, I knew someone'd tell you about that," Phillips complained. "Well, you'll be pleased to know, these rock-solid abs are one hundred percent cabbage free. I went on strike, the last time I was forced to eat the stuff, and, besides, the neighbours were startin' to complain."

He winked, to make her laugh.

"God, have mercy," MacKenzie said, and hid her eyes in embarrassment. "Excuse my husband, Charlie. He's got a way with words."

"That's what all the lasses say," came the quick reply. "D'you fancy that muffin, then? It's got blueberries in, so it's like havin' one of your five a day."

"Since you put it like that," Charlie said. "I'd better have one for my health."

"See?" Phillips said to MacKenzie. "I knew, the minute I met her, this lass was one of us."

He placed their order, and, while they waited for it to be made up, talk turned to murder.

"I heard from Neil Jones just now," Phillips said. "The Ministry of Defence finally came back and confirmed the explosives used in that car bombing at Frankland Prison were military grade, just as he thought."

"Any idea where they came from?" MacKenzie asked.

"Not yet," he replied. "Could be all manner of illegal sources, which we'd never trace in a million years, or something stolen from a military site…Jones is checking for any reports of stolen explosives, but, if they're smart, they'll have bought off the Dark Web, not from some legitimate source."

"Look out," Charlie said. "The Chief is on her way over, and she doesn't look happy."

They followed her line of sight and spotted Morrison striding towards them with an expression of extreme annoyance written all over her face.

"Hold my hand," Frank whispered to his wife. "I'm scared."

"Get a grip on yourself," she whispered back. "She's probably just coming over to get a coffee."

"I want a *word* with the three of you," Morrison said, without preamble. "In my office, in five minutes." She turned away—then, thinking better of it, paused to nab the muffin from Frank's hand before stalking off again.

"Okay, you might have been right to be scared," MacKenzie acknowledged.

"I've got an affinity with women," Frank said. "I just seem to know what they're thinking. It's a gift, really."

MacKenzie turned to him with an arch expression. "Is that so? What am I thinking now, all-seeing prophet that y'are?"

"That you'd like to give us a kiss?"

"Close, but no cigar."

"Well, it comes and goes."

CHAPTER 28

Four and a half minutes later, they stood in front of Morrison's desk, this time with the addition of Jack Lowerson, whom they'd intercepted in the corridor as he'd tried to make a run for it.

"You might well be thinking I look a little *tired* this morning," the Chief Constable said.

Phillips and Lowerson opened their mouths, and MacKenzie put a staying hand on both of their arms, to prevent whatever they'd been about to say—no good would come of it.

"That's because I took a personal call, in the early hours of this morning, from an extremely persistent American lawyer based in Tampa, Florida." Morrison lanced them all with a look. "Florida is five hours behind us," she added. "In case you were wondering."

Once again, MacKenzie gave a small shake of her head, to indicate the question had been rhetorical and did not require any smart alec responses.

"It turns out, the UK distributor of that health drink company, Green Power, contacted their head office in Tampa and told them that some detective in the North East of England had ordered them to stop selling their powder."

They looked amongst themselves, then back at her.

"I see they weren't mistaken about that," she said. "Well, I won't bother asking which of you made the call, because it hardly matters. What *matters* is that some trumped up tart was spouting a load of legal mumbo-jumbo at me, at a time when I should have been tucked up in bed, not being harangued by someone called Tammy Tuffman!"

"Sorry, ma'am," Denise said.

"The upshot is, according to Ms Tuffman, her client's powder is made in a medical-grade controlled facility in the United States and shipped around the world—tonnes of the stuff, every week—and no other problems have been reported. She's insisting on their supply resuming sale as normal and, what's more, she's demanding samples of the contaminated powder, threatening us with court injunctions and a multi-million-dollar lawsuit for unlawful restraint of trade. Oh, and a defamation claim, if the press hears about any of it." Morrison paused to check the clock on the wall. "All of this before nine o'clock," she said. "Not bad."

There was a short silence, during which they each considered alternative careers, should that lawsuit happen to go ahead, then Lowerson stepped forward.

"I was the one who spoke to the UK distributor, last night—" he said.

"No, I'm Spartacus," Phillips said. "We're all Spartacus, when it comes to somethin' like this, lad."

"That's great, Frank, but who's Spartacus?"

Phillips was astonished. "D'you mean to tell me, you've never seen one of the greatest films ever *made*?"

"Was it made before I was born?" Lowerson queried. "Because it helps if I was alive—"

"This isn't a film club!" Morrison almost roared. "You can talk about Kirk Douglas and classic cinema on your own time—which you'll all have a lot more of, if you carry on at this rate. Jack? What did you actually say to the UK distributor, when you spoke to them?"

"I explained we'd already had one death and another severe case of poisoning, both after drinking some of the Green Power, and that it might be advisable to stop selling the powder until we could sure that a full batch hadn't been contaminated, causing further risk to life."

Morrison considered his explanation, and relaxed slightly. "That puts a different complexion on matters," she said. "That was a sensible course of action, to protect public health, but, unfortunately, we don't have the power to order this company to stop supply with the evidence we have. It's a matter for the Food Standards Agency Enforcement Team, now—unless you have some reason to think there's any other connection between George Masters and Stacey Hitchens?"

"The only present connection is that they both attended the same gym in Alnwick," Charlie said. "The staff there have confirmed they both trained there at the same time, over the past few weeks. It's circumstantial, but—"

"It's a start," Morrison said, with a decisive nod. "Any suggestion of a personal relationship between the two victims?"

"Only inferences, at this point," Jack said. "No evidence whatsoever."

"See if you can find some, or rule out the possibility for good," Morrison suggested. "Then, report back to me. I want to be prepared the next time that attorney rings, which will probably be around three o'clock in the morning."

There were murmurs of assent.

"Right, then," she said. "I've got to call the legal department, to put them on notice of a possible claim, so it's probably best if you're nowhere within striking distance while I do that." She gave them a dangerous smile. "That means, piss off, the lot of you."

"Yes, ma'am—"

"Absolutely—"

"Yes—"

The four of them each babbled something unintelligible and made for the door, like rats fleeing a sinking ship.

———

In Devon, Ryan was reading a copy of *The Tiger Who Came to Tea* with Emma, when a call came through to the burner mobile in his pocket.

"Sorry, princess," he said, pressing a kiss to her cheek. "I'll finish the story with you soon, but I have to take this call because it's important."

Anna stepped in, scooping up their daughter and the book in her capable arms, before suggesting they make some cakes themselves in case a tiger should come to tea. This was met with excitement, and Ryan blew his wife a grateful kiss before answering the call.

"Yes?"

"Ryan? It's Hassan."

"Do you have any news for me?"

"Possibly," he said. "It could be nothin', or it could be somethin'."

"All right."

"Well, Chiyo's team in Digital Forensics has made some good progress, even since yesterday," Hassan said. "There were forty-eight potential cases fitting the bill, as of our last discussion…now, there are hundreds."

Hundreds? Ryan thought, horrified. "Is that nationwide?"

"Mostly the London catchment," Hassan was sorry to say. "Factor in the numbers we're getting in the provinces, and you're looking at *several* hundreds. They're all potential matches between classified ads in a print media database, which correspond with a death certificate from around the same time as the advert."

"Which publications have they appeared in?" Ryan asked.

"Obviously, you already know about *The Northern Fisherman* in your part of the world, and *The Weekly Wanderer,* which I was telling you about yesterday. Since then, Chiyo's found three more small magazine publications that are London based, and we've heard from colleagues around the country with details of seven small publications based in Devon and Cornwall, Wales, Somerset, Cheshire, Lancashire, Yorkshire, Midlothian and The Highlands." Hassan listed their names, which Ryan noted down. "There are bound to be more that come through," he said. "I'll admit that, at the start of this, I didn't really think this network or scheme or whatever you wanna call it was quite as big as you all seemed to think. I guess I didn't like to imagine somethin' so big could have slipped past us. It makes you realise how vulnerable the system is, after all."

"We're still fit for purpose," Ryan told him. "We could always use more staff, or more money, but until that utopian day comes around, we just need to manage ourselves and our resources to focus on the priorities."

"It won't be easy," Hassan warned his friend. "So far, the matching's been done with the help of computer search functions, but every one of those potential matches will need to be manually checked out. With such a large sample size, it's always possible some or all of those names are legitimate deaths, where people have happened to die shortly after placing a genuine ad. It's that kind of detail we need to look at."

"Did you speak to Chiyo about my idea for an embedded link with a tracker?"

"Yes, he thinks it's possible," Hassan replied. "He's got someone working on it, now."

They spoke for a while longer, until Ryan ended the call and immediately put another call through, this time to his friend in the north.

At his desk at Police Headquarters, Phillips spotted the 'NO CALLER ID' pop up on his smartphone, and remarked to the others about the number of cold calls he still received from solicitors looking to help him claim back mis-sold PPI insurance.

"You'd think all the cases would be done, by now," he muttered, and binned the call.

After a moment, it rang again.

He sighed, and decided to give the call centre operator a piece of his mind. "Now look," he said, as soon as he answered the phone. "I don't know how you got this number, but I don't want to claim back PPI or any other insurance. Nobody's mis-sold me anythin', so that's an end to it—"

"I don't know about that," Ryan said, once he could get a word in edgewise. "Whoever sold you that mountain bike saw you coming a mile off, for one thing."

"Oh! It's you—" Phillips said, and quickly left the room to find a quiet spot elsewhere.

Charlie watched him leave with a degree of interest, never having seen Frank behave in such a clandestine manner. On the other hand, he was at the age where a lot of men began to suffer issues with their prostate, so it was possible he'd taken a call from his local GP surgery, and he simply preferred to talk about his arse end without the rest of the office listening in.

Fair enough, really.

Phillips found a cupboard at the end of the corridor and ducked inside.

"Okay," he said, keeping his voice low. "What's up?"

"I've just spoken to John Hassan. The number of potential cases around the country is unbelievably high…at this rate, we'll be investigating every one of them for the next decade, unless we can get to the source. I was wondering how far back our Digital Forensics team have managed to go, based on classified ads at *The Northern Fisherman?*"

It was something Phillips could answer, having conversed with the team only minutes before.

"The magazine only went digital fairly recently, as you know—that was how Marcus Atherton was alerted to the unusual correlation between deaths and classifieds. He searched the name of some previous victims, and they flagged on the magazine's site."

"That's right."

"The team up here have been concentrating on hard copy records of the magazine before then, which is more labour intensive," Phillips said. "They've still uncovered plenty more potential names, going all the way back to June 2007."

"That's a long way back," Ryan muttered.

"Actually, there was a funny discrepancy that month," Phillips said. "Two names appeared in the June 2007 edition, and one of them was quite well known. One bloke, Edward Delaney, died of a drug overdose after advertising a selection of flies and fishing lures. Another one, Kyle Rodgers, died of a heart attack in what was presumed to be undiagnosed Sudden Death Syndrome, after advertising a top of the range fishing rod."

"It's unusual to have two names featuring in the same month, isn't it?"

"Well, Rodgers was a footballer who was known to like a bit o' fishing," Phillips pointed out. "He was a famous face, a local lad and all that. Could be a coincidence."

Ryan smiled to himself. "Knowing how I generally feel about coincidences, I think we should concentrate our efforts on those two cases," he said. "Unless the team update us with any earlier ones, they're currently the earliest we've found, and to have two of them in the same edition is strange. I want to know the full background, the police reports, the coroner's reports, media coverage…everything."

Phillips nodded. "Will do."

"Oh, and Frank?"

"What?"

"I heard that."

"Heard what?"

"A fart of such magnitude, it could have hit Factor Ten on the Richter Scale," Ryan said. "Wherever you're hiding, for God's sake just remember to crack open a window for the next poor sod who goes in."

"I had baked beans, this mornin'—"

"How *many*?" Ryan asked. "On second thought, never mind. Just try not to gas anyone, at least until I'm back in the office."

Phillips ended the call, grumbling about friends with better hearing than a bat, and looked around for a window in the little stationery cupboard.

There wasn't one.

The next person would just have to take their chances.

CHAPTER 29

"If I'd known we'd be spending so much time in Alnwick, I'd have saved myself the trouble of moving to Newcastle," Charlie said, as they motored northbound for the third day in a row. "I feel like I've never been away."

"Do you miss living in the countryside?" Jack asked, as they approached the slip road that would take them into Alnwick town centre.

"Yes and no," she said. "It's a beautiful place and the people are so friendly, but there aren't as many job opportunities. I have to do what's best for Ben—and my mother, too."

Jack glanced across at her from the passenger seat, and wondered if she ever did what was best for herself. "You work very hard," he said.

"Don't we all?" she replied, with a cheerful smile. "You worked late last night, and I know you won't be claiming overtime."

"I enjoy my work."

"So do I, but I enjoy lie-ins and lazy weekends more."

He conceded the point. "I guess the house has been a bit quiet without Mel," he said, as they turned into the car park. "It's lonely, so I've been spending a bit more time at my desk."

Just nod sympathetically, Charlie thought. *Or say something non-committal.*

"You'd always be welcome to come and have dinner with us," she said. "Any time you need a bit of company, or feel inclined to help put some pictures up..."

"Ah, *now* we get to the truth of the matter," he said, with a smile. "But, thanks, I might just take you up on that."

"I'm not much of a cook, but I can make about five things really well."

"And they are?"

"Macaroni cheese, Victoria sponge cake, fishfingers, banoffee pie, and any kind of soufflé."

"You're not much of a cook, but you can make a soufflé?"

"Weird, isn't it?"

They parked, and made their way towards the entrance of the Alnwick Garden, this time bypassing the tall iron gates of the Poison Garden in favour of the main entrance, which, Jack was relieved to see, didn't bear a skull and crossbones but rather a set of automatic glass doors leading to a large gift shop and the gardens beyond. There was a queue to enter, so they decided to use their official privilege to jump it and go in search of a manager.

"You should see some of the filthy looks we're getting," Charlie said.

"Just don't make eye contact with anyone," he said. "You know how much the Brits like to queue—we don't want to be responsible for starting a riot."

"That'd send Morrison right over the edge—"

"*Excuse me*! Sorry, but there's a *queue*." A woman bustled over with a determined smile on her face, prepared to dispatch them, if necessary.

"We're from Northumbria CID," Jack said, keeping his voice low. "We'd like to speak to the manager, please?"

She took her time checking their warrant cards, then held up a finger while she spoke into her radio. A moment later, another woman appeared from behind a side door.

"Thanks, Jan," she said, and turned to the pair of them. "I'm the duty manager, here. I understand you're from the police?"

"DC Reed and DC Lowerson," Charlie said. "Is there somewhere quiet we could talk?"

"Of course, please follow me." She led them back towards the side door, which led into an office. There was no space for any visitors' chairs, so they remained standing.

"I'm Hilary," she said. "How can I help you, today?"

"We're investigating what we believe to have been the murder of a local man," Jack said.

"George Masters? Yes, I heard about that," she said. "My husband's sister's daughter works as a receptionist at Masters Estate Agents, here in town, and she happened to mention it to her mother who mentioned it to Dave, who mentioned it to me."

They looked at each other, then back at her.

"That's quite an active grapevine," Jack said. "Did you happen to hear anything else about the late Mr Masters from your…niece, was it?"

"On my husband's side, yes. Well, according to her, he was a decent enough employer, but…" She pressed her lips together.

"But?" Charlie prompted.

"I don't like to speak ill of the dead."

"They're not here to complain about it," Jack said.

"Well, when you put it like that—I was only going to say, my niece thought George had a bit of a roving eye. A bit flirtatious around the office, that sort of thing."

"This is a bit of a delicate question, Hilary, but I'm afraid I do have to ask: do you think anything happened between your niece and Mr Masters?"

Hilary shook her head. "I can tell you Imogen—that's my niece—certainly never thought *twice* about him," she said, with a sniff. "She has a gorgeous boyfriend; he plays for the Newcastle Falcons, you know."

The Falcons were the region's premier rugby team, and boasted a squad of young, physically fit players with far more stamina than the late George Masters could ever have matched, even with a HardBody Gym membership.

"I see," Charlie said. "In that case, perhaps you might be able to help us with our enquiries—we need a list of your annual ticket holders, or those who've paid using their card to enter the Alnwick Garden over the past six months, as well as a list of names for anyone who completed a tour of the Poison Garden."

Hilary was crestfallen. "Do you know how many visitors we get over a six-month period?"

They could hazard a guess.

"We appreciate it could be a long list," Jack said. "We wouldn't ask, if it wasn't important."

"I suppose it may not be so bad, if you're only interested in the people who completed a tour of the poison garden, because people do have to book that part separately," she said.

"Even season ticket holders?" Jack queried.

"You don't have to pay twice, but everyone has to book their tour for the Poison Garden," she said. "It's a safety matter—nobody goes in without being on a pre-booked tour, or at any time without supervision."

"In that case, it would be helpful to have that list of pre-booked visitors who've taken a tour."

"There *is* the matter of data protection," Hilary said, doubtfully.

"There's an exception to the ordinary rules in an active criminal investigation, especially where the release of personal data might prevent further loss of life," Charlie said, pre-empting any difficulties on that score.

Hilary nodded, seeming as relieved as they were to be able to cut through a bit of red tape. "It might take me a little while to pull that list together," she said. "Would you like to have a walk around the gardens, while you wait? I could meet you at the bottom of the cascade in twenty minutes?"

It was a fine morning, and it seemed as good an idea as any, so they took themselves off into the sunshine. Outside, the first thing to greet them was an enormous water feature known as the 'Grand Cascade'. In contrast to the castle, the garden had evidently been designed along more contemporary lines, with a bamboo labyrinth and plenty of hidden corners for children to play in, as well as the fountain which drew the eye—not to mention the ducks, who'd taken up residence nearby.

"There's a cherry blossom orchard, over that way," Charlie said. "Or we could wander through the rose arbour?"

"Let's go for the roses."

They wandered past the cascade towards the arbour, which happened to border the entrance to the Poison Garden, separated by a high stone wall.

"Security is high," Charlie said. "But, if someone was really determined, they could find a way in. You could say the same of almost anything, mind you."

Jack agreed. "I've seen some cases where burglars have been pretty imaginative," he said. "It would take a bit of physical strength to scale that wall, but it's not impossible."

"There are cameras dotted around, but there might be a blind spot somewhere," Charlie added. "A local person with an annual pass to use to the garden might come to know the ins and outs of the place and, as we've already established, whoever poisoned George and Staccy put a bit of thought and preparation into doing it. They wouldn't necessarily be put off by having to break in and steal some plants."

They continued onward, following a pathway through beds of roses of varying size and colour.

"They're beautiful, aren't they?" she murmured, brushing a gentle finger over the petals of a pale pink rose.

Jack nodded, and thought of the last bouquet he'd bought for Melanie. "Um, Dean mentioned something about there being a hidden service access to the Poison Garden, yesterday," he said. "It runs beneath the cascade."

"It's possible that someone could gain access that way," Charlie said. "Especially if they work in the garden. We're still going through the list of staff to check if there's any connection between them and George or Stacey."

"My gut is telling me the Poison Garden was just the inspiration," Jack said, and took a seat on one of the benches beneath a rose arch. Charlie hesitated, since the bench was rather small, but then he patted the space beside him, and she realised it would look odd to refuse.

She perched on the end, leaving as much of a gap as she could.

"It seems like too much effort for somebody to break in and steal a cutting from one of the plants in the Poison Garden, especially considering the risk of being seen, and the safety measures they'd have to take to protect themselves from being poisoned," he continued, stretching an arm along the back of the bench to work out an ache in his shoulder. "It would've been much simpler for someone to take a tour, make a note of the most efficient poison to use, especially one that could be bought online, and then to go away and order it from a herbalist or wherever."

Charlie nodded, and tried not to think about his arm, which lay along the back of the seat, inches away from her skin.

"We'd better be getting back to meet Hilary," she said, standing up again. "It's been—"

Five minutes, she realised, and sat down again.

"Cool your jets," Jack said, with a smile. "You know your problem? You're so used to running around like a blue-arsed fly, you can't relax for a minute."

"Yeah," she said. "It's a hard habit to break."

"What d'you think of my theory?"

"I think it's the most likely possibility," she said. "The most dangerous plants have iron fencing around them, anyway, so, even if somebody gained access to the Poison Garden and protected themselves from any adverse effects, they'd still be faced with the problem of getting past those bars. There's a few entrances, but all of them are secured—including the ornamental gate in the middle, which is the Duchess's private entrance, and only she has the key."

"You don't think Her Ladyship could've—?"

"Already checked out that possibility," she said, being as cynically minded as he was. "The Duke and Duchess are travelling abroad, at the moment, and, in any event, there doesn't seem to be any motive for either of them to bump off a local estate agent or a newly qualified solicitor."

"Good point," Jack said. "I guess that brings us back around to the same question, then. If we work from the assumption that the sachets of Green Power weren't contaminated in bulk from the supplier, then it must have been someone at an individual level, here in the area. Theoretically, almost anybody might have been able to procure the poisons, but who would've had the motive, means and opportunity to actually contaminate those sachets of Green Power?"

Charlie thought about it. "The only connection between the two victims is the HardBody Gym," she said. "It's the obvious place to look."

"Their sachets weren't delivered there," Jack argued. "They were delivered direct to George and Stacey's homes."

"But how could anyone intercept a delivery?" she wondered aloud.

"Maybe they work for a delivery service, or—"

Just then, Jack's phone began to ring. "Lowerson," he said, and his face became animated. "Really? That's fantastic news. We'll be there as soon as we can." He ended the call and turned to Charlie. "That was the RVI," he said. "Stacey Hitchens has come out of her coma, and she's conscious—for now."

They stood up and managed to bump hips.

"Sorry—"

"Oops—"

They looked at one another beneath the arch of roses.

"Let's find Hilary and tell her she can forward that list of names on to us, instead," Charlie suggested.

"Yeah," Jack mumbled. "We should speak to Stacey as soon as possible."

They both stepped forward at the same time.

"After you—" Charlie said.

"No, no, after you."

They both gave a nervous laugh, and then Charlie strode quickly through the carpet of fallen rose petals and back towards civilisation.

CHAPTER 30

"Thank you for the lift."

Alex Gregory hadn't expected to be driven to the station by Lady Summersley, but Ryan's mother had overruled any objection and insisted upon hopping behind the wheel of her jazzy little runaround to take him back to Totnes herself.

"I needed to get out of the house," Eve confessed. "It's amazing how large places can start to feel small."

He looked across at her. "The feeling won't last forever," he said. "As soon as the threat has lifted, you can start living normally again—and grieve properly, too."

Eve kept her eyes on the road ahead, which cut a beautiful, treacherous path through acres of ancient woodland. "Every morning, I wake up and turn over to find an empty space where Charles should be," she said. "We spent so many years sharing a bed, and a life, together. It's as though I'm suffering from amnesia; I go to sleep and dream of him, then wake up and feel shocked all over again."

She braked sharply as a deer pranced out of the woodland to run across the road, then accelerated again without batting an eyelid.

"When we lost Natalie, Charles and I consoled each other, and we tried to console our son whenever he'd let us," she said. "Charles was my rock."

As a clinician, Alex hadn't dealt exclusively with abnormal minds; in the early days, he'd often helped people coping with grief and other kinds of everyday trauma, so he drew upon those rusty skills to do what he could.

"Distraction can be very useful," he said. "Exercise, creative endeavours such as painting or crafting, gardening… or, simply talking about Charles with Ryan and Anna— sharing the grief with somebody close to you can be very cathartic. A counsellor could be another useful tool, if and when you're ready to step outside the family unit. It all helps to come to a stage of acceptance about his loss."

Eve nodded. "Emma is a natural distraction," she said. "Whenever I find myself starting to dwell on the past, she runs into the room and sweeps me off to play with the puppy, or to make a cake. Then, there's Anna and Ryan. I know the wider situation isn't ideal for them but, I don't mind telling you, having them here with me has been a godsend. I don't know how I'd have coped without them both."

Alex thought she was the kind of person who could cope with almost anything, if she had to. "You've helped each other."

"True," she said. "I'm conscious that I don't want to be guilty of leaning on either of them too much. Ryan isn't a proxy for Charles, although, at times, when the light falls in a certain way, it might be his ghost standing there, rather than his son." She slowed to make a sharp turn before hurtling downhill.

"I can see where Ryan gets his driving skills from," Alex said, and was pleased when she laughed.

"Actually, I *did* teach both of my children to drive around the service roads on the estate," she said. "Most people assume it was Charles to blame."

"Clearly, most people miss the devilish glint in your eye," he said, risking another little tug of humour, to lift her spirits. "Ryan has the same one."

Eve smiled again. "As does Emma," she said. "Then again, she has her mother's sweet nature, to temper it." She looked across at him, briefly. "I'm sorry, I haven't asked—do you have children yourself, Alex? You're very good with Emma, so I presumed—"

He shook his head. "No, I haven't," he said. "Not yet, at least."

Eve was a perceptive woman. "There's still time to meet the right person," she said.

"I have," he said, and felt his chest tighten as it always did when he thought of Naomi. "Things are...difficult, at the moment."

"I hope they resolve soon," she said, kindly.

They reached the outskirts of Totnes, and Eve drew the car to a stop in the station car park. She turned off the engine and turned to Alex with a smile that crinkled the delicate skin on either side of her silvery blue eyes. Charles had been fifteen years older than his wife, which meant that Eve was around sixty-five, by Alex's reckoning, but could easily have passed for five years younger than that. She'd lost weight, recently, and her skin was paler than it might usually have been, but he could still see where her son had inherited his bone structure and lust for life.

"Thank you again, for all your hospitality," he said, and held out a hand.

"You're welcome, Alex. Thank you for your friendship."

She ignored his outstretched hand and drew him in for a motherly hug. Not having been fortunate to receive much in the way of maternal affection, Alex wished he could bottle the memory. He started to get out of the car, only for her to stop him.

"They're going to come for him again, aren't they?" Eve said, quietly. "Whoever tried to kill Ryan before, and whoever murdered Charles. They're going to try again, until they succeed."

Alex opened his mouth to issue a denial, but couldn't force himself to lie. "Yes," he said instead. "I think they will, if they can. They mustn't find out he's alive, at least not before the police find their whereabouts, first."

Eve nodded, and clasped her hands together. "Thank you for telling me the truth," she said. "I know Ryan thinks I'm too fragile at the moment, but not knowing the true danger makes matters worse. It's better to be prepared, as Charles always used to say."

"I can stay on, a bit longer," Alex offered. "If it would help?"

She reached across to pat his hand. "It's good of you to offer," she said. "But no. You have your own life to lead. We can handle things from here."

Yes, Alex thought. *He was right about Eve Finley-Ryan.*

She could cope with just about anything.

CHAPTER 31

Stacey Hitchens might have survived two of the deadliest poisons to be found in nature, but she still looked like death warmed up— though none of the small crowd gathered at her bedside would ever have dreamed of saying as much. Her skin was pale beneath a layer of flaking artificial tan and her slim, athletic body was now gaunt, her system having expelled as much of the toxins as it could over the course of the past couple of days. Her lips were dry and cracked, and her eyes bore the fuzzy, unfocused expression of one who hadn't quite returned to full consciousness.

"Stacey? I'm Detective Constable Reed," Charlie said. "This is my colleague, Detective Constable Lowerson. We're investigating how you came to be in the hospital."

She didn't say, 'How you came to be poisoned', because none of them could be sure how resilient Stacey's psyche would be after such an ordeal.

"*Water,*" she croaked, and her mother reached for the jug beside her bed to slosh some inside a cup with a long, bendy straw.

"Here," she said. "Have some of this, love."

Stacey's mother, Jeanette Hitchens, turned to Jack and Charlie with the tired expression of one who hadn't slept a wink for two days.

"Do you know what happened to her?" she asked them. "The doctors say it was some kind of poison—resin, or something?"

"*Ricin*," Jack said, keeping his voice low. "And aconite. We believe the poison was mixed in with a health drink Stacey often has—Green Power?"

The woman on the bed coughed, and managed a nod. "I drink it all the time," she whispered.

"Take it easy, sweetheart," her mother said, and wiped away fresh tears. "The doctor said you should relax."

She flashed a warning glance towards the two detectives, and Charlie nodded.

"We won't stay long," she assured her. "If we can just have the answers to a few important questions, that'll be an enormous help."

"I don't kn—" Jeanette began, but Stacey squeezed her arm.

"I want to help," she managed, and took another sip of water.

"Okay," Charlie said, and drew up a chair near to Stacey so that she wouldn't have to raise her voice. "Do you remember what you did on Sunday, before this happened?"

Stacey swallowed painfully. "I—I went to the gym," she remembered. "But I didn't—didn't stay long because—"

"Take your time," Charlie murmured.

Stacey nodded, and took another drink. "I had a call from my boss, about some overtime," she said, and they nodded, having already confirmed it themselves. "I left the gym early and—and had the Green Power in the car on my way home. I parked the car but—" She paused and swallowed again. "I didn't go home, I went straight to the office. It's really close to where I live."

Jack remembered their infamously short getaway drive, and looked across to find Charlie smiling, too. "Where did you make up the powder into a drink?" he asked.

"At the gym," Stacey replied. "It just needs water. I drank some in the car…but, I didn't finish it."

"Why not?"

"It—it tasted bitter."

"Thank God you didn't," her mother said, and kissed her daughter's hand. "The doctors say that's the reason you're still—still alive—"

She began to cry again, and they gave mother and daughter a moment to compose themselves after what had been, by any metric, an extremely worrying ordeal.

"Did you leave the drink unattended at any time?" Charlie asked.

Stacey shook her head. "Never," she said.

"What about the powder?" Jack said. "Did you use some from the gym, or bring your own?"

"My own," she rasped. "I get it delivered, and I use my own shaker bottle, too."

It corresponded with what they'd already been told.

"How often do you have the powder delivered?"

"Monthly," Stacey replied. "But…" She drank thirstily to relieve the pain in her throat. "It arrived a week early, this month."

Their ears pricked up at that.

"Does that often happen?"

"Never," she replied.

"Was there anything else unusual about the delivery?" Charlie asked, sensing they were finally onto something important. "Anything at all?"

Stacey thought again, and nodded. "The envelope," she whispered. "The sachet usually arrives in a branded green padded envelope…this time, it arrived in a normal white padded envelope."

"Did that worry you?"

"Not at the time," she said, and tears pooled in her eyes. "I just—I emptied the sachet into the Tupperware container, where I keep the powder, and then spooned it out into the shaker bottle to take with me to the gym."

The effort was beginning to take its toll, so they moved on to the next important line of questioning, before they could leave her to recover in peace.

"I don't know if anyone has told you, but another resident of Alnwick—George Masters—was also poisoned," Charlie said.

"Is he okay?"

"I'm afraid not," she replied. "We believe Mr Masters ingested a much larger dose of the poison, and sadly he passed away."

Stacey closed her eyes and, when they opened again, they were filled with tears. "That's awful," she whispered.

"Did you know Mr Masters?"

Recognition flickered in the woman's eyes, but Stacey glanced across at her mother, who was still in the room.

"Do you think it would help to have something warm on your throat?" Charlie suggested. "How about lemon and honey tea?"

Stacey nodded. "Yes," she said. "Mum, would you mind?"

"Of course, love, I'll get it now." Jeanette raced out of the ward, glad to be of use to her daughter.

"Thanks," Stacey whispered, after she'd gone. "I didn't want to say anything...in front of her."

"Say what?" Charlie asked.

"About—about George," Stacey said, and raised a shaking hand to wipe an errant tear from her cheek. "I met him at the gym, and we've been seeing each other for a couple of months, now. He's in the middle of divorcing his wife, but, technically, they're still married."

They hadn't heard anything about a pending divorce, Charlie thought, and she'd put money on Mrs Masters not knowing anything about it, either.

"Do you know of anyone who'd want to hurt you or George?" Jack said.

Stacey shook her head. "His wife didn't know anything about me," she said. "Even then, he told me she's the one who had an affair, that's why they were separated. She wouldn't have any reason to hate us, if she was in the wrong, first."

Did she really believe that? Jack thought. "Okay, how about anyone else? Has anyone been giving you trouble, at the gym, for example?"

Stacey shook her head again. "No," she said, and her eyelids began to droop. "Sorry, I—I feel tired now."

"That's okay," Charlie assured her. "You've been very helpful. Get well soon, and we'll come and see you again, when you're feeling stronger."

Stacey nodded, and was asleep by the time they'd reached the door.

Outside, they ran into her mother, who was returning with a small cardboard cup filled with herbal tea.

"Did you get what you need?"

"Yes, thank you, Mrs Hitchens," Jack replied.

Jeanette looked through the small window of the private room, where her daughter had recently been transferred. At first glance, Stacey's inert body looked just as it had done for the past two days, which was to say, closer to death than to life.

"Call a doctor—" she said, in a choked voice.

"She's sleeping," Jack assured her, and put a gentle hand on the woman's arm. "Why don't you try to get some rest in the chair beside her?"

Jeanette nodded. "The doctors say she's come through the worst, now," she said. "But I don't think I'll ever be able to sleep again. I'll worry for the rest of my life."

And *that*, they thought, was the long-term impact on a victim's family. Trauma never ended with death, or even when a loved one survived an attack. Either way, people lived in a state of purgatory, their lives never the same again, often stuck in an endless limbo where they couldn't move past the memory of what had happened. It made their job all the more important, because justice could bring a degree of closure.

"That's why Ryan used to fight so hard to avenge the dead, isn't it?" Charlie said, as they made their way back out of the hospital. "He understood what it meant to the living."

Jack kept his eyes straight ahead. "Charlie…"

"Yeah?"

"Never mind."

She gave him a funny look, but any further conversation was interrupted by the sound of her smartphone. "Sorry," she said, and fumbled to see who was calling her. "Oh, it's Ben's nursery…this can't be good. Hello?"

Jack listened with half an ear while the manager of 'Little Tykes Nursery' informed Charlie that her son had a fever, and needed to be collected straight away.

"I'll be there as soon as possible," Charlie said, and ended the call.

"Everything okay?"

She lifted a hand in mute resignation. "Some weeks, it just feels…relentless," she said, and immediately felt guilty for the admission. "It's fine, I shouldn't complain."

"You're allowed to rant sometimes, you know. Besides, I don't have kids, so I'm not part of any parental militia."

She had to smile. "You heard about that, huh? There's a Breast Brigade—"

His eyebrows flew into his hairline. "There is? I feel like that's one brigade I'd like to be part of."

"It isn't as exciting as it sounds. This brigade likes to lecture new mums about 'breast feeding being best', so that you feel like a terrible person if you can't manage it, or need to bottle feed."

"You're right," he said. "That's definitely not as exciting as I hoped it would be."

Charlie laughed, and then her face fell.

"Is there anything I can do?" Jack asked.

"No, thanks," she said. "My mum isn't well, today, so I can't ask her to collect Ben…he's becoming too energetic for her, anyway. I'll need to take some personal time off, to go and collect him. I'm sorry—"

"Why are you apologising?"

"I—well, I don't know. Because I feel like I'm leaving you in the lurch."

Jack shook his head. "You're always the first one in the office, Charlie," he said. "You work at home, even when you don't have to, and you give the job everything you have, on the ground, despite everything else you've got going on. You don't need to apologise for leaving work an hour early to pick up your sick kid."

Charlie knew he was right, and yet… "It's hard not to feel like I'm doing many things, but none of them very well."

"I don't have kids, and I still feel that way," Jack replied. "Trust me, you're winning."

"Remind me of that later, when I'm covered in snot and watching the ten millionth episode of *Bluey*."

CHAPTER 32

"Hello, hello! Come in Prince Charming? This is Silver Fox calling—" Detective Sergeant Phillips affected an upper-crust accent and adopted the persona of a wartime radio operative.

"Frank, you daft article," MacKenzie muttered, from across the conference room table. "Stop messing around."

This is Prince Charming, receiving. Over.

"For the love of God," she said to Jack. "They're as bad as each other."

MacKenzie leaned forward, and spoke into the microphone in the centre of the table.

"This is Irish Harpy intercepting," she said, dryly. "Have you and Silver Fox finished playing bloody silly beggars with the conference call facility? Some of us have homes to go to."

At the other end of the line, Ryan grinned. "Sorry, Mac. Your husband's a bad influence."

"Don't I know it."

"Spoilsport," Phillips muttered, and folded his arms across his burly chest.

"Right, let's get down to business," Ryan said. "What's the status of Operation Strangers?"

"Frank and I have been working on those two names from the June 2007 edition of *The Northern Fisherman*," MacKenzie said. "Edward Delaney and Kyle Rodgers."

"And?"

"We've managed to cobble together a few more interesting details," she said. "Edward Delaney died of an overdose in *The Blue Bamboozle* nightclub in the Bigg Market back in April 2007. He was the only son of Crispin Delaney, a wealthy local businessman who used to be a second-hand car salesman but founded an online retail business back in the noughties, which he sold for a pretty penny."

"And the son was his pride and joy?" Ryan said, and caught sight of a framed picture of himself and his late father sitting on one of the bookshelves across the room.

"Seems that way," MacKenzie said. "He attended the best private schools, but it seems he wasn't all that smart, if his grades were anything to go by. Still, he managed to get into university—"

"His dad probably greased the wheels a bit," Phillips put in.

"That's not all he had to do. Delaney Junior was tried and acquitted of a rape charge in September 2006—not long before his death."

"Who was the victim?" Ryan asked.

"I've requested the file from Archives," Phillips said. "For some reason, it wasn't transferred onto the online database with the rest of the old files, so I've asked them to hunt out the paper file, instead. The name of the alleged rape victim wasn't reported in the press."

"The victim and her family would certainly have an obvious motive," Ryan said. "Especially, if he was acquitted—"

"Unfortunately, young Delaney had a bit of form, in that area," Phillips said. "We found two other complaints of sexual assault from his first year of university, but neither of them wanted to proceed with a prosecution. They'd have just as much motive as the lass who took him to court, though."

Ryan agreed. "All right," he said. "Start looking into everyone who has a potential motive, especially the woman who accused him of rape. In the meantime, what did you find about Kyle Rodgers' death?"

"He died in June 2007. There were plenty of articles in the press, at the time, what with him bein' a premiership footballer," Phillips said. "I remember everyone bein' a bit shocked at him dyin' after a heart attack, because he was only twenty-six."

"What did the coroner have to say about it, and the pathologist?" Ryan asked. "It seems too much of a coincidence that both were listed in the *Northern Fisherman*—especially since they were already dead by the June 2007 edition."

"Well now, speaking of coincidences," MacKenzie said. "What would you say if I told you that, of all the cases in 2007, Rodgers' death was the only other one, aside from Delaney's, not to be transferred onto the digital record?"

"I'd say that's very interesting, indeed."

"Aye, which is why I've *also* requested Rodgers' file from Archives," Phillips said. "There must be a reason why somebody didn't want to make it easy for anyone to access either of those files."

"Yes," Ryan agreed. "Do we have any idea who might've had a motive for killing Rodgers?"

"The write-ups were all glowin', after he died," Phillips said. "They were full o' stories about his football skills and his charity work with the kids, and all that. But you know what these young lads can be like. There's bound to be some skeleton or other, rattlin' around."

"The thing is—" Ryan began.

There came a peremptory knock on the conference room door, before Neil Jones let himself in.

Quickly, Phillips jabbed the 'MUTE' button on the conference call.

"Hello there!" Jones said, jovially. "Sorry to barge in, but they told me I'd find you lot in here."

"What's the trouble?" Jack said.

"No trouble," he replied. "Just thought I'd let you all know, the MOD have come back with some further confirmation—not only was the explosive used at Frankland a military grade, they've also confirmed that some of its components match items listed as 'missing' from the army training base at Otterburn."

The last time they'd been called out there, Phillips had nearly done himself an injury on a quad bike, if he recalled. "Thanks, Jonesy," he said. "Let us know if you hear anything else."

244

"No bother," he said. "I'm going to take a run up there and see if anyone on base can tell me how someone gave them the slip, or whether one of their own is earning a few extra bob, hocking explosives on the black market. You never know, someone might be able to tell us something useful." He gave them all a mock salute. "Cheerio, then!"

They waited until the door closed behind him, and then Phillips unmuted the conference call. "That was close," he said.

"I don't think Neil heard anything," MacKenzie said. "But it'll be good when we can dispense with all this cloak-and-dagger malarkey."

"I couldn't agree more," Ryan said.

"Which reminds me to ask about Charlie," Jack said. "Look, I know she hasn't been with us long, but she's one of the team and I feel pretty bad about lying to her."

There was a long silence at the other end of the conference call, while Ryan thought about it. "All right," he said, eventually. "Bring Charlie in, if you have to—but only if necessary. Knowledge can be powerful, but it also carries risk in this case."

"Thanks, boss," Jack said.

"While you were talking to Jones, a message has come through from Digital Forensics in London," Ryan said, and scrolled down the e-mail on his laptop. "A new classified advert has been placed on the *Northern Fisherman*."

"Another one? Who does it name, this time?"

"Two names," Ryan said. "George Masters and Stacey Hitchens. Aren't they the poisoning cases you're dealing with, Jack?"

Lowerson came to attention. "Yes," he said. "We don't have a prime suspect in either case, yet."

"Don't you?" MacKenzie said. "It seems to me, the obvious bet would be Masters' wife. Remember, if she's used the killing scheme, she doesn't need to have administered the poison herself. Most likely, she'll have an alibi in both cases."

"She was staying at her mother's house, over the past few days, so she wasn't physically in the house while her husband would have ingested the poison in his Green Power drink," Jack said. "However, she could conceivably have been the one to doctor the powder and send it to him, as if from the company. As for Stacey Hitchens, she could have found out where the woman lives and sent the powder, in the same way. The fact that the poison was mixed in with their Green Power powder means that whoever was responsible wouldn't necessarily have been there at the time either George or Stacey drank it."

"Who else is likely to have ordered the hit, though?" Phillips asked. "You told us that Stacey has come clean about havin' an affair with George, which makes it all the more possible someone would've known about it and that someone could have been Masters' wife, or someone who told her about it."

"It's worth ruling it out, at the very least," Ryan said. "Why not bring her in for questioning tomorrow, Jack, and see what that throws up?"

"Aye, if she's got a new baby, she's less likely to abscond," Phillips added.

"All right," Jack said. "It's our best bet, at the moment."

"I've asked Digital Forensics, to implement a tracing link on the *Northern Fisherman* website, to simplify the process of tracking down whoever places a classified ad," Ryan said. "It's possible he managed to do that before this particular ad went live, so I'll check in with him and see if we can get a name, or an IP location for the computer that was used."

"As for Operation Strangers, hopefully Jones will get a lead from the army base at Otterburn, when he talks to them tomorrow," MacKenzie said. "Frank and I will hurry along the Archives department and dive straight into those historic files on Delaney and Rodgers when they come through. Frank? Have the team thrown up any earlier names from the print editions of *The Northern Fisherman*?"

Phillips shook his head. "No, they haven't come back with any new names, today," he said. "So far, Delaney and Rodgers are the two earliest red flags. There aren't any other matches with accidental deaths or suicides before the June 2007 edition of the magazine."

"How about other cases around the country, in different magazines?" Jack said. "Have they found any matches prior to June 2007?"

"No," Ryan said. "Hassan says the earliest potential cases date back to September 2007, but nothing before then. We might have traced the spider's web, right to the centre."

"It seems like the centre's right here, in the North East."

"I always knew you were a nefarious lot," Ryan said.

"Aye, that's why you love us, so much," Phillips shot back. "Howay, let's catch these spiders, whoever they are."

After they'd made their farewells, Ryan remembered something.

Spiders didn't share a web.

There was only ever *one*.

CHAPTER 33

Tom Faulkner stood in his polypropylene overalls and stared at the floor of Ryan's former home. Chief Constable Morrison had given him permission to go over the scene again, on his own time, and this had been the first opportunity. He'd been inside the house several times as a guest, over the past few years, and his forensic mind told him there was probably a quantity of his own DNA knocking around the place, somewhere or other. He'd already found several alien DNA samples, which he'd matched to Phillips, MacKenzie and Lowerson, as well as the larger quantity he'd expected to find of Anna, Emma and Ryan. However, there was one sample he was struggling to account for.

Ryan's father.

Tom hadn't needed to obtain a blood sample from Charles in order to know it was his DNA spattered in tiny fragments all over the floor of Ryan's conservatory; the lab tests he'd run himself had confirmed a male familial match to Ryan's own DNA, which was already on file. He might have expected to find a small quantity of leftover DNA belonging to Ryan's extended family, but not in the form of blood spatter, and not in such large quantities. If he didn't know better, he'd have said—

He'd have said Charles died on that floor.

But that wasn't possible.

Was it?

No, he thought.

It was Ryan who'd died from a fatal gunshot, not his father.

Tom turned to look at the large window to his right, which had been boarded over, temporarily. It was an easy shot for anyone with experience of a long-range rifle, which could include any number of farmers, police personnel, ex-military or security staff with a license, discounting everyone who handled a gun illegally, too.

He thought of the trajectory, and of the position of the sun at the time Ryan died—which had been early morning. The sun would have been rising behind the house, and could have posed a problem for anyone trying to take a shot from a westerly position, in the trees visible from the conservatory window.

They could easily have mistaken Ryan for his father, and vice versa.

A sick, churning feeling spread through his stomach, and the truth hit him like a sledgehammer.

Ryan was still alive.

Ryan found his wife sitting in the library, with a half-drunk glass of wine in one hand and an open book in the other. Her dark hair shone in the lamplight, and music played softly—something by Gershwin, he thought—while the puppy snored gently on the rug at her feet.

"What're you reading?"

She looked up, and smiled at him over the top of the paperback. "It's an epic adventure novel, set in the Borderlands of England and Scotland in the sixteenth century," she said. "It's all about murder and intrigue—and a bit of bodice ripping, which never hurts."

"Oh?" he said, with a sudden, renewed interest in historical fiction. "I might have to read it, after you're finished."

"Ha," she said. "I thought you weren't interested in the Border Reivers."

"You never told me there was bodice ripping," he countered.

Anna laughed, and marked the page with a bookmark before setting the novel down. "How are the gang?" she asked, and enjoyed the simple pleasure of watching him move across the room towards her.

"Things are progressing," he said, coming to sit next to her. "Just not fast enough, for my liking."

"Nothing ever is," she said.

"That's true," he said, and wrapped one strong arm around her shoulders while she rested her head on his chest. "The good news is that we might have found the first two casualties of the murder scheme. If we're right about that, it won't be long until we can isolate the most likely suspects who'd have wanted them dead; and perhaps they'll turn out to be the founders of the network."

"That's good news," Anna said, and listened to the strong thud of his heartbeat against her ear. "Well, not 'good', exactly, but you know what I mean."

"Yeah," he murmured, and ran his hand over her hair. "I think we're running out of time, Anna. I can feel it."

"We've been very careful not to let anybody know you're still alive," she said, turning her head up to look at him. "None of your friends would have told anyone."

"No, but accidents happen," he said. "Today, for instance, on the conference call. We were talking and then, suddenly, somebody else walked into the room. Phillips muted the call, but you never know what might have been overheard."

"Do you mistrust the person?"

"Not particularly, but it's just an example. Another one is Samantha," he said.

"*Sam*? What does she have to do with it?"

"Frank and Denise told me that she overheard their conversation," he said. "She's a teenager, so they do listen at doors, sometimes."

Anna sighed. "Sam's a good kid," she said. "I'm sure she won't tell anyone you're alive."

"Not maliciously, no," Ryan said. "But what about her best friend, at school? She may think it wouldn't hurt anyone, since her schoolfriends don't have anything to do with anything, that we know of. But what if one of them goes home and repeats her story to their parents, one of whom happens to be affiliated with the murder scheme? It only takes one careless voice to undo weeks of careful silence."

"The chances of that are—" Anna began to say, before tapering off.

"Quite high," he said. "Yes. Anybody and everybody could have been involved in this scheme, because it was open to all. That includes the parents of Samantha's schoolfriends."

"I take your point," Anna said and nestled closer against his chest, for comfort. "What can we do?"

"Nothing," Ryan said. "We're already doing everything possible to mitigate the risk but, if someone were to find out I'm alive, and happened to know my full name, it would be easy to find out where we're staying."

"Then we should move—"

"And run, for the rest of our lives?" he said, with a shake of his head. "We can't do that to ourselves, or to Emma. She deserves to live freely, to play with other children and go to nursery, as she normally does. That won't happen, if we keep moving around from place to place, hiding all the time."

"But here, we're like sitting ducks."

"We also have the advantage of knowing the terrain," he said. "I know every door and window of this house, every entrance and exit. Tomorrow morning, I want to show you some different escape routes, to use with Emma and my mother, if and when the time comes. They lead out into the courtyard, where a car will always be waiting, stocked with a tank of fuel."

"Ryan, I'd never think of leaving you behind."

"If it was a question of survival, we have to think of Emma and my mother, first, and ourselves second."

"I could be helpful," she argued. "You know I can fire a gun, for one thing."

"I do," he said, remembering the last time she'd discharged a weapon, to save his life as he'd fought a madman atop a raging waterfall. "You're an asset in any situation, Anna; I value you, immeasurably, and I hope you know that. It's because I trust you above all else that I'm asking you to ensure the safety of my mother, our child—and *her* mother, too."

Anna closed her eyes, and held onto him. "It won't come to that," she said.

"But, if it does?"

"I'll do the right thing."

It was all he could ask.

CHAPTER 34

Jack Lowerson pulled up to the kerb a few doors down from Charlie's new flat, and wondered if coming to see her had been a bad idea, after all. Her son was sick, and she was probably up to the eyeballs in dirty nappies and Calpol.

He checked the time on the dashboard.

Eight-twenty-three.

Most young children tended to be asleep by eight, he thought, but it was still a dangerous time of night for any parent. He mulled over the pros and cons, and decided that she'd rather know the truth about Ryan sooner rather than later. That being the case, he hopped out of the car and trundled up the short pathway to her front door, where he was about to press the buzzer, before remembering there could be a sleeping child inside. He leaned across and tapped on her living room window, instead.

After a few attempts, the curtain flicked back to reveal her surprised face.

"Can I come in?" he mouthed.

She nodded, and pointed towards the door. A moment later, she opened it, dressed in stained jogging pants and a vest top with no bra underneath, her hair bundled atop her head in the ubiquitous 'mum bun' worn by harassed mothers the world over.

"*Jack*? What are you doing here? Has something happened?"

"Sorry to disturb you at home," he said, keeping his voice down. "I won't stay long. I just needed to tell you something—it's important."

She put a self-conscious hand to her hair, before crossing her arms over her chest, the night air having reminded her that she wasn't wearing any undergarments. "Come in," she said, and led him through to the living room.

There, he found an older woman seated on the sofa, engrossed in a book of crosswords while her small grandson slept with his head resting on her lap.

"He fell fast asleep, after the last crying jag," Diane Reed told them, in a stage whisper. "You must be Jack?"

Lowerson stepped forward and took her hand. "And, you must be Mrs Reed," he said. "Pleased to meet you."

"Diane," she said. "Sorry, I can't get up, or I'd offer to make you a sandwich."

Jack grinned across at Charlie, who watched their interaction with a nervous eye. "You had me at 'sandwich'," he said, and she smiled, revealing the same dimples as her daughter.

"I'll take Ben and put him to bed," Charlie said.

"Do you need any help?" Jack found himself asking, and Diane smiled again.

"Thanks, but I can manage," Charlie said. "He's getting bigger by the day, but I'm stronger than I look."

She leaned down and carefully plucked her son off the sofa, cradling his sleeping body in her arms with infinite care. Jack looked on and watched a toughened murder detective brush her lips over her son's soft head, murmuring gentle words in his ear as she walked down the corridor towards his bedroom.

"He's a sweetheart, isn't he?"

Jack had forgotten Diane was there, for a moment. "Ah... yes, she is. I mean, he is."

"Especially when he's sleeping," she said, with a wink. "Would you like that sandwich now?"

"Oh no, please don't go to any trouble," he said. "Can I get you anything?"

Diane's legs were aching badly, as they'd done every day for the past month, which didn't bode well for the progression of her illness.

She'd worry about that tomorrow.

"Well, perhaps a cup of tea would be nice. Milk, one sugar, please."

Jack nodded, and walked through to the kitchen to begin boiling the kettle and helping himself to tea bags. Diane decided to walk through and join him, her muscles having seized up after sitting still for too long.

"How's Ben doing?" Jack asked her. "Charlie said he had a fever."

"It's his age," Diane said, with the wisdom only a grandmother could bring. "Sometimes, a fever denotes something nasty, so you have to take it seriously every time, just in case. Most of the time, it means a new tooth's coming in, or he's got some passing virus or tummy bug. Kids his age are riddled for the first couple of years which, of course, means their parents are, too."

"Charlie never seems to be ill," he remarked.

"She always had a strong constitution, even as a baby. She takes after her father, for that."

Charlie never mentioned her father, so Jack was intrigued.

"Derek was injured at work," Diane said, reading the question on his face. "He worked as a master builder, but one of the scaffolding towers hadn't been put up properly. It collapsed and he happened to be underneath it. He suffered a huge brain haemorrhage, and died the next day. Charlie was five, at the time."

"I'm so sorry," Jack said.

"We managed," Diane said, and gave him one of her warm smiles when he handed her a cup. "My girl can manage almost anything."

Jack thought of something similar Charlie had said the other day, and wondered if she ever had an opportunity to loosen the reins.

Probably not.

"I should be getting home, soon," Diane said. "I expect the two of you will want to discuss work."

"I can give you a lift?"

Before she could answer, Charlie came back into the room, this time wearing an all-covering sweatshirt—*to go with the rest of her glamorous attire*, she thought, sourly.

"Why don't you stay here tonight, Mum? It's getting late."

Diane knew her daughter was angling for her to move in and, so far, she'd resisted the idea. However, as her illness became harder to manage, and travelling became more of a chore, she began to see the sense of it.

"Well…if it isn't too much trouble?"

"Never," Charlie said, and leaned over to kiss her mother's cheek, then whisper in her ear to ask whether she needed any personal help.

Diane shook her head, grateful for her daughter's tact.

"I'll be fine," she said. "It was nice to meet you, Jack. Come back, sometime, for one of my famous BLT specials."

Jack didn't have the heart to tell her he was vegetarian, so he nodded and kissed the cheek she offered up to him.

"Goodnight, then."

"Goodnight, Mrs Reed—Diane."

"So," Charlie said, helping herself to the mug of tea he'd made her. "What brings you here, aside from an urgent need for a cup of Yorkshire tea?"

"There's no good way to say this, so I'll just say it. Ryan's still alive."

Charlie almost choked. "*What?*"

"I know," Jack said. "I told you, there was no good way to say it."

"I don't understand."

Jack gave her an executive summary of the situation, and she set her tea down on the counter.

"You mean to say, the rest of you *knew* about this?"

"Not everyone," Jack said, quickly. "Faulkner, Pinter, and lots of other people don't know anything about it. Frank and Denise only found out on Sunday, and the only reason I know is because—"

"You witnessed his father's murder," she finished, softly.

He nodded. "Yes. It was awful. When Ryan saw his dad lying there...it was heart-breaking."

Charlie watched pain flit over his face, and experienced a sudden, strong urge to comfort him. "I thought I was a member of the team," she said, and turned away to go in search of the biscuit tin. "I thought you trusted me."

"We do. *I* do," Jack said. "But you have to understand, the threat against Ryan and his family is severe. So long as nobody knows he's alive, there's a bit of a security net which allows us to investigate. As soon as his cover is blown, that security net goes with it."

She thought about that, selected a Viennese swirl, and then passed the tin to Jack, who helped himself to a bourbon.

"Okay," she decided. "How can I help?"

CHAPTER 35

Wednesday

"Don't even think about it." Denise MacKenzie saw the words forming on her husband's lips before they were spoken aloud.

"Eh? I didn't even *say* anythin'."

"No, but you were thinking it," she growled. "And, the answer is *no*, I won't swap with you, Frank. It's your turn to go along and talk to the school kids about the dangers of drug use and online abuse."

"Aww, howay man, you're so much better at it—"

"Flattery will get you nowhere, this time," she said.

"But we've got more important things to be doin'," he argued.

"More important than protecting the next generation?" she countered. "Try telling Samantha that, when you cancel."

Phillips sulked for a moment, then an idea popped into his mind. "Can I take a friend?"

She eyed him closely. "Which one?"

"I reckon it's Jack's turn to face the teenagers," he replied.

MacKenzie was happy with the arrangement, and thought that it would give her a chance to get to know Charlie Reed better. "That's settled, then," she said. "You'd better call Jack and tell him the bad news, before he evades you and gets an early start on the road to Alnwick."

"Aye, good point," he said, and hurried off to find his phone.

Samantha entered the kitchen a moment later, and cocked a thumb in the direction of Phillips' back. "Where's the fire?" she asked.

"No fire, but plenty of brimstone," MacKenzie laughed. "Your dad's worried about having to give a talk at your school, this morning. He managed to wriggle out of it, last time, because Ryan did most of the talking."

"Sneaky," Sam said, with approval. "I guess he won't want to answer any awkward questions about periods, then?"

MacKenzie pointed a finger at her daughter. "Now, go easy on him," she said, and then spotted the trail of destruction her husband had left around the toaster, including a mountain of crumbs, smears of butter and jam on the counter.

Jam? That definitely wasn't on their Approved Diet Plan.

"You know, on second thought, have at it."

Samantha smiled like an angel.

"And, if your dad has anything to say about it, just say these two words and he'll understand…"

"Which words?"

"*Strawberry jam.*"

An hour later, DS Phillips and DC Lowerson were seated on a couple of plastic tub chairs outside the headteacher's office at Samantha's school, fidgeting, nibbling their fingernails and generally looking guilty as sin.

"Now, in these situations, the trick is to admit *nowt*," Frank whispered. "You didn't smoke behind the bike sheds—"

"Vape," Jack corrected him. "The naughty thing to do is *vape*, nowadays, not puff on a pack of Marlborough Lights."

"*Eh*?"

"Never mind," he said. "Anyway, we haven't done anything, Frank. We're here to talk about drugs and—"

"Aye, well, you can't be too careful," Phillips said. "Whatever you're accused of, you didn't do it, and that includes cheatin' on any maths tests, peekin' down Mary Malone's top—"

"Who's Mary Malone, when she's at home?" Jack interjected.

"Never you mind," Phillips muttered, and thought fondly of his first girlfriend in high school. He cast an eye in either direction down the corridor, which smelled strongly of shepherd's pie and featured display boards filled with paintings of trees, which had apparently been the topic in science class, that term. "Now, just listen to me, and you'll be alreet—"

"Detective Sergeant Phillips?"

"What? *No!*" he said, and nearly fell from his chair.

The school's headteacher, who had joined the faculty after the recent retirement of her predecessor, looked at Frank as though he might have been lost on his way to a mental institution.

"Er, yes, he *is*," Jack said, and stood up to shake her hand. "I'm his colleague—and sometime carer—Detective Constable Lowerson."

Phillips shot him a fulminating glare. "I was caught off guard, that's all," he said. "It's been a while since I found myself sittin' outside the Head's office."

"It's nice to meet you," she said. "I'm Avril Stephenson."

"Aye, nice to meet you," he mumbled.

"*Well*," she said, hiding a smile. "Are you boys ready to face the music?"

"As ready as I'll ever be," Phillips said, and they followed her down the corridor towards the dining hall, which doubled as an assembly room.

He put a hand on Jack's arm. "Remember my advice, lad," he said. "Approach this just as you would a hostage situation, or an interview with a hostile witness. Don't negotiate, don't show any weakness, and don't let them see your fear. They can smell it a mile off."

Jack gave a funny, nervous laugh. "I'm not frightened of a bunch of school kids, Frank."

"You should be," Phillips said, and gave him a gentle shove through the double doors. "Break a leg, son."

"How d' you think they're getting on?"

MacKenzie glanced across at the woman seated beside her in the car, and smiled. "It'll be character building," she said.

Charlie laughed, but any sympathy she might have expressed was forestalled by a phone call from an unknown number, which came through to the hands-free system and was answered with the click of a button on the steering wheel.

"DI MacKenzie."

"It's Ryan."

She and Charlie had already held a discussion before starting their journey to Alnwick, so MacKenzie knew his existence was no longer a secret.

"Good morning," she said, injecting a bit of cheer into her voice. "I have Charlie here with me. We're on our way to bring Amanda Masters in for questioning in that poisoning case."

"Hi, Charlie," he said. "Sorry for all the underhanded business—"

"I understand completely, sir," she said, because she did. "You have to do all you can to protect your loved ones, as well as yourself."

"Thanks. I'm glad I caught you both," he said. "I had a communication from DCI Hassan, early this morning. I contacted him last night, following our discussion about that ad having been placed in the classifieds, featuring Stacey Hitchens and George Masters. I asked him to check with Digital Forensics to see whether they'd managed to install a tracking link, and, if so, where it led."

"Any luck?" MacKenzie asked.

"Yes," Ryan said. "The team managed to trace the physical address of the computer used to place the ad—it's the HardBody Gym, in Alnwick. Charlie, I'm going to forward the long, numerical IP address to you, by e-mail, but I can tell you the server description of the terminal is 'Reception Desktop'. Hopefully, that will help to narrow things down, when you check it out."

"You think we should divert our attention from Amanda Masters, for now?" Charlie asked.

"It seems unlikely she'd have found a way to use the reception desktop to place an ad," Ryan said. "That being the case, I think you should sweat a few people down at the gym—pun intended."

"Har har," MacKenzie said, obligingly. "We'll head straight there, and seize that computer terminal, so we can work out who's had access."

"All right, let me know how you get on," Ryan said.

Before he could ring off, Charlie spoke up again. "Sir?"

"You don't need to call me 'sir', all the time," he reminded her.

"Sorry, force of habit. I was only going to say…it's good to have you back."

Ryan smiled. "It's good to be back, Charlie. I hope to see you all again, very soon."

He ended the call, and looked at the little block of plastic he held in his hand before slipping it back into his pocket. Across the room, a large, ornately carved clock hung above the mantelpiece of a marble fireplace. It had been made in the Netherlands, and given to his father as a gift by the Dutch government, one Christmas. It was beautifully made, with a strong *ticking* sound and a resonant chime that sang out every half hour. He'd always liked it, even as a boy, but now the endless ticking of the clock served only to remind him of time that was slipping away.

Tick tock, tick tock.

The beat matched the sound of his racing heart.

CHAPTER 36

MacKenzie and Reed stepped into the foyer of the HardBody Gym, where they were greeted by an oily grin from the manager, Steve.

"*Welcome*, ladies—" he started to say, before recognising Charlie from the previous day. "Oh, Detective Reed, how—er—how nice to see you again. Have you made any progress with the case?"

"We're pursuing all avenues of enquiry," she said. "This is my colleague, Detective Inspector MacKenzie."

MacKenzie held out her warrant card, which he ignored in favour of getting an eyeful of her face and figure, which set her teeth on edge.

"How many computers do you have in here?" she said, choosing not to bother with any of the usual niceties.

"Er, just this one in reception," he said, tapping the monitor in front of him. "Oh, and the one in the manager's office. There's another one in the main gym, which is sometimes used by the trainers to track progress charts and so on, but the screen is broken on that one, at the moment. Why do you ask?" He looked between their bland faces with a growing sense of unease.

"We suspect one of them has been used for an illegal purpose," MacKenzie replied. "Do the staff have access to all the computers?"

Steve began to sweat, thinking of the stash of porn he'd saved on the desktop in his office, for when things were slow at the gym. It was just regular, heterosexual nudity, he thought, but...what if he'd accidentally downloaded something awful—or underage?

He began to shake.

"The—the staff can only access this one in reception," he said. "Not—not the one in the manager's office. That's just for management staff."

"You look unwell, Mr Purdie," Charlie remarked. "Are you feeling all right?"

"*Me*?" he squeaked. "Yes, yes, I'm fine."

"Oh, good. For a moment, I could have sworn you looked nervous about something."

He shook his head, and wiped his hands on the back of his shorts.

"May we check the browsing history of the computer here?" MacKenzie said. "It seems a quiet moment."

Steve looked past them to the empty foyer, and nodded. "Yes, um, okay," he said, and held open the security gate so they could slip behind the front desk.

MacKenzie thanked him, and set about searching the browsing history on the computer, but there was no listing for *The Northern Fisherman.*

"Some people use 'private' mode to hide their browsing history," Charlie said, and cast a telling glance towards Steve, who looked as though he was about to pass out.

MacKenzie sighed. "Of course," she muttered. "What time was the ad posted?"

Charlie checked the message Ryan had sent her, and read out the details.

"Who would have been on reception at that time?"

They turned expectantly towards Steve, who held up his hands in mute appeal. "Not me!" he declared. "I have a regular session with a client at that time."

"If not you, then who else?" MacKenzie said.

"I—well, it could have been anyone, really," he stammered. "Any member of staff can jump onto reception. They take it in turns, whenever one has a PT session another one hops on."

"Don't you have a permanent receptionist?"

"No, it's a *concept* thing," he muttered. "At least, that's what the owner says. Members can just scan through the automatic gates, so they don't really need to speak to anyone. New members can ring the bell for attention, and one of us responds."

"I see," MacKenzie said. "Don't you have a log of some kind?"

"No, I mean it's just a general password for this monitor…" he said, knowing fine well that was against company policy, but it just made life easier than having to change the passwords every three months, or log off and on again with each new user.

"What about CCTV?" Charlie said, and pointed at the camera on the wall, which was trained on the front desk where they now stood.

"Yes," Steve said. "Yes, we could check the footage, if you like?"

"We like," Charlie confirmed.

They watched as he fiddled with the computer again, this time bringing up a live video feed which showed the three of them standing there.

"Okay, we need the footage from...when was it, again?"

They told him, and Steve clicked on a file marked with the date. He dragged the time of the recording forward to the time they'd requested, and swallowed hard when he recognised the figure on the screen.

"I'm sure there's some explanation," he said, and stepped aside so they could see for themselves.

"Who is it?" MacKenzie asked, not having met any of the staff at the gym.

"It's Fiona Duncan," Charlie said, remembering the woman instantly. "Do you know of any reason why she would seek to harm George Masters, or Stacey Hitchens?"

They turned to look at Steve, who decided it was the opportune moment to disclose everything he knew, or face the consequences.

"I—I might have heard that Fiona and George had something going on, previously," he said.

"How do you know that?" MacKenzie asked.

"Well, to put it as delicately as possible…I walked into the back office, a few months ago, and found Fiona…on her knees, you might say."

"With George?"

He nodded.

"Isn't that against company policy?" Charlie said, tartly.

"Yes, but…er, when we first opened, I might have been in a similar situation with Fiona, a couple of times." He looked pained. "Please, don't tell my wife…"

They folded their arms.

"Well, the timing matches the record we have, so it seems fairly certain Fiona placed that ad—" MacKenzie broke off, catching sight of an attractive woman walking towards them from the direction of the main gym, a friendly smile on her face until she noticed her image on the reception monitor.

There was a second where the two women locked eyes, then Fiona turned and ran.

"Charlie—"

"On it!" she said, and flew after her, vaulting over the turnstiles to give chase down the corridor.

———

"I don't think I'll ever be the same again."

"Don't say I didn't warn you," Phillips said, and put a hand on Jack's head as he sat down in the car's passenger seat, to make sure he didn't bang it on the doorframe, in his traumatised state.

"All these years, I always thought you and Ryan were exaggerating," Jack muttered. *"They're just kids,* I told myself. *What harm can they do?* But now…"

"Now, you know better, eh?" Phillips chuckled, and put the car into gear.

"There were so *many* of them," Jack said, eyes still wide with terror.

"Imagine how I feel, when they all descend on the house for a bloody party or play date," Phillips said. "It's nowt but gigglin' till the early hours, and they eat us out of house and home."

Jack nodded. "One of them asked me if I was married," he said, and turned to his friend with a look of incomprehension. *"Married?* Frank, I could be their dad."

"A young dad, but aye, still possible," Phillips agreed. "It's the hormones, lad. They don't discriminate."

Jack wasn't sure if that was comforting or not.

"Anyway," he said. "It's definitely Denise and Charlie's turn, next time. See how she likes it, having a bunch of teenage boys leering at her and asking all kinds of questions."

Phillips laughed. "I've got a feelin' the lass can handle herself," he said, and then added, "She handles you, well enough."

Jack didn't pretend to misunderstand; not with Frank. "I like her," he said, quietly. "I like her a *lot.*"

"Aye, lad. I gathered that much."

"Is it that obvious?"

Phillips shrugged, and accelerated to forty miles per hour along the coast road.

He could live dangerously, too.

"Aye, lad—well, to me and Denise, it is. Maybe not to anyone else."

"How about to Charlie?"

"Couldn't say," Phillips replied. "I think she likes you too, though."

Something leapt inside Jack's chest, and then flattened again, like a burst balloon. "What about Mel?" he said. "I still love her."

"Have you heard from her, lately?"

"No, nothing."

Phillips ran his tongue around his teeth, thinking about the best advice he could give. "She told you not to wait for her, didn't she?"

"Yes, but…"

"Well, then?"

"I don't want to rush into anything, unless I'm completely sure things are over between us," Jack replied. "I owe it to Mel, and to Charlie, too."

And her son, he might have added.

"That's the honourable way," Phillips agreed. "But, remember lad, the heart doesn't always heed what the mind tells it. Don't be afraid to follow your heart, sometimes."

It was good advice.

CHAPTER 37

Fiona Duncan would have a shiner in the morning.

At least, Charlie could only hope so, considering she was also likely to have one, after tackling the woman to the ground at a run, with considerably more brute force than finesse.

"D' you want some ibuprofen?" MacKenzie held out a mug of tea and a packet of anti-inflammatories, both of which Charlie accepted with thanks.

"You were pretty fast, back there," Denise said, and couldn't help but remember a time when she would've been the one tackling a suspect to the ground, in the days before she was attacked. Her leg gave a twang of remembered pain, around the area where scar tissue had formed, and she rubbed it with her free hand.

Charlie caught the motion, and offered the pills back to her. "Do you need some of these, too?"

"No," Denise said, waving them away. "It's psychosomatic, mostly."

Charlie knew what had happened to MacKenzie, a few years before, and of her epic escape from the clutches of a serial killer known as 'The Hacker'. Looking at her, you'd never have known Denise had ever been through anything like it, but then, she also knew that some scars were invisible to the naked eye.

"Well," she said. "I think we've let her stew in her own juices for long enough. What do you reckon?"

"I agree," Denise replied. "Better go in and put her out of her misery."

The two women left the observation room, where they'd kept an eye on Fiona Duncan through a sheet of protective, one-way glass. She'd demanded a lawyer as soon as they'd slapped the cuffs on her, and one of the duty solicitors from a local firm had rocked up to the station smelling faintly of last night's booze and old aftershave. Still, it was better than no representation at all.

"DI MacKenzie and DC Reed entering Interview Room B, at twelve-oh-seven p.m.," Denise said, for the benefit of the recording equipment, and proceeded to give the date and to read Fiona Duncan the standard caution. "Do you understand, Ms Duncan?"

Fiona looked across at her lawyer, wrinkled her nose, and then nodded.

"If you could reply audibly, for the benefit of the tape?"

"*Yes*," she snapped. "I understand."

"Good," Denise said, with a smile. "Let's get started, then."

She opened a laptop, and brought up the image of an advert placed in *The Northern Fisherman*, which she described and labelled 'Appendix A'.

"Do you recognise this, Fiona?"

The other woman's eyes flicked onto the screen, then away again.

"No comment."

"You didn't have time to read the wording," Denise said, with a tut. "Is that because you're already familiar with the contents of this advert?"

"No comment."

"Did you know a man by the name of George Masters?"

Fiona had already admitted as much, so she gave a reluctant nod. "Yes. I've already told you, he was a member of the gym, where I work."

"Indeed, I understand you're employed by the HardBody Gym as a personal trainer. Is that correct?"

"Yes."

"Did you ever train George Masters?"

"Yes."

"Did you know he was married."

"Yes."

"And yet, you had an affair with him?"

"Y—no. I…No comment."

Denise leaned in, as if they were having a chat, woman-to-woman. "Fiona," she said. "We already know you did. We have a *witness*."

There were no prizes for guessing who, but they couldn't help that.

"Fine, then. Yes, we had a thing going on for a while."

"How long?"

"None of your business."

"Oh, it is our business," Charlie said. "It's very much our business, when we're investigating the man's murder."

MacKenzie brought up the next round of images on the laptop screen, this time showing a log of the time and date when the classified advert was placed on *The Northern Fisherman,* as well as details of the IP address and computer location at the gym.

"Where were you, at this time, Fiona?"

"I don't remember. Working, probably."

"You're sure you didn't place this ad?"

"No comment."

This time, they rolled the CCTV footage, and watched her solicitor's face fall.

"Is that you, Fiona?"

"No comment."

"More than one witness has identified the woman on the screen to be you, Fiona Duncan," Charlie said. "The time of the footage exactly matches the IP record for when that advert was placed. Do you still deny having done it, Fiona?"

"No comment."

"Who's behind the murder scheme?" Charlie asked. "Tell us who runs the network."

This time, confusion passed over Fiona's face. "I don't know about any scheme," she said.

"I'm not inclined to believe that," MacKenzie said. "You know how the scheme operates…quid pro quo, isn't it? You kill someone, then someone kills for you, isn't that it? Who were you working with— was it Amanda Masters?

Did you find you had something in common with his wife, when he moved on to the next woman—is that it?"

Fiona's lip wobbled.

"Am I getting closer?" Denise rolled on. "He rejected you, didn't he, Fiona? Someone *younger* came along, and George forgot you existed, didn't he? Did you and Amanda concoct this plan, together?"

"I've never met his idiot wife," Fiona snarled. "I've only seen her in the street."

"All right, if it wasn't her, then who did you do it for?"

The confused look passed over her face, again. "It wasn't for anyone else," she said. "It was for me."

Which didn't fit the scheme, they thought, but said nothing.

"Did he hurt you, Fiona?" Charlie said, injecting a note of sympathy into her voice. "Did he deserve to pay?"

"*Yes,*" she replied. "The bastard deserved everything he got, and so did she. I gave him a year of my life, and he gave me nothing. *Nothing!* The lying, cheating, bastard."

Neither Charlie nor Denise bothered to mention the hypocrisy on display, since obtaining her confession was far more important.

"How did you do it, then? How did you teach him a lesson?" Charlie asked.

"I'd like a moment to confer with my client," the solicitor said, having apparently been napping throughout the interview thus far.

"It doesn't matter, now," Fiona said. "They've got me on CCTV, anyway."

He scratched his chin, and wished for a pint. "Your choice," he muttered.

"How did you poison the powder sachets, Fiona?" Denise asked her. "It was clever, however you managed it."

Narcissists loved to be flattered, she thought.

"I doctored a couple of sachets and sent them a week early," Fiona replied, with a self-satisfied air. "It was easy, because I knew their home addresses from the membership database and I was the one who recommended Green Power, in the first place." She spoke the words without a hint of remorse.

"What about the poison? How did you acquire it?"

"I went for a tour around the Poison Garden a few months ago, when I found out George was shagging on the side. I didn't know who he was seeing, but I didn't believe him when he said he was going back to his wife, that's for sure." Fiona snorted. "I was planning to grab a few bits and pieces, while I was in there, but I didn't have a chance," she said. "They keep watch, the whole time."

"Bad luck," Charlie said. "So, what did you do?"

"I just went to the herbalist," she said, and mentioned the name of an outlet in an area of Newcastle known as 'Chinatown'. "They had castor beans, and dried aconite…I had to be a bit nifty, getting the ricin from the beans, but it's not that hard. It took a few goes, but I got there, in the end."

The solicitor, who'd given up entirely, stared off into the distance.

"What about this advert," Denise said, picking up that thread now that Fiona was feeling talkative. "If you say you know nothing about a network of any kind, why did you place that advert in *The Northern Fisherman*?"

"Well, I just saw that vlogger on TikTok," she said. "It's all over there, about killings being advertised in that magazine, so I thought it'd be a good way to cover my tracks."

"Pity you didn't think about IP addresses or CCTV," Denise couldn't resist saying.

They questioned her for a while longer, and then charged her with the murder and attempted murder of George Masters and Stacey Hitchens. As the custody sergeant took her away to the cells, Denise turned to Charlie. "It feels like we got lucky there—Fiona isn't very tech savvy."

"Yeah, I think it must have spooked her when Jack and I turned up at the gym—she panicked and tried to throw us off the scent by placing the ad. Sadly for her, it backfired and led us straight to her," Charlie replied.

"She is pretty savvy when it comes to social media, though. Fiona said something there that struck a chord—the part about TikTok. It occurred to me that most people of my generation—maybe Ryan's too, since he's a few years younger—wouldn't use TikTok. Would you or Jack? You're in your early thirties, right?"

Charlie nodded. "I'm sure some people use it," she said. "But, speaking for myself, I'd rather scoop my own eyeballs out with a blunt spoon than film myself. I can't speak for Jack, but he doesn't seem the type to bother with it, either. It makes more sense that Fiona might use it, given that her profession is very public facing. She needs to sell herself, to sell personal training sessions, and it's all about social media presence, nowadays."

"It's another world, to me," MacKenzie said. "And I wonder if it also might be to whoever is running this murder scheme."

"What makes you say that?"

"Well, we've managed to keep most of it out of mainstream media," she said. "But, obviously, we can't stop people blabbing and, apparently, coming up with 'reels' about it online. If the founder of this network had seen the TikTok reels, they'd know their platform was under far more scrutiny by us than they might otherwise imagine. If you only looked at mainstream press, you wouldn't think we'd made half as much progress with our investigations."

"And so you're thinking whoever started all this might be—"

"Careful, young gun, careful," Denise warned her, with a smile.

"—of a certain age?"

"It makes sense." Denise nodded. "As for Fiona Duncan, she seemed to be genuinely confused by any mention of a network. Either that, or she's a good actress."

"Which means George and Stacey aren't connected to Operation Strangers, after all?"

"I don't think so," Denise said. "But we never make the facts fit the crime. Let's keep an open mind, but work on the basis they're potentially distinct. That takes us back to those first two cases, in the June 2007 edition of *The Northern Fisherman*."

"Has there been any progress, finding the family of that rape victim?"

"Let's go and find out."

CHAPTER 38

While his mother entertained their young daughter, Ryan and Anna took a tour around Summersley House, this time with an eye for exits and escape routes.

"There are ten potential exits on the ground floor," he told her, as they stood in the centre of the hallway, which was tiled in chequered marble that had been worn underfoot by past generations of Finley-Ryans. "Obviously, the front door, there. After that, there's the kitchen door, which leads out onto the back terrace, the utility room—or butler's door—which leads to the side of the house, where the garages are. There are three sets of double French doors, all leading out onto the terrace, which run along the back wall of the house from the library, my father's study and the dining room, which is next door to the kitchen. At the other end of the house, there's another utility exit, which leads onto the side terrace, and there are two more sets of French doors to the front, leading out onto the circular driveway, and which aren't used very often."

"What's the tenth?" Anna asked.

"The basement," he said. "Technically, not the ground floor, but it leads from the coal store up a short flight of stone steps adjacent to the butler's exit."

"Okay, I think I'll remember that. What about upstairs?"

"We'll get to that in a minute," Ryan said, and took her hand. "First, I need to show you some hidden routes, here on the ground floor."

They walked towards the library, where he led her towards one of the shelves on the side wall.

"*The Importance of Being Earnest,*" Ryan said, pulling out the worn leather copy his father had loved. "Behind it, you'll see a lever."

Sure enough, Anna could see a worn brass lever, which, when pulled, opened the panelling beneath the shelves.

"A priest's hole, from the old days," Ryan explained, and they crouched down to look inside. "Originally, it didn't lead anywhere, but, at some point over the past few hundred years, my ancestors added a passageway. Natalie and I used to play in here, and hide from our parents, just to wind them up."

Anna wondered how long it would be until Emma was doing the same thing. "Where does it lead?"

"I'll show you," Ryan said, and, to her delight and dismay, began to clamber inside. "Are you coming?"

Feeling like the sixth member of *The Famous Five*, Anna crawled inside the open panel to find Ryan a short way ahead of her, inside a narrow tunnel. Lighting had been fitted, at some stage, and illuminated the length of it.

"Follow me," he said, and began to crawl along the tunnel.

Anna followed him until, a couple of minutes later, he stopped at another switch on the wall. It was beside another brass lever, which he pulled, and she heard the *click* of a door unlocking.

"This way." Ryan pushed open another panelled door and, to her delight, they emerged into the morning room, where she'd spent many a day writing her book.

"I had no idea," she said. "Why didn't you mention it, before now?"

"Slipped my mind," he said. "It isn't as if we normally use it, nowadays."

"It's great," Anna said, and watched him lean down to flick the lights off, before returning the panel to normal. "Are there more like this?"

"Yes, there's one that runs from the study to the cupboard in the hallway," he said. "It's the same idea, only you need to look behind *The Quiet American* for a lever to open the panel."

Anna nodded, and felt her stomach quiver. "I won't need to use any of these passageways," she said.

Ryan said nothing, but took her through to the utility corridor and opened another old door, this time to reveal an old-fashioned dumbwaiter, on a set of pulleys.

"This runs from here to the first floor, and you access it via the door next to the linen cupboard, near my mother's bedroom," he said. "It runs alongside the servants' back stairs. From here, the closest exit is the utility door, there." He pointed to a door less than two metres away. "The Land Rover is full of petrol," he told her. "So is my mother's car; I saw to that, this morning."

"Ryan—"

"Please, just let me get this out," he said, quietly. "Both cars will be kept unlocked, and a set of spare keys are in each glove compartment."

Her eyes filled with tears, but Anna held them back. "Go on," she said.

"There's also a car seat fitted in each, for Emma," he said. "I've put a bag of essentials for each of us in both cars, as well as some money in the central unit, just in case. There's a fob for the electric gates in there, too. In case they malfunction, you can manually override the gates using the electrical box, which is inside the gatehouse. There should be one of the security staff there at all times, but—"

"Yes," she said. "In case anything should happen."

Ryan nodded. "Now, as for weapons, I know you can handle a pistol," he said. "Can you handle a rifle?"

"Yes," she said. "My father taught me."

"Good, they're this way," he said, and led her to a locked gun room, off the butler's pantry. "The old lock has been upgraded, since this was first built." Sure enough, an electronic lock kept the weapons safe from young or inexperienced hands, and Ryan told her the code. "I don't like guns," he said. "But they have their occasional uses. Ammunition is kept separately, here."

They went through everything, until Anna could stand no more, and walked away, back through to the kitchen where she could watch her daughter playing on the lawn outside.

"Why are you so certain they'll come for you, again?" she asked Ryan, when his arms wrapped around her. "Why won't they just leave us alone?"

His chest lifted, and fell again. "Anybody who becomes embroiled in the scheme is desperate," he said softly. "There could be a hundred reasons why they need somebody dead, but the deal is the same for everyone who signs away their soul; to receive a death, they have to perpetrate one themselves. If they don't, the consequences are probably fatal. If they don't finish the job and see me off, they won't fulfil their own part of the bargain—or, if they've already received a death, that means they'll be in arrears. It's a kind of debt to the network."

"So, when it comes down to it, you mean it's your life, or theirs?"

"Yes."

They were quiet for a long moment, then Anna broke away. "I'm going to call Emma inside," she said, and Ryan nodded while his eyes swept over the far line of trees, on the edge of the lawn.

"Good idea."

CHAPTER 39

"This is Emily Charteris."

The team assembled again, this time with the addition of Chief Constable Morrison, who'd returned from a few days of hobnobbing with The Powers That Be, and was glad to be back amongst ordinary folk who spoke in clear sentences and didn't dally with the truth.

"Emily made an accusation of rape against Edward Delaney towards the end of her second year at university, here in Newcastle, back in September of 2005," Phillips said. "There was some forensic evidence of rough sex, and the case went to the Crown Court, where it was tried in September 2006. From what I read in the file, it looks like it came down to her word against his; Charteris says she told him to stop, and that she didn't consent to all the stuff that went on. Delaney said she told him 'yes' to all of it, then felt embarrassed in the mornin', and called a bunch of witnesses in to support his character. Cut a long story short; Delaney was acquitted of all charges."

Phillips nodded towards the young man's picture, which he'd stuck on the wall.

"Now, as I said yesterday, the lad had already been accused of sexual assault, but none of those lasses took it any further and the court ruled those complaints 'inadmissible' in the rape trial," he continued. "As we *also* know, Edward died in April 2007, from a massive drug overdose."

"What were the circumstances?" Morrison asked.

"Dodgy batch of cocaine, according to the toxicology report," Phillips replied. "It'd been cut with all kinds of crap which, put together, brought on a fatal cardiac arrest."

"Any ricin or aconite in there?" Jack asked, just in case.

Phillips shook his head. "Neither of those," he said. "There were a bunch of chemical compounds, mostly stuff you'd get from a dealer, or hocked from the medicine store at a hospital. Everythin' from sleepin' tablets to beta-blockers."

"And there's no suggestion that he took his own life?" Morrison asked.

"Nah," Phillips replied. "Delaney was a known user and had plenty of stuff in his bloodstream and in his hair follicles to show long-term use. There were a couple of witnesses who say he was chattin' up a good-lookin' blonde lass, before he died, but she was never found. It was a busy nightclub, so that's hardly surprisin'."

"It depends how much effort they made to find her," Ryan said, his voice coming down the line through the mic in the centre of the table. "What happened to Emily Charteris— where is she now?"

"All Saint's Cemetery," Phillips replied. "She took her own life in October 2006, a few weeks after his acquittal."

There was a long silence in the conference room.

"Poor girl," Ryan said, and, although his voice was carefully devoid of emotion, they still heard anger simmering beneath it. "What about her family?"

"No brothers or sisters," Phillips said. "She lived at home, with her Mam and Dad—Kevin and Janet Charteris. Janet still lives at the same address."

"And Kevin?" Ryan asked.

"Is beside his daughter, at All Saint's," Phillips said. "He topped himself four years after she went. Drove his car into a tree, near where they live, up near Bellingham."

"That's tragic," Jack said. "How old is the mother, now?"

"She's in her early seventies," Phillips replied.

"But she was younger, then," Ryan said. "And she lost the two people closest to her, thanks to Edward Delaney. Where was she, when he died?"

"She and her husband were at grief counselling retreat, in Wales," Phillips said, having spent most of the day finding answers to the same questions. "The investigating team didn't cover it, at the time, but I called Mrs Charteris today, to check everythin' out. She was happy to tell me, and seemed a nice woman. I called the organisers of those retreats, n'all, but the only answer I got from them was the usual ramble about protectin' personal data."

"Even if you can't confirm her story, it wouldn't be surprising if Janet Charteris has an alibi, would it?" Charlie said. "The point is, if she has anything to do with the scheme, she wouldn't have been the one to harm Delaney—if we're thinking his drink was spiked, or he was deliberately sold a bad batch of cocaine. A second person would have done that, while Janet was miles away in Wales."

"Who'd be the second person?" Morrison wondered aloud. "It could be anyone, given the way the scheme works."

"Not if these two cases involve the founding members of that scheme," Ryan said. "In the beginning, the network was begun by two people who knew one another, somehow, and had a shared interest. It can't have been Kevin Charteris, because he also had an alibi for when Edward Delaney died, but it seems plausible it could be somebody else connected to the Charteris family. Perhaps the answer lies with Kyle Rodgers, once we find out who had a motive to kill him?"

Phillips smiled. "That's what I thought, so I did a bit o' diggin' around. It seems Rodgers had an eye for the young lads," he said. "Apparently, he wasn't very gentlemanly about it, either."

"I seem to remember he was always seen with a harem of women around him," Morrison said, having been a lifelong fan of the Beautiful Game.

"Ever heard of a closet?" Phillips quipped.

"Good point," she said. "Appearances can be deceptive."

"If the rumours I've heard about Rodgers are true, it was more than just a case of not bein' ready to tell people he was gay," Phillips continued. "It was more a case of coverin' his tracks, so nobody would find out what he was really up to."

"I'm almost afraid to ask," Ryan said. "What was he up to?"

"Preyin' on young men," Phillips answered. "A lot of 'em still teenagers, n'all. You can imagine the sort o' thing. The investigatin' team found all sorts, when they went through his house…recreational drugs in a locked box, hidden cameras—"

"Cameras?" MacKenzie jumped in. "What about footage?"

"Already tried to get my hands on it," Phillips said. "Archives are gonna come back to me by the end o' the day, but accordin' to the file, there was a load of explicit footage of his bed partners—most o' which they couldn't identify, otherwise they'd have let 'em know. On the day he died, Rodgers didn't do much; he was movin' house, so a woman from a cleanin' company came round to look at the place, but that's about it."

"Could any of the men on the screens be identified?" Ryan asked.

"Only a couple, accordin' to the old file," Phillips said. "One lad brought a civil claim against Rodgers' estate, which settled out o' court. The other lad was dead, by the time all this came to light."

"Dead?" Jack repeated. "How?"

"Well, funny you should ask that, because I wondered the same thing myself," Phillips replied. "He was a seventeen-year-old by the name o' Stuart Atkinson. He killed himself towards the back end of 2006, a couple o' months after the camera captured him spendin' the night with Mr Rodgers."

"Was the connection made, at the time?" Charlie asked.

Phillips shook his head. "Even if it was, both parties were dead, by that point," he said. "Rodgers and Atkinson. However, I did find somethin' they might have overlooked."

Ryan smiled to himself, and thought that his friend was like a bloodhound.

"When I looked into the lad's family background, I found out Stuart had a sister, Marie. He was livin' with his mother and sister, at the time he died, and occasionally did a bit o' part-time work for his Ma's business. She ran a cleaning and housekeepin' operation, mostly around Darras Hall and Ponteland."

He referred to an affluent area, west of the city.

"Lo and behold, I find that his Ma used to housekeep for Kyle Rodgers—until Stuart killed himself, that is."

"That must be how Rodgers came to meet him," Jack said. "If Stuart's suicide was anything to do with the experience he had with Kyle, then his mother might have found out about it and that would be a good enough motive to want him dead."

"Exactly," Phillips said. "Now, lookin' back over the file, I can see that the *new* cleanin' woman who came around on the day Rodgers died gave a statement to the police sayin' he was alive and well, when she left him. D'you want to guess what her name was?"

"Janet Charteris," MacKenzie said, before the rest of them could finish thinking about it. "She tampered with something, somehow, while she was in there."

Phillips pointed a finger. "Close," he said. "She gave her name as Janet Rusk, but, me bein' the bloke that I am, I wondered whether that might've been her maiden name. Turns out, it was. Janet Rusk and Janet Charteris are one and the same, if y'ask me, but the footage'll confirm it for us, when it comes through."

"That's good work," Ryan said, and felt his spirits lift for the first time in weeks. "So, we have two families both dealing with the suicide of a loved one—or, in Janet's case, two suicides—after sexual assault or something similar. Is that correct?"

"Aye, that seems to be the link," Phillips said.

"In which case, we have to ask ourselves how Janet and— Who? Atkinson's mother?—met."

"I had a think about that," Phillips replied. "It could've been the mother, and I s'pose the father, but accordin' to her social media pages, Stuart's sister, Marie, is a slim, attractive blonde lass."

"Just like the one Edward Delaney was seen chatting up before he died, you mean?"

"Exactly like that one, aye. Marie Atkinson's a bit older, now, but she would've been in her twenties, back when Delaney was prowlin' round the clubs. She's Marie Everett now, since she got married a few years ago."

"So, we think Janet and Marie met one another, somehow," Morrison said. "But where?"

They all considered it, and then Charlie spoke up. "Counselling, or grief therapy of some kind? They tend to offer group sessions, as well as one-to-ones, for the families of suicide victims."

"That has to be it," Ryan agreed.

"One other thing that might be of interest," MacKenzie said, having performed a quick search of the database of members provided to them by *The Northern Fisherman*. "Didn't you say that Kevin Charteris died—back in 2007 or 2008?"

"Aye, he did," Frank said. "Why?"

"Funny that his subscription to the magazine is still active, wouldn't you say?"

They looked amongst themselves.

"I think it's time you paid a visit to Marie Everett, née Atkinson—and Janet Charteris," Ryan said. "Bring them in and ask them a few pertinent questions about what they do in their spare time."

"I say we put out an All Ports Warning and call in the Firearms Unit before any of you so much as step within thirty yards of either woman," Morrison added. "They might seem like ordinary people but, as we said at the start of this conversation, appearances can be deceiving. If we're right about them, then this scheme of theirs has been running for more than ten years, and has spread nationwide. We aren't dealing with a couple of grieving women, any longer, but the heads of a serious and organised criminal organisation. I won't take any chances, especially since this could be our only opportunity to apprehend them without them being forewarned."

"The only people who know about this are the folk in this room," Phillips said.

"And the archivist you spoke to," Morrison said, mildly. "People talk, even when they don't mean to. I say we act swiftly, before they've had time to scratch their arses let alone anything else."

"I'll contact Firearms," MacKenzie offered.

Phillips was unusually quiet, while they discussed strategy.

"Everything okay, Frank?" his wife asked. "This could be the moment we've all been waiting for, especially Ryan—"

"Aye, I know," he said, and worked up a smile. "And I hope we're right, if only so as that workshy Southern pansy can get himself back into the office."

Ryan swore at him, very politely, from Devon.

"But I was just thinkin' there, about Stuart Atkinson and Emily Charteris," Phillips continued. "Then, I was thinkin' of Samantha, and of what I'd do if anyone hurt her like that. I'd rip the bloody limbs from their body, and that's a fact."

It was no idle threat.

"Gregory said there would be some sort of vendetta against the justice system, or against society, as well as a hatred of the people who hurt their loved ones," Ryan said, and his voice was soft and serious now. "We've come across perpetrators on a mission before, only they operated on a smaller scale than this. They didn't expand their mission to include strangers, for one thing. Still, they all shared a sorry back story, often a heartbreaking one of loss or abuse." Ryan paused, while their faces swam in the forefront of his mind. "I remember them all," he said. "It isn't that we don't mourn the loss, or feel sorry for what happened to them, but we uphold the banner of the

Law. We have to believe in it, Frank, or render everything we do worthless. There has to be a standard that we bear."

They listened to his voice as it carried around the conference room and were, as always, inspired to carry on and be the example to others.

"See you on the other side," Ryan added. "Over and out."

CHAPTER 40

"I couldn't get hold of Jones."

It was shortly before three o'clock, and MacKenzie was about to leave to collect Samantha from school. She slipped on her coat, made a grab for her bag, and repeated her statement to Phillips, who hadn't caught it, the first time around.

"I couldn't get through to Neil Jones, in Firearms," she said again. "I spoke to his colleague, instead. They're going to arrange the support you need for this evening."

"Right-o," Phillips replied. "See you later on, love."

Still, MacKenzie hovered by his side, and he looked pointedly at Jack, who was seated across the table.

"Pet, y'nah I can't be givin' you a smooch, here in the office," he whispered. "I thought we agreed—"

MacKenzie gave him a clip on his dozy ear. "I'm not after a sloppy kiss from you, Frank Phillips," she said. "I was just thinking...I wonder where Jones could be?"

"Does it matter? The lad's probably taken the day off, like some people do," he said.

She nodded, started to turn away, then turned back again. "No, I think he said he was going to speak to someone up at Otterburn and get back to us," she said. "His colleague doesn't know where he's disappeared to, either."

"I'm sure it's nothin' to worry about," he said.

"You're probably right," she said, and gnawed at her lip. "I'm looking for baddies behind every corner, just because he walked in our meeting the other day, has a military background and knows how to plant an explosive device… but, as you say, it's probably nothing to worry about."

Phillips heaved a sigh, and tapped the table to get Jack Lowerson's attention.

"Hm?" he said.

"Do us a favour, will you? Track down the whereabouts of Neil Jones—nobody's seen hide nor hair of him."

Jack needed no further bidding.

"I'll be off, then," MacKenzie said, and, this time, she leaned down to bestow a kiss upon her husband's upturned face. "Be careful, Frank."

"I will."

In the years since her brother's death, Doctor Marie Everett had married and moved to the sleepy village of Stamfordham. She practised general medicine, and was mother to twin boys, who'd never be the same again, once the events of the day unfolded—nor would their father, who'd fallen in love with Marie Atkinson almost as soon as they'd met.

Phillips and Lowerson were aware of some of this, as they drove along the Stamfordham Road, west of the city of Newcastle and into the folds of Northumberland.

"Even knowin' what she might have done, I can't help thinkin' of her boys," Frank said. "I have to keep remindin' myself, it's thanks to this lass that I almost died outside Frankland Prison. Ryan lost his father, and many more families lost people they cared about. So many, it'll take us months, if not years, to get through them all."

Jack continued to drive at a steady pace—not the kind of speed Ryan could command, nor with the snail-like caution that was Frank's preferred level, but somewhere in between. "I know what you mean," he said. "But I lost any sympathy I might have felt, after what happened with Jen."

He thought of the woman who'd almost ruined his life—and of his mother, who'd killed her. The intention might have been to protect him, but the execution was misguided, to say the least.

"Aye, can't blame you for that," Frank muttered. "I s'pose, maybe, it's not *them* I feel sorry for, but the ones who took their own lives. If the system had worked, and justice had prevailed, then they might not have been driven to do somethin' so drastic, and none of this would've happened."

"What do you think, Frank? Are they 'mad' or 'bad'?"

Phillips pondered the question. "Both," he replied. "Driven mad by grief, but turned bad by their own choices."

Jack nodded, and took a call from the Firearms Team, who were already in position in the back lane behind Marie Everett's home.

"Almost there," he said, tugging at the bulletproof vest that covered his torso.

"I reckon the diet's paid off a bit," Frank remarked, and tapped his own vest. "This thing used to pinch a bit more than it does now."

Jack didn't have the heart to tell him that the one he wore was a size larger than usual, which meant it was the *correct* size for a change. "You can be the one to chase after Everett, if she makes a dash for it," he said.

Phillips made a quick re-evaluation. "With my dodgy ticker?" he said, and patted his chest for effect. "I wouldn't dare—"

"Uh huh," Jack said. "I thought the doctors said you were completely fit and healthy?"

"It never hurts to have a second opinion."

They laughed, and then sobered quickly as the sign for 'Stamfordham' came into view.

"Showtime," Jack said.

The Everett family lived in a beautiful, stone-built former schoolhouse, which overlooked the green in Stamfordham village. It was a pretty place, with a strong community of people who knew one another by name and held raffles for worthy causes. There was a pub, a convenience store, and a string of bunting hanging between the trees lining the main road, which flapped in the wind.

Phillips and Lowerson were joined by two members of the Firearms Unit, whilst the remaining two stayed in position at the rear of the property.

"Ready?" Frank asked them. At their affirmative, he raised a fist to knock on the front door, painted in a pretty shade of navy blue. Behind them, several pedestrians paused to watch what was happening, from the other side of the road.

"Rubberneckers," Jack muttered.

The door was opened by a good-looking blonde woman in her early forties. The moment her eyes registered who they were, they caught the momentary panic, which extinguished any remaining doubt they might have had about her involvement.

"Dr Everett?" Phillips asked.

"Y—yes," she replied, while her hand gripped the edge of the door. "What do you want?"

"We're DS Phillips and DC Lowerson, from CID at Northumbria Police. We have some questions we'd like to ask you, in regards to the death of Edward Delaney in April 2007."

"Who is it, Mummy?" A young boy came to the door.

"I'm just helping these policemen to answer some questions," she told him. "Go and find Granny."

When he skipped back down the hallway, she turned back. "I'd like a solicitor," she said.

No denial that she knew Delaney, Jack thought.

"My husband isn't due home until later," she said. "Can it wait?"

"No," Phillips said, hardening his heart. "I'm afraid it can't. Do you have childcare for your son?"

"Yes," she said, thinking fast. "I can ask my mother."

"Do that, please. It would be easier for all concerned if you agreed to come in for questioning without our needing to make an arrest, but we're prepared to do so if necessary."

No questions about what the charge would be, either, Jack noted. *She knew her time had run out.*

They accompanied her into the house, where she spoke to her mother. They watched the older woman's eyes turn round like saucers, obviously shocked by the turn of events, and, unlike her daughter, she put on a good show of having no idea why they were there.

"What's going on, here?" she demanded. "Marie says you're taking her in for questioning? What for? Has there been an incident at the surgery?"

She thought of the local health centre, where her daughter worked as a doctor and dealt with sick and dying people, every day.

"Mum—" Marie tried to quell the tide.

"No, Marie, this is outrageous," she stormed on. "My daughter is a hard-working, upstanding member of the community, and you're treating her as if she was some sort of *criminal!*"

They watched Marie's eyes close, as if the weight of the world was upon her shoulders.

"I'm ready to go," she told them, after pressing a kiss to her mother's cheek. "Mum? Tell Mark—just tell him I'll be home as soon as I can."

She bade her mother and son a tearful farewell, and allowed herself to be led away.

CHAPTER 41

"Sir?"

It took Phillips a moment to realise the young constable was speaking to him.

"Oh. Aye? What is it?"

"The team went to pick up the other suspect, Janet Charteris, but I'm afraid she wasn't at home. Should they wait, in case she turns up?"

Phillips nodded. "She's a major flight risk," he said. "Tell them to wait at the property, at a safe distance, and keep it under surveillance. If she comes back, let us know straight away. Meanwhile, we've got the ports covered."

"Thank you, sir."

Phillips resumed his task, which was to fill a couple of cups with instant coffee. There was a time, before he'd met Ryan, when Maxwell House would've been fine, and he'd have chugged it down without a second thought. That was the problem when you made friends in high places, he thought. You started getting highfalutin ideas about coffee, and all sorts.

"Still no word on Neil Jones," Lowerson said, coming to join him in the break room. "Is Janet on her way in?"

Phillips shook his head, and handed him one of the mugs. "No, she's not at home," he said. "I've told them to stay put and let us know when she comes back."

"Frank, you don't think Neil had anything to do with this, do you?"

Phillips took a swig of coffee, winced, and thought back to MacKenzie's warning, earlier. "He has the skillset," he replied, with none of his usual 'happy-go-lucky' humour. "He has the connections to pull off an explosion, for one thing, and the experience to take the kind of long-range shot that killed Charles Ryan. We don't know what his motive would be, for turnin' his back on his duty and wantin' to become a part of the scheme, but there's always somethin'. Addiction, gamblin', money, women…"

"I—er—had a quick dive into Jones's personal life," Jack said, keeping his voice low. It never sat well with any of them, to investigate one of their own, but they did what was necessary. "He got divorced, last year, and the ex-wife has the marital home and the kids, most of the time."

"Is she dead?"

"Nope, but Jones's father died suddenly, a few months ago," Jack replied. "He was old, but healthy, as well as being very wealthy. Now he's gone, Jones inherits the lot, because his mother died years ago, and his father never remarried. He doesn't have any siblings to share the inheritance with, either."

"How'd you find all *this* out?" Phillips had to ask.

"Canteen," Jack said, and Frank nodded, sagely.

"Well, let's not go jumpin' to any conclusions," he said. "Aside from our suspicious natures, we've got nothin' to suggest Jonesy's had anythin' to do with all this. On the other hand, we've got one woman sittin' in the interview suite downstairs, and I reckon she's got a few secrets to tell us."

Jack checked the time on the wall, which was shortly after five-thirty.

"She's had plenty of time to confer with her solicitor," he said. "Let's go."

———

Eve Finley-Ryan watched her son from a distance, as he made the rounds speaking to the security personnel he'd hired to watch over them, night and day. In addition to that, he liked to make a daily check that each of the cameras in the CCTV network was in working order, so that any intruder who made it past their security staff would be captured on screen and picked up by the gatekeeper or Ryan, each of whom could log into the live stream at any time. Despite these precautions, and the fact nothing had happened during the day, it seemed to her that Ryan was more anxious than usual. Oh, he was trying to hide it, of course; but there were some things a mother could always see.

"I just took a call from Jack Lowerson," Anna said, coming to join her at the window while Emma watched an episode of her favourite show.

Eve turned to her. "Have they found the people they're looking for?"

"He's hopeful," Anna said, and relief made her voice wobble. "They've brought one woman in for questioning, and will probably charge her, and they're waiting to bring another one in as soon as they can."

"Oh, thank goodness," Eve said, and drew Anna into her arms for a tight embrace. "Finally, this will all be over."

Anna held her mother-in-law, inhaling the delicate scent of her perfume and enjoying the warmth of her body. Eve was a generous woman, in word and deed, and that had never been more apparent than in the way she'd welcomed Anna into their family. Eve had lost her own daughter, while Anna had lost her mother, so it seemed the universe had brought them together; two strong, intelligent women who shared a love for the same wilful, raven-haired man.

"I don't want to get too excited, but we might finally be able to sleep properly, again. Ryan can live an ordinary life, and so can we."

Eve nodded, and rubbed a comforting hand over her back, which had grown slender of late. "You need fattening up," she said.

Anna laughed, and pulled away. "I'd never say 'no' to a scone," she said. "You stay here, with Emma, and I'll put a tea tray together. This news is worth celebrating."

Eve looked across at the little girl who was sitting cross-legged on the carpet in front of their old television.

She thought of Natalie, as she always did, and tried not to mourn her, or the children she might have had.

My beautiful girl, she thought.

Then, she closed the door to grief, and thought not of all that she'd lost, but all that she still had. There was much to be grateful for, including the little pixie bopping along to the theme music of a television show featuring a selection of cartoon animals.

Eve put a smile on her face, jiggled her hips, and moved across the room to join her.

"Sit beside me, Grandma!" Emma patted the carpet.

"I'm not sure my hips can manage it, darling—"

"Is that because you're *old*?"

Like hell I am, Eve thought. "I'm older than you," she said, coming to sit beside her on the carpet. "But I'm never old."

Emma smiled, and rested her head on her shoulder.

Marie Everett had chosen one of the city's premier solicitors to represent her, which led Phillips and Lowerson to wonder just how long she'd had the number on speed-dial. Laura Sayle was a sharp woman with an experienced background in criminal defence, whom they'd met dozens of times over the years and—it had to be said—respected far more than some of her peers, for her professionalism and straightforward attitude. They might have been coming at the case from different sides, but each one understood the other's role in the justice system, which included the fact that everyone was entitled to a defence, even the most heinous of criminals.

They made the introductions, read aloud the details of the interview and case number for the record, and prepared to interrogate a woman who may very well have been partly responsible for masterminding a nationwide murder scheme.

"Dr Everett, thank you for agreeing to come in and answer some questions for us, today," Jack began.

"My client would like to have it restated, for the record, that she is here voluntarily."

"That's true," Frank said. "At least, for now."

That was met with stony silence, so Jack pressed on. "We'd like to begin by asking you some questions about your family, Marie. May I call you, Marie?"

She nodded.

"Thank you," Jack said. "Now, then. We understand that, very sadly, you lost your brother, Stuart, to suicide several years ago, in 2006. Is that correct?"

Marie glanced at her solicitor, then nodded. "Yes, that's correct."

"We're sorry to hear it," Jack said, sincerely. "Can you tell me why your brother might have taken his own life?"

"Detective, my client understands she's here to help with an active investigation," Sayle chimed in. "Her late brother's untimely death has no bearing on any active case."

"We disagree," Jack said. "In fact, we believe Stuart Atkinson's death might have been one of two catalysts which started a chain reaction, leading to the active and cold case investigations we are now pursuing."

Sayle leaned in, to whisper in Marie's ear.

"He was ill," she said. "Most people who take their lives have some form of mental illness, in my experience."

"We understand you're a General Practitioner?"

"Yes."

"But we're not talking about the cases you might've seen in the years since he died, but specifically about Stuart," Jack said. "You say he was unwell—did he have a diagnosis? Was he always that way?"

She hesitated. "No," she said. "He wasn't."

"Detective—" Sayle said, irritably.

"We're getting to it," Jack said, with his own measure of irritation. "Marie?"

She stared at him, from a set of pale blue eyes that held a flat, faraway expression. "Stu had begun taking anti-depressants, but they weren't working," she said. "He—he couldn't hold on." Marie swallowed, and reached for the glass of water beside her.

"And did he always suffer from depression?"

"No," she said.

"Something more recent had upset him, then?" Frank put in. "Do you know what that could've been?"

"No comment," she said.

"Touched a nerve, have we?" Frank said. "How about I tell you what we think happened, and you can tell me if it's correct?" He didn't wait for an answer, but folded his hands

POISON GARDEN

on the table. "Your mam used to run a cleaning firm, before she retired, didn't she?" he said.

"That's a matter of record," Marie said. "You can see it on Companies House."

"You can, indeed." Frank nodded. "Another thing we know is that she used to housekeep for a famous footballer, Kyle Rodgers, before he died, in 2007. Did you know that?"

"No comment."

"Well, she did, right up until your brother passed away," Frank continued, nonplussed. "Now, if my son had died, I wouldn't want to go back to work straight away, either. I'd take some time off to grieve and try to pull myself together, hard as it may be."

She nodded.

"Here's the thing, Marie. When we looked at your ma's records, we could see she started back at work a few days after Stuart died," Frank said. "She might've wanted the distraction, or many a thing. But she didn't start back to work for Mr Rodgers, even though she knew he might've needed the help since he was movin' down to Bournemouth. Now, why d'you think that was?"

"No comment."

"I think she knew Rodgers had been...unkind, let's say, to your brother, after they'd had a night together. I think that's what tipped Stuart over the edge, and left you and your family devastated."

Marie's eyes filled with tears, but they didn't fall. "No comment."

"People who lose loved ones to suicide often go to group therapy, don't they?" Jack said, and she turned to him with glazed eyes.

"I—yes, they do."

"Did you?"

That, too, was a matter of record, so she nodded. "Yes, I did."

"Do you have the details of where and when?"

They could easily find that out, she supposed, and gave them the address at the hospital.

"Do you remember having met Janet and Kevin Charteris, while you attended these support group meetings?"

They'd find a list of attendees, she thought. "Yes."

"Do you remember why Janet and Kevin were at the group?"

"It was a group for the surviving family members of suicide victims," she said, evasively.

"Yes," Jack persisted. "But do you remember who they lost?"

"I…think it was their daughter."

"Really, this is getting beyond a joke," Sayle interjected. "So far, I've heard nothing whatsoever that relates to an active or past investigation. All you've talked about is the highly emotive subject of my client's brother having passed away, causing her extreme distress, I'm sure. As for the Charteris family, there isn't any connection to my client or any known offence. State your case, or I'll be advising my client to walk."

"All right," Jack said. "It is our belief that you and Janet Charteris became friends, after she lost her daughter, and you lost your brother. You both felt let down by the system, for similar reasons—she, because her daughter brought a rape case that led to the acquittal of her attacker, Edward Delaney, and you, because your brother was sexually assaulted by Kyle Rodgers and groomed in such a way that he felt he couldn't make a complaint, or he'd be publicly humiliated or disbelieved." He paused. "How am I doing, so far?"

Marie said nothing, but her eyes burned.

"Here's where our investigation comes in," Jack continued, before Sayle could utter a word. "Delaney died following an apparent overdose. Are you aware of that?"

"No comment."

"On the evening of his death, several witnesses say they saw him with an attractive blonde woman, who matches your description. Were you at the nightclub when Delaney died, Marie?"

"No comment."

"Have you ever met Edward Delaney?"

"No comment."

"Did you spike Delaney's drink, or anything else?"

"No comment."

"Did you kill Edward Delaney to help your friend, Janet, in the belief that she would then do the same for you?"

"No comment," Marie said, but this time her throat bobbed as she tried to swallow the fear that stuck her throat.

"As for Janet, she returned the favour, didn't she? Janet Charteris posed as a woman from a cleaning company and went along to Kyle Rodgers' house under the pretext of looking it over ahead of a big cleaning assignment. Instead, we believe she planted a toxic substance in his food, or some other ingestible, which led to him having a fatal cardiac arrest. Isn't that true?"

"No comment."

"After Edward and Kyle were killed, that wasn't the end, though, was it, Marie? You and Janet conspired to create a network, a scheme, if you will, which allowed other people who felt wronged and impotent, to kill the people who had harmed them or their loved ones. Didn't you?"

"No."

Phillips looked up at that, noting the difference to her previous 'no comment' answers.

"The system you created has allowed hundreds, possibly thousands, of people to arrange a murder—and all they had to do was commit one themselves. Isn't that right?"

Marie shook her head. "No."

Sayle looked at her client, and then at Jack and Frank. "I think we need another moment to confer—"

"You've had plenty of moments," Frank said. "So has your client."

"What about *The Northern Fisherman*, Marie?" Jack persisted, giving no quarter now. "Was it your idea to use Janet's late husband's membership to start posting the classified ads?"

"*No.*"

"I think we've heard enough," Sayle said. "Unless you're going to charge—"

"Rodgers had cameras in his house," Frank said, softly.

Marie's eyes widened, a fraction.

"Yes," he said. "It's true. He had hidden cameras all over the place, but then, I think you knew that already, didn't you? Did Stuart find out?"

She said nothing, but a single tear fell down her cheek.

"We'll find out if Janet's on the camera footage," he said. "Somebody managed to prevent the file from being uploaded to the digital system, but we keep the original, y' know. There'll be a USB memory stick with that footage on it, in the archives, and I'm going to go through it, personally, to see if the woman who paid Rodgers a visit that day is Janet Charteris. You know what else I'm gonna look at?"

Frank paused, and leaned forward.

"The old footage from the nightclub," he said, and she turned a paler shade of grey. "We still have the recordings. I'll bet I see you on it, somewhere, Marie—which would be awfully strange, wouldn't it?"

"You sure there isn't anything you want to tell us?" Jack asked.

"No—no comment."

"Alreet," Frank said, and turned to his friend. "D'you wanna do the honours?"

"Don't mind if I do," Jack said, and went through the formalities of charging her with murder.

Further accusations of conspiracy to murder would follow, but not until after Ryan was safely home, and not until they'd made a full account of all the people who'd died, thanks to this woman's scheming.

CHAPTER 42

"I thought you'd be happy?"

Anna put a gentle hand on her husband's back, and tried to soothe the tension she found there. Upstairs, Eve was reading her granddaughter a bedtime story, while the sun disappeared behind the trees on the far side of the lawn. But Ryan wasn't watching the sunset, no matter how beautiful the sky looked, as it melted into deep shades of lilac and navy blue.

"This could mean the end of all our worries," Anna continued.

Ryan's eyes were a deep, stormy blue when he dragged them away from the garden, and the look in them made her shiver. "Even if these women are responsible for starting the scheme, they're unlikely to talk," he said. "They'll drag everything out for as long as possible, to cover themselves, because that's what they've been doing for years. The hit has already been put out, as we all know, and so the threat remains; whoever thought they'd been the one to kill me has a vested interest to see the job done properly, because they won't have any idea that the people behind it have been apprehended."

"You mean...they won't know there's been any change in the guard?"

"Exactly," Ryan said, and turned back to the garden, where his eyes searched the gathering darkness. "There've been a couple of potential leaks, so I have to remain vigilant."

"We both will," she said, and took his hand.

Ryan looked down at their entwined fingers, then raised hers to his lips. "I love you," he said. "I know we say it all the time, but it costs nothing to say it again."

She smiled. "I love you too, Ryan. I'm worried about you, today more than ever. You seem agitated...Is there anything you're not telling me?"

He put an arm around her, and drew her into the warmth of his body. "I'm sorry to worry you," he said. "I just can't shake the feeling."

"What feeling?"

"I've just had a feeling that something's going to happen, today."

"The day is almost over," she said.

"And night is only just beginning."

They looked out at the shadows, which stretched into contorted shapes across the lawn, mirroring every bush and tree. A person could hide in and behind any of them, Anna realised, and it sent a chill through her veins.

It was after eight, by the time Phillips and Lowerson finished booking Marie Everett into her new lodgings for the evening, and writing up their reports for the Crown Prosecution Service, including the many reasons why bail should be refused when her solicitor applied for it.

Jack yawned, and checked his e-mails one last time. "Jonesy's ex-wife hasn't heard from him," he said. "He isn't due to collect the kids until the weekend, so she wouldn't expect to."

"No help there, then."

"He lives alone," Jack said. "I can drive over and see if he's at the address?"

"Not without me, you won't," came the rejoinder. "We all hope to be wrong, lad, but we can't take any chances with this. I'll come with you."

"Has the surveillance team been in touch about Janet Charteris?"

Frank shook his head. "They're still up there, waiting for her to reappear," he said. "She could be anywhere."

"Or she could be at the most obvious place," Jack said.

"Which is, Smarty-Pants?"

"The cemetery."

Janet Charteris looked up at the sky, and knew it was time to go home. The wind was picking up, colder now that the sun had gone down, and the cemetery gates had already closed for the day. Of course, she had a set of keys for her own personal use, procured by a very grateful patron a few years earlier.

"I had a call from a police detective," she told her husband, and smoothed the grass over the spot where he lay. "He wanted to know what we were both doing, on the day Edward Delaney died."

Janet stood up, and moved to the headstone next to his, the same shade of weathered white marble and inscribed with her daughter's name.

"I told him the truth," she said, conversationally. "Your father and I were away in Wales, at that grief retreat. Do you remember, Kev? You couldn't stand it, could you? You said going there was a waste of time."

Janet chuckled, as if they were sitting around the kitchen table, as they used to.

"I think they must be getting closer to finding out the truth," she said, with genuine sadness.

She stroked her daughter's headstone, and imagined it was her hair.

"I miss you," she whispered. "I miss both of you."

The old, familiar anger rose up again, as fresh as it had been all those years before. Time hadn't diluted its potency; in fact, killing Kyle Rodgers had unlocked some hitherto unknown part of herself that was brave, and fearless. She fancied herself as a kind of anonymous superhero, crusading for justice, but, she knew, there were plenty of others who'd killed simply for money or some other base cause.

She didn't think about that.

All organisations were prone to hiccups, especially as they grew in size and strength. If one or two less worthy members slipped through the net, that was to be expected.

Still, she was getting tired.

She could admit that to herself, in the company of her family, beneath the blanket of stars that began to pop in the night sky overhead. Time wasn't on her side, anymore. Having a mission had given her the strength to get up each day, and carry on living. Becoming an angel of death had gifted her with new life, and the irony of that wasn't lost on her.

But now?

Now, her energy was waning, not because she no longer believed in the cause, but because it didn't provide the same distraction for her as it once had. Besides, the hourglass was running out and perhaps that wasn't such a bad thing. Her anger was uncontrollable, as was the compulsion to kill. Not with her own hands, necessarily; she found an almost equal rush in killing by proxy. Every time a new request came through, she felt a little buzz of exhilaration.

How would they do it? she wondered. *Would the police find out?*

Then, there'd been that photographer, in Dunstanburgh. It was bad luck, the way all the dots seemed to have joined, despite best efforts to conceal them. The police were, for the most part, a collection of useless, morally defunct clods, but occasionally Lady Luck threw them a bit of good fortune.

Janet leaned down and kissed each headstone in turn.

"I have to go now," she said. "I'll see you both, very soon."

She forced herself to turn away, hating the part where she had to leave them but knowing there would come a day when they'd be reunited. Before Emily died, she hadn't been a believer of any kind, but it was funny how the prospect of Heaven became more palatable than the alternative, which was unthinkable. Never to see Emily again, or Kev? Janet shook her head, the keys to the cemetery gate jingling in the pocket of her overcoat.

Lost in thought, she didn't see the shadows until they were almost upon her.

"Janet Charteris?"

She saw a man of average height, with a stocky, boxer's build and thinning grey hair. Behind him stood a younger man, with pleasant features she might have approved of, had Emily brought someone like him home for tea.

"So, you've come for me, then?" she said.

Phillips looked into the eyes of an ageing woman, whose papery skin crinkled into wrinkled fans as she spoke. She was dressed in hardy trousers and walking shoes, and her hair was cut short in a practical, no-nonsense style designed to be functional rather than decorative. She carried a small rucksack on her shoulder, which contained a selection of gardening and other tools she used to maintain her family's gravesites.

"We have," he told her. "Are you going to come with us, and have a chat?"

Janet looked back over her shoulder at the empty cemetery, and nodded. "It's getting late," she said.

CHAPTER 43

"She doesn't look like a criminal mastermind."

Chief Constable Morrison stood between Phillips and Lowerson in the observation room at Police Headquarters. Unlike her confederate, Janet Charteris had no solicitor at her fingertips, and seemed happy to accept the services of whichever one happened to be available. It was after nine o'clock on a match day in the city—which usually brought with it a higher volume of assaults, batteries and cases of grievous bodily harm—so Janet would likely have to wait a while.

"She looks like she's a couple of sandwiches short of a picnic, if y'ask me," Frank pronounced.

"Thank you for that insightful analysis, Doctor Freud," Morrison drawled.

"I dunno, boss," Jack said. "I agree with Frank. On the way over here, she was muttering away to herself. I only caught the odd word, but it sounded like she was talking to her husband, who's long dead."

Morrison sighed. "If you're right about that, any lawyer worth their salt will request a psychological evaluation," she said. "They'll try to argue diminished responsibility."

"What can we do?" Jack said.

"Hope they're not worth any salt at all," Morrison muttered. "At least, not until you've elicited some answers. We need to know how Janet's been running her organisation, who else is involved, and how the hell to put a stop to it without any further loss of life— especially the life of one pain-in-the-arse detective, in particular."

"Ryan loves you, too," Frank said.

Morrison snorted, and then stifled a yawn. "We're going to need more coffee."

After a couple of seconds ticked by, she and Frank turned to look at Jack.

"Why do I always have to get it?" he complained.

"Because you're the *youngest*," Frank said, as if to a slow child. "We don't make the rules, lad, we merely follow them."

"Yeah, right," Jack mumbled.

As he reached the door, Frank's voice stopped him. "None o' that instant muck, neither," he said. "I've got standards to uphold."

"You've got a *nerve*, that's what you've got," Jack told him. "Where am I supposed to find fancy coffee at this hour of the night?"

This time, they slowly turned to look at Morrison.

"*Fine*, use the coffee machine in my office," she said. "Break it, and I'll demote you."

"Understood."

An hour later, a young man who looked barely old enough to be out of short trousers presented himself as the duty solicitor assigned to Janet Charteris. He sat on a chair at the table opposite his new client and opened a dog-eared notepad. "Right, Mrs Charteris," he began. "Perhaps you could start by telling me—"

"I did it," she said.

He stared at her. "Sorry, did you say—?"

"I *did* it," Janet repeated, obligingly. "The police are probably going to charge me with the murder of Kyle Rodgers, and something like accomplice to, or conspiracy to murder, a total of four hundred and seven other people—depending on how many they've managed to uncover. Incidentally, the number might have risen in the past few hours, but I'm afraid I haven't had a chance to check my e-mails."

She spoke in the same tone she might have employed at a meeting of the Women's Institute, which was all the more unsettling.

"I want to be very clear," he said. "Are you saying you'd like to confess to—did you say forty-seven murders?"

"No," she said, and thought the poor lad must be hard of hearing. "*Four hundred and seven*, is the most recent figure, according to my records. However, I was more of a guiding hand in most of those, rather than the one holding the dagger, as it were."

He looked at her in mute disbelief.

"Oh, I know, it's an impressive number," she said, with a touch of pride. "Far more efficient than the court system, for one thing."

"And—how are you planning to plead, if charges are brought?"

"*Guilty*, of course," she said, and gave him a beautiful smile.

He removed the lid from his biro, and wished he'd brought more than one notepad.

"Good evening, Mrs Charteris."

After much discussion, Frank and Jack had decided to play it suave with the lady sitting demurely in Interview Room 4. After a lengthy chat, she'd eventually dismissed the young solicitor, who'd left Police Headquarters shortly afterwards looking shell-shocked but relieved.

"Good evening," she replied, politely. "We met in the cemetery, didn't we?"

"That's right," Jack said. "I'm DC Lowerson, and this is DS Phillips."

He recited their details fully for the recording, gave their warrant card numbers, and restated her decision to waive her right to legal representation.

"Goodness, how do you remember those numbers off by heart?"

"Well, now, I was goin' to ask you the same thing," Frank replied. "Do you remember the exact number of murders you've had a hand in, or are you up to approximate figures?"

She waggled a finger as if he'd been a naughty boy. "Now, now," she said. "Just because I'm getting on in years, that doesn't mean I'm going to make this easy for you, sergeant."

"That's a shame," he said. "We're both very interested to know how you managed to pull off such a scheme. She's had us on the run, hasn't she, Jack?"

"You have indeed, Mrs Charteris."

She smiled, coyly. "I thought you'd have cottoned on long before now," she said. "But then, it was intended to be *fool*proof."

They both smiled, and took the insult on the chin.

"We're both very sorry about what happened to your daughter, and to your husband," Frank said. "That must've been very difficult for you."

Her fingers clasped together tightly beneath the table. "It should never have happened."

"No, it shouldn't."

Janet stared at Frank, into eyes that were full of compassion, and felt inexplicably angry. She didn't *want* sympathy from the police, nor any kindness. They were incompetent *morons*, liars, deadbeats. The fact they'd let her and her family down so grievously was all the proof she needed of that, and meeting so many others with similar experiences had only solidified that opinion.

"Is that why you and Marie decided to do an exchange?" Jack asked her. "Because you felt wronged by the system?"

Wronged, she thought. *What a quaint way of putting it.*

"You could say that," she replied. "It was clear to both of us that those men would've carried on hurting other people like my Emily, or like Stuart, and the justice system would've let them."

"Kyle Rodgers was never brought to court," Frank said. "The system wasn't given a chance to work."

"It was perfectly *obvious* how things would have been skewed in his favour," she snapped, all vestiges of the calm, older lady disappearing without a trace. "Those young men were too frightened to make a public complaint, for fear of what he'd do to discredit them. The power balance was completely in his favour."

They couldn't argue with the likely truth of that, but it didn't justify murder.

"How did you kill him, Janet?"

"How do you think?" she replied, with an unexpected playfulness.

They looked at one another, then back at her.

"Well," Frank said, folding his hands across his chest. "To be perfectly honest, Janet, we think you dressed up as a cleaning lady, knocked on his door, then found some way of contaminating his food so that he'd suffer a huge heart attack."

She inclined her head. "But you couldn't have proved it, unless I'd told you," she said.

Now, it was Phillips who waggled a finger. "Ah, that's not quite true," he said. "I'm expectin' a very interestin' delivery from our archives department, with the original recordings taken from Rodgers' house."

She didn't look perturbed. "I'm well aware that he had cameras hidden in some of the rooms, including the bedroom," she said. "Stuart told Marie all about it."

"So, you kept your head down, you mean?"

Janet nodded. "I don't suppose it matters now," she said. "I put a toxic dose of beta-blockers into his toothpaste. Stuart told us he used the powdered stuff for smokers, to keep his teeth from yellowing, so Marie swiped some from the medical store at the teaching hospital and I crushed them up. Nothing simpler, really."

They knew that, in high enough doses, beta-blockers could slow the heart to such a degree that it went into cardiac arrest.

Why hadn't it shown on the autopsy report?

They made a note to check the name of the pathologist who'd handled the case.

"I suppose Marie did the same thing to Edward Delaney and used crushed up beta-blockers to spike his drink?"

"I can't recall exactly what she ended up using, because it was so long ago," Janet said, as if they were talking about an old recipe for Victoria sponge. "Whatever it was, it did the trick, though, didn't it?"

They said nothing to that.

"How long have you and Doctor Everett been running this...what would you call it? An enterprise?"

"I like to think of it as a judicial co-operative," Janet said. "And, since you ask, I must say Marie hasn't been terribly helpful in running it. I'm afraid she wasn't really committed to helping others."

"What makes you say that?" Jack asked.

Janet folded her arms. "Marie was quite angry, when she found out I'd advertised their names in *The Northern Fisherman*," she remembered. "She said it wasn't part of our bargain, and it was only supposed to be a one-time thing, which we were meant to keep to ourselves. Well, naturally, I told her that other people would trust our system a lot more if they could see some sort of proof that we'd had a hand in it, and what better way of doing that than to publish their names?"

Janet looked at them, affronted all over again.

"Marie said she'd never agreed to broadening the scope of our little co-operative, and that it was *wrong*," she continued, using her fingers to put the word in quote marks. "I told her, in no uncertain terms, that it was a bit late for her to start making claims about what's 'right' or 'wrong', and she didn't like that very much, either. In the end, we parted ways."

"So, Marie was only involved in the murder of Edward Delaney, and as accessory to the murder of Kyle Rodgers? Is that what you're telling us?"

Janet nodded.

"If you don't mind us askin', how many others have there been in your co-operative since then?" Frank said, with no small amount of trepidation.

"Four hundred and seven," she said. "That's FOUR, ZERO, SEVEN."

"That's a lot of deaths," Frank said, once he could trust his own voice. "One of our own is part of that number—"

"Oh, come now, sergeant," Janet interjected. "You and I both know your detective friend, Ryan, is still alive."

Frank and Jack strived to keep the fear from showing on their faces, in case it broke the flow of conversation or—worse still—encouraged her to clam up, out of spite for them and all they stood for.

"Do you have the time?"

Her question was unexpected, and caught them off-guard.

"Yes, it's…" Jack checked his phone. "Nine-forty-seven. Are you feeling tired?"

A suspect had rights, after all.

"Me? Oh, heavens, no, I'm wide awake, dear. I was just wondering whether what I'd just said was still accurate. I suspect I might have to change my statement, because one of your own may very well be part of that number, after all," she said, with obvious relish. "I'll have to update the tally to four hundred and *eight*."

Jack's stomach performed a slow flip. "What do you mean, Janet?"

She looked at him with eyes that were no longer clouded by age, or blunted by grief, but clear and calculating.

"I mean, constable, that somebody will have rectified their earlier error."

"Who?" Frank managed. "*Who*?"

"Gosh, I wouldn't dream of telling you that!" she exclaimed. "Where would be the fun in that?"

Frank wondered how a person could fall so far, and how he could ever have imagined himself feeling sorry for her.

"Jack—" he said, but Lowerson was already halfway out of his chair.

"Interview terminated," he said, and hurried from the room to make an urgent call.

CHAPTER 44

Ryan watched his daughter sleeping from the doorway to her room, which had once been his nursery. It had been redecorated, since then, his mother and father having taken great delight in creating a little girl's dream, without any deference to political correctness whatsoever. It was unapologetically girlish, in shades of pale pink and cream, with a mountain of fluffy toys and a gauzy chiffon canopy above her bed, fit for a princess. They'd even found Natalie's old doll's house, which Emma loved to play with.

A wet nose nudged the back of his hand, and he looked down to find the puppy sitting there with a dopey grin on its face, having followed him stealthily from his bed in the utility room.

"Hey," Ryan whispered, coming down to the dog's level to scratch his ears. "What d' you think you're doing up here? Are you lost?"

The puppy licked his chin, and Ryan was about to scoop him up when the animal's body became very still.

"What is it, Rascal?"

The dog turned and raced back along the corridor, yapping so loudly Ryan was surprised he didn't wake the whole household. He followed him towards the stairs and managed to catch him before he ran down them.

"What's the matter?" Anna said, stepping out onto the landing.

Ryan opened his mouth to reply, but then noticed something odd. Behind her, the door to their bedroom stood open and he saw a large, impressive window whose curtains hadn't yet been drawn. In the evenings, they could usually see the comforting yellow glow of light from the gatehouse at the end of the driveway, faint and indistinct, but always there, like a lighthouse. Now, there was no yellow glow, only a whisper of moonlight to relieve the unrelenting darkness.

"There aren't any lights on, in the gatehouse," Ryan said.

Anna moved to the window to look for herself.

He was right.

"What's happening?" she asked, in a hushed whisper. "Why are the lights off?"

Ryan followed her into the bedroom and crossed the carpet in a couple of strides. He made for the bedside cabinet, inside of which he kept a locked box containing his service weapon, which he checked and then tucked into the waistband of his jeans.

"I don't know, but we have to move quickly," he told her. "Wake my mother and Emma, and, if everything looks clear, head for the utility exit. Get in one of the cars and drive. I'll follow, as soon as I can."

"Shouldn't we call the police?"

"Yes, but only once you're safely out of here," he said. "It'll take them at least fifteen minutes to get here from the nearest station, and that's on a good day. A lot can happen in fifteen minutes."

He handed the puppy to her, and Rascal burrowed into her chest.

"Ryan, I can't leave you—"

"We talked about this," he said. "There's no time to argue."

Anna knew it was true.

"Please, do as I ask," he said, and pulled her in for a hard, passionate kiss. "I love you."

"Wait—where are you going?"

Ryan's voice was grim. "To check the doors."

Ryan stood very still at the top of the wide, carved staircase, keeping to the wall as he strained to hear any unusual sounds coming from the ground floor. The landing lights shone above him, which were kept on so that Emma could go to the bathroom if she needed, but there were only a few night lights shining around the house downstairs, which was alarmed at night.

Ryan reached for the radio in his pocket.

"This is Ryan," he said quietly. "All units please respond. Over."

There came a crackling reply.

This is Bell. The lights are out in the gatehouse and Finch isn't responding. I'm going to go and take a look. Please remain where you are until—

Ryan heard a gunshot, and his heart slammed against the wall of his chest.

"Bell?" he said. *"Bell!"*

The radio was dead in his hand.

Ryan drew out his smartphone and accessed the security app, which allowed him to check the CCTV livestream.

Deactivated.

Multiple screens, which normally fed a clear stream of footage from key points around the house and grounds, were now blank. The security staff knew how to access the system from their devices and from the main terminal in the gatehouse. They were trained to withstand terror threats, but this wasn't a military base in the desert; nowadays, you could be dead, and your assailant could access your phone device using facial recognition long after you'd stopped breathing. It would be simple enough for someone to deactivate the alarm and—

Ryan heard it, then.

Glass breaking, somewhere downstairs.

They'd found out he was still alive and had come for him. Security personnel, expensive alarms, and acres of grounds hadn't been enough to stop an assassin hell-bent on completing their mission. It was no longer a case of wondering which unknown stranger sought him out, which malevolent being had murder in mind, somewhere out there in the wild. It didn't matter who they were; it only mattered that time had run out and the threat was there, knocking at his door.

The fortress he'd built was only made of sand, after all.

The phone he still held in his hand began to vibrate, and a glance told him the caller was Jack Lowerson, who was probably calling to warn him.

Too late, Jack.

The wolf was at the door.

Anna shoved her feet into a pair of trainers and, together with the puppy, hurried to her mother-in-law's room. She didn't bother to knock, and went inside to find Eve sitting up in bed, still awake and reading her husband's old journal.

"Anna?" she said, and set the book aside. "What's the matter?"

"It's time to go," Anna said, and grabbed the dressing gown Eve had draped over an occasional chair. "Here, put this on, and grab a pair of shoes—anything will do. We have to get Emma and make our way to the car."

"What about Ryan?" Eve said, anxiously.

"These are his instructions," Anna said, and held out the puppy. "Take Rascal, while I go and get Emma. Stay in here and we'll go together."

Eve nodded, and sat down on the edge of the bed, cradling the dog in her arms.

Ryan moved downstairs, a police-issue Glock in hand. He moved softly in his bare feet, while his eyes darted around every corner of the hallway. Reaching the bottom of the stairs, he paused, standing perfectly still in the semi-darkness while his ears strained to hear every sound, every whisper, until—

There, he thought.

Splintering wood, as a door came off its hinges.

The side door, he thought. The one at the far end of the corridor, in the opposite direction to the kitchen and utility room.

That was good.

If he could distract the intruder, Anna could get everyone out of the house via the utility room door and head for one of the waiting cars, assuming they hadn't been tampered with.

Ryan steadied himself, thought of those he loved, and then crossed the hallway with light-footed steps, heading directly into the path of danger.

There was no choice.

Both security personnel were unresponsive and, he feared, either dead or seriously injured. Even if Anna managed to get out and escape quickly, the police would take at least fifteen minutes to arrive once she managed to call them. There was no way to be sure they'd get there in time.

Ryan knew one thing for certain.

They were on their own.

Emma opened her sleepy eyes when Anna lifted her from the warmth of her bed.

"Mummy, it isn't morning yet!" she protested.

"Shh! Be quiet, Emma," her mother replied, and coaxed her arms into a warm coat.

"Why?"

"*Shh*! I'll tell you, when we get to the car," Anna whispered. "Now, promise me, you won't say a word?"

Emma nodded. "Okay," she said, and rested her head on her mother's shoulder.

"Let's go and get grandma, too," Anna said, and checked the coast was clear before hurrying back along to Eve's room.

Her mother-in-law had changed into more practical clothing, and tucked the puppy into one of her larger bags, which she'd lined with a towel.

"Grandma!" Emma exclaimed. "Are we going to have a midnight feast?"

"Shh, quiet, sweetie!" Anna reminded her, and then met Eve's eyes across the room. "Are you ready?"

The other woman nodded. "I'm ready."

Anna hitched Emma more comfortably into her arms and waited for Eve to lift the bag with the puppy.

"Let's go as fast as we can," Anna said, and opened the door to check the landing again.

It was clear.

"Follow me," she whispered, and headed for the servants' stairs.

Ryan thought he heard the dog whimpering, and Emma's voice, but put them both out of his mind. He trusted Anna and his mother to look after themselves, and the precious cargo they carried, just as they trusted him to ensure their safe passage.

He forced himself to keep moving down the corridor towards the side door, Glock held tightly in his outstretched hands. There was a slight breeze on the air, coming through the side door directly ahead of him, but no sign of the person who'd broken the glass. Ryan moved very slowly, his bare feet inching along the polished marble floor, keeping his eyes sharp as he moved through the semi-darkness and his ears trained on the sounds of the old house, from the creak of its radiators to the groan of floorboards moving beneath the weight of a man—

Ryan saw the figure emerge through the open doorway of the library, weapon poised to fire. He swung his Glock, but was seconds too late to discharge it before another bullet came whizzing through the air towards him.

There was no time to think, only to act.

Ryan threw himself against the opposite wall, jarring his shoulder badly. Instead of hitting his chest, the bullet skimmed his upper arm, burning a pathway through his skin. He didn't stop to think of the pain, because there was no time.

They were coming for him again.

He rolled in the opposite direction on the floor, narrowly missing another bullet, then lifted the Glock and opened fire.

As Anna and Eve reached the bottom of the old servants' stairs, they heard a succession of loud *pops* coming from the direction of the main hallway.

"*Max!*" Eve said, forgetting that her son no longer used the name she'd given him. She began to turn, maternal instinct taking over.

"It's too dangerous!" Anna whispered, but knew that, had Emma not been in her arms, she'd have gone to help him, herself. "We have to carry on this way."

Anna moved towards the utility room door, away from the gunfire, feeling her daughter shaking in her arms.

"It's okay," she said, and kissed Emma's cheek. "You're safe with me."

She waited while Eve fiddled with the lock on the door, her hands trembling badly.

Finally, the key turned in the lock and they hurried outside, where they found two cars waiting, just as Ryan had promised.

"We'll take my car," Eve said. "You get in the back with Emma and strap her in, while I drive."

"I can drive—"

"I'll be fine. Get in!"

Anna looked back at the house, and thought of the man she loved.

She couldn't leave him.

Then, she remembered what he'd told her, felt the child in her arms, and knew she held Emma's life in her hands. Anna bundled them both inside and, a moment later, the car surged forward, accelerating down the driveway into the night.

———————————

Ryan heard a car's wheels crunching against the gravel driveway outside, and hoped it was Anna and his mother, taking Emma and the puppy to safety. It bolstered his strength, which was waning now that his arm was bleeding heavily. He'd pushed back the assailant but knew that the fight was far from over; he was weakened, and the other man knew it.

Was it a man?

He'd seen a figure around five feet ten, dressed entirely in black, with a balaclava covering his face except for the eyes. Ryan had taken up a position behind a large wooden chest positioned against the wall in the hallway corridor, but he couldn't stay there forever. If he didn't seek out his opponent, then they would seek him out.

CHAPTER 45

Eve's car tore up the driveway towards the main gates, and came to a stop with a skid of tyres against gravel. The gatehouse stood in darkness; its door wide open. Anna watched for any signs of life, while Eve pressed the fob to open the electronic gates.

"They're not opening," she said. "Why won't they open?"

"They might have been tampered with—or maybe the power's been shut off, same as the gatehouse."

Eve looked back at her, in horror. "What do we do?"

"Mummy, I'm scared!"

"Shh, it's okay, Emma. It's okay."

Anna lifted the puppy onto her daughter's lap. "Here," she said, and stroked Emma's hair. "Cuddle Rascal, while I go and open the gates."

"Anna!" Eve said. "Where are you going?"

"There's an electrical box with a manual override inside," she replied, and slid out of the back seat of the car.

"Be careful!"

Anna nodded, and moved towards the open doorway of the stone gatehouse, her breath coming in short bursts as adrenaline rushed through her system. The house was in darkness, but she gathered her courage and stepped inside, into the blackness beyond. She reached for the light switch on the hallway wall and flicked it on and off, but nothing happened.

Had the fuse gone?

Anna made her way down a narrow hallway, the soles of her shoes crunching against the wooden floor at her feet, and she realised the sound was shattered glass. She lifted her smartphone and used its torch to look above her head, where she saw the remains of a bulb hanging loosely from a pendant.

She sank back against the wall, more frightened at the sight of that deliberate act of destruction than the darkness.

Move, her mind whispered. *There's no other way.*

Move!

She carried on down the hallway, passing a toilet and a bedroom, then a small galley kitchen until she came to the main room, which held a long desk with a bank of monitors, all turned off. But it wasn't that which held her attention.

It was the body of a man, lying outstretched on the floor at her feet.

Anna gasped, and her bowels wanted to loosen.

It wasn't the first time she'd experienced terror, but the feeling never diminished. Her stomach quivered as her body dealt with fresh waves of fear, and the very real prospect that whoever had attacked the security guard could be waiting nearby, ready to strike again.

It was enough to propel her into action.

Anna rushed forward and placed two trembling fingers against the man's neck.

There was a pulse.

It was weak, but it was still there.

Shining her torch over him, Anna found the wound at his upper arm, which could be fatal if he lost any more blood. She rushed into the kitchen and grabbed a tea towel, then grappled with his muscular weight so she could tie it tightly around the wound and try to stem the flow of any further blood.

Then, she rang the police.

Having made the security guard as comfortable as she could, Anna found the fuse box and tried to work out which switch would open the gates.

"Stuff this," she muttered, and flipped all of them on, filling the room with light and a cacophony of various electronic *bleeps* as the equipment came back online. Another look at the unfortunate man on the floor told her he needed urgent help, or wouldn't last another half hour. She ran outside, and pulled open the car door.

"Oh, thank God, I wondered what was taking you so long," Eve said.

"There's a man badly injured in there," Anna said. "I recognise him, he's the security guard—Finch, I think?"

"How badly is he hurt?"

"Fatally, if we can't get him out of here. I rang the police and the ambulance service, but the operator told me it would be at least twenty minutes before the paramedics could get to us, which is too long."

"We could take him to the nearest hospital," Eve said. "There's an urgent care unit in Newton Abbott, or a community hospital in Totnes, but they might not be open at this hour."

"Still closer than the nearest major hospital," Anna said.

They looked at one another, and then Eve nodded.

"It's worth a try," she said. "But we can't leave Emma—"

"No, you stay with her, and put this back as far as it'll go," Anna said, tapping the front passenger seat. "I'll drag him out."

"How will you manage?"

"Willpower," Anna said, and hurried back inside the gatehouse.

A minute later, Anna emerged from the gatehouse again, having learned that willpower alone couldn't solve every problem.

"Where is he?" Eve asked.

"He's dead." Anna peered inside the car and was pleased to find her daughter had fallen asleep with the puppy in her arms.

"There's nothing more we can do for him, now."

Eve covered her mouth, and said a silent prayer for the man and any family he might have had.

"We need to get you out of here," Anna said, pushing the image of his body to the farthest recesses of her mind, until a time when she could safely process it.

Eve nodded and started the car, before realising Anna wasn't moving.

"Why aren't you getting in?"

"Ryan's alone back there, and he might be injured. I couldn't live with myself, if I don't go back, now."

"I can't let you go back!"

"Yes, you can. Take Emma and keep her safe. We'll meet you at the Imperial Hotel in Totnes, just as we planned."

"What if something should happen to you?"

"It won't. Trust me, Eve, this is for the best."

It took a few more minutes to convince her of that, but Eve knew when she was beaten. The gates opened after a few frantic attempts clicking the fob, and Anna waved them off, watching the red taillights of her mother-in-law's car until it disappeared. Then, the gates clanged shut again and she turned back to the long driveway, which was at least half a mile long and swathed in darkness.

Ryan heard the creak of floorboards, as his assailant crept forward and prepared to mount another attack. Gunfire was dangerous enough, but Ryan knew that, if it came to physical combat, his chances were now limited by the excruciating pain and growing numbness on the left side of his body.

He needed a clear shot.

Just one.

Ryan sucked air into his lungs, and positioned himself as best he could. "Come on, coward!" he called out. "What are you waiting for?"

As expected, another shot rang out, spinning somewhere to his left, and Ryan countered with a solid shot against the edge of the doorway. He heard a muffled expletive as the other man jumped back, and decided to take a chance, moving forward, away from his cover and towards the doorway to get a better shot.

He took it, but knew he'd missed.

Ryan backed away, flattening himself against the side wall as counter shots came thick and fast, and dust filled the hallway. There was a short, intense exchange of fire, then he heard the click of an empty weapon, followed by another low expletive from the other side of the wall.

"It's over for you!" he called out. "The police are already on their way. There's no way out of this! Lay down your weapon, come quietly and I'll bring you in!"

There was a tense silence.

"Surrender now, and maybe we can make a plea deal!"

Ryan had no intention of bargaining with the person responsible for killing his father, but he'd say whatever was necessary to buy himself more time. He bore down against the pain in his arm and, when he touched the spot, his hand came away slicked with blood.

He waited, but no sound was forthcoming.

"We can—"

A sharp kick caught him off-guard, winding him so that he fell forward, followed by a brutal punch to the wound in his upper arm. Ryan cried out, then reared up and used his body to slam the other man back against the wall. It only stunned them off for a moment before they came at him again, gloved hands pummelling his face, his ribs and the sensitive area around his vital organs until he fell to his knees.

He spat blood onto the floor, but dragged himself up again and came back with a series of sharp jabs left and right, ignoring the singing pain on his left side to keep going, keep defending himself until the last ounce of fight had left his body.

Anna was breathing hard by the time she reached the utility room door. It was still open from earlier, so she took a deep breath and stepped inside.

The first thing she heard was Ryan's voice.

He was alive.

A sob escaped her lips, and she followed the sound, then came to a shuddering stop as his voice became a sharp cry of pain, followed by a series of grunts and the hollow sound of fists meeting flesh.

Ryan's flesh.

Anna spun around, searching for a weapon.

There was the gun cabinet, but that would take time to unlock. Instead, she ran into the kitchen and grabbed one of the butcher's knives from the block beside the oven, its blade gleaming silver in the moonlight that shone bleakly through the window. She took it in a hard, downward grip, and then hurried to help her husband.

She saw two figures at the other end of the long marble corridor, and, for a moment, they looked like they were dancing. Ryan had a firm hold on the other man's neck, while his assassin punched him again and again, knowing that it would eventually wear him down. Anna saw all this in the seconds it took her to move, running towards the two men who were so engrossed that neither heard her presence until she was almost upon them.

The hooded stranger turned at the precise moment her knife came down in a smooth arc, and she felt the edge of the blade connect with his body in a long slice of flesh, though not deep enough to kill.

He stumbled backwards.

Anna saw his eyes through the slit in his sweat-soaked balaclava and she raised her knife again, but then there came the sound of a siren at the head of the driveway, signalling the arrival of the emergency services. He turned and ran towards the open side door, and disappeared into the night as quickly as he had come.

She turned to her husband, who was propped against the wall, one hand clutching his arm. His face was beaded with sweat, his black hair matted with blood and his eyes, normally so clear and incisive, stark with pain.

She took his hand and held it tightly.

"I thought I asked you to drive away," Ryan gasped. "Emma—"

"She's safe, with your mother," Anna reassured him.

"You should have been with them."

"Since when do I take orders from you?" she said. "Besides, you're lucky I came back when I did."

Ryan wheezed out a laugh, which turned into a guttural sound. "Ain't that the truth," he mumbled.

CHAPTER 46

Thursday afternoon

On the orders of their Chief Constable, the entire Criminal Investigation Department had assembled at Northumbria Police Headquarters, including Frank Phillips, Denise MacKenzie, Jack Lowerson, Charlie Reed, Tom Faulkner and Neil Jones—who apologised for his recent absence, but explained that he'd been pleasantly occupied with a female squaddie from the Otterburn ranges, whom he'd met the other day. They told him he looked worn out, and Phillips advised him to be careful in future or he'd do himself a mischief.

While they waited for the Chief to arrive, they discussed the status of Operation Strangers.

"We interviewed Janet Charteris again, this mornin'," Frank said. "She's singin' like a canary, except when it comes to tellin' us the names of people who've used her scheme, or 'co-operative', as she likes to call it. The only one she's happy to name and shame is Marie Everett, but that's because she feels betrayed by her."

"Who's Marie Everett?" Faulkner asked.

"Her partner in crime, back in the early days," Frank replied. "She murdered Eddie Delaney for Janet, and Janet murdered Kyle Rodgers for Marie, like those two blokes in *Strangers on a Train*. Janet was thrilled with how easy it was, so she decided it was worth expanding the idea. Apparently, she was miffed when Marie told her that setting up a nationwide murder network was goin' a bit too far," Frank explained. "Then again, I've got a strong suspicion wor Janet's off her chump."

"She's certifiable, as far as I can tell," Jack agreed. "She talks to dead people more than that kid from *The Sixth Sense,* and she genuinely thinks she's done the world a favour. She reckons there've been more than four hundred deaths, thanks to her."

"Good God," Jeff muttered. "Please tell me they don't all need exhumation and post-mortems."

"No idea," Phillips replied. "We'll have to go through every case and connect the right people to the right murders."

"What does Everett have to say?" Charlie asked.

"She isn't admitting to anything, but Janet's grassed her up, anyway," Jack said. "Even if she hadn't, Everett made a curious distinction between 'no comment' and a plain 'no' in her interview. The current thinking is that she killed Edward Delaney in a kind of pact with Janet, who, in return, killed Kyle Rodgers—just as we thought. However, Marie seemed very keen to tell us she didn't know about anything that happened *after* those deaths. That would corroborate Janet's version of events."

"What about Ryan's murder?" Jeff asked them. "Have you found the person responsible?"

"I'm afraid you'll only be able to charge them with *attempted* murder," Ryan said.

"But surely—" Jeff began to argue, and then he spun around. "*Ryan!*"

There was a short, charged silence as his team looked at a man who, until that moment, they'd believed to be dead. Now, Ryan stood there, tall and vital as ever—even with a sling on his arm and bruises all over his face.

"Well?" he said. "Somebody had better say something."

"I'll say somethin'," Phillips volunteered, and made his way through the crowd. "You look rough as a badger's arse."

Ryan grinned, despite the bruises. "It's good to see you, Frank," he said, and gave him a strong, one-armed hug. "It's good to see all of you, again."

The dam broke, and the staff of CID rose to their feet and crowded around him, touching his arms to be sure he real. Ryan was overwhelmed by the outpouring of affection, which he dealt with by claiming they'd gone soft, in his absence, and that he'd have to toughen them up again.

"Aye, that'll be the day," Phillips said. "You look like somebody dragged you through a hedge, backwards. Rough night?"

"You could say that."

"If I've told Anna once, I've told her a thousand times, she needs to be more gentle with you."

Ryan laughed. "Reprobate," he said, but his eyes were shining. "Jack, Charlie, you're a sight for sore eyes."

Charlie held out a hand, not entirely sure how to cope with moments such as these, but Ryan overrode the Human Resources policy and gave her a quick hug, which he offered to Jack, and then every other person in the room, bar one. Questions flew back and forth, and he held up his hand to stave them off.

"Some of you might be wondering who died, in my place," he said.

Their faces grew solemn.

"Your father," Faulkner said quietly, and Ryan turned to look at him. "I'm sorry."

Of course he'd worked it out, Ryan thought. Tom Faulkner was a first-class forensic examiner, so it was obvious he'd have picked up on any evidential discrepancy. He'd likely noticed a large quantity of DNA belonging, not to him, but to his father, and put two and two together.

"Yes," he said.

There were murmurs of sympathy, which Ryan accepted with as much grace as he could.

"Thank you," he said, briskly. "We've been searching to find the people behind this network, and I'm glad to say we've achieved that, thanks to the dedication of everyone in this room. However, we've also been searching for the person or persons responsible for the car bomb that injured Frank, and for firing the bullet that took my father's life, at my house in Elsdon," he said, and then paused. "There's also the small matter of the armed home invasion and murder of two security personnel at my mother's home in Devon, last night, as well as another attempt to kill me off."

"They'd need a nuclear explosion to see you off," Frank joked, and drew good-natured laughter from around the room, which was much needed after weeks of working long days and nights.

"I'm confident Janet Charteris will tell us, in time," Ryan said.

"What if she doesn't cough it up?" MacKenzie said.

Ryan smiled, but there was a hard edge to it. "I don't need her to tell me," he replied. "I *know* who tried to kill me, last night, and succeeded in killing the security guards."

Beside him, Morrison's eyes strayed to the person he'd already named, and hoped Ryan was wrong. Unfortunately, he seldom was. Her eyes fell, and her heart was heavy as the truth stood on the edge of a precipice, ready to fall.

Ryan walked through the crowd until he approached the small group of people he called 'friends'.

"I asked myself: who knew my address in Northumberland and in Devon? Who had a reason to want somebody dead, and wound up being the one assigned to kill me, because they had the right skills? Who could have found out that I was still alive, despite it being a closely guarded secret?"

He walked past Phillips and MacKenzie, past Reed and Lowerson, and came to stand beside Tom Faulkner.

"You had a reason, didn't you?"

Faulkner was shocked. "*Me?*"

"Not you," Ryan said, and turned to look at the man standing beside him. "*You*. Neil Jones."

A collective gasp went up around the crowd, and Neil looked amongst them with a look of total bemusement. "What are you *talking* about? I had nothing to do with your father's death!"

"You came into a lot of money recently, didn't you, Neil?"

He raised a hand to his hair, and let it fall away again, looking for all the world like a wronged party. "Ryan, mate, I know you've been through a lot, but you're way off base with this one," he said. "I promise you, I had nothing to do with it. Frankly, I'm hurt that you'd even think it."

He was good, Ryan thought. "You're very convincing," he said. "Let's settle this, shall we?"

"How? I can give you the name of the woman I spent the night with," he offered. "She'll tell you I was with her, the whole day and overnight, too."

"I'm sure she will," Ryan replied. "Now, remove your shirt."

Neil laughed, but the sound was forced. "Come on—"

"Remove your shirt, or I'll do it for you."

Frank stepped forward. "Howay," he said. "You heard what the man said."

"Chief?" Neil appealed to Sandra Morrison, who looked at him with flat, unrelenting eyes. "Have a word, will you?"

In answer, she nodded to Ryan, whose good arm shot out and, with one hard motion, tore the front of Neil's shirt open. There was another rumble of shock, which was quickly silenced when they saw what Ryan knew they would find beneath the cotton shirt—a long, white bandage, covering the superficial knife wound Anna had inflicted upon him, the previous evening.

He tried to hide the wound, but it was too late, and his arms fell limply to his sides.

"How did you come by that wound?" Ryan asked, in a voice as hard as granite.

"I—" Neil swallowed, his Adam's apple bobbing up and down as he tried to formulate an excuse. "I—I fell—"

"You killed my father," Ryan snarled, danger in every line of his body. "You shot him, as if he was nothing."

"No, I—I never meant—"

"You almost killed me," Frank said, conversationally. "I could've done without that, Jonesy."

Neil looked between them, and then at all the other eyes that looked upon him with disappointment and disbelief.

"You don't understand," he said, defiantly. "I was in debt…that's why my wife divorced me. I—I have a gambling problem."

"Boo hoo," Jack said. "We've all got problems, but we don't resort to killing people."

There were murmurs of agreement.

"It was crippling," Neil argued. "I had to borrow from the Feeney brothers—" He referred to a notorious family who, amongst other things, loaned money at astronomical interest rates. If a person couldn't pay, they were punished without mercy. "They said it was my last chance, or they'd come for me," he said, and, to their disgust, began to cry. "I-I had no choice. I needed the inheritance money."

"I see, so it isn't just other people's fathers whom you were willing to kill, or have killed," Ryan said. "You were quite happy to arrange your own father's death, as well."

"He was old!" Neil shouted, eyes wide and appealing for understanding. "He'd already lived a good life—"

"A better one than you ever will, no doubt," Ryan said, and then turned his back on the man. "Lowerson? Reed? Would you take Mr Jones downstairs, please, and book him in?"

"With pleasure, sir—and, welcome back."

Ryan turned to his staff, and found he could still smile. "As for the rest of you…get back to work, or you'll feel my boot up your arse!"

There was a ripple of happy laughter around the room, and they began to disperse, chattering about the work that lay ahead.

"Try not to get into any more scrapes, will you?" Morrison said, with a smile in her eyes. "Oh, and Ryan?" He waited. "It's good to have you back."

To their surprise, she cocked a cheek, and he leaned down to peck it. With a satisfied grunt, she moved off, already thinking of the next fire to fight.

"Reet, lad, I've got a bone to pick wi' you," Frank said, once they were alone.

Ryan looked at his friend and wondered what he'd done, now. "If it's about the proposed ban on Lycra around the office, then I have to tell you, the motion's already been passed."

"Har bloody har," Phillips said. "Actually, I wanted to check how you'd like to be known, from now on?"

Ryan frowned.

"Well, since you've inherited a title, me and some of the lads were wonderin' if you'd prefer us to call you His Lordship, or maybe Your Grace, or His Greatness... how about, His Baronet-ness?"

Ryan swore to hunt Alex Gregory down, but that would have to wait. "You can call me, Your Boss, for one thing."

"I already call you, Your Bossiness," Phillips said. "Is that close enough?"

"You're never going to let me forget this, are you?"

"Not while there's a breath left in my body, Your Worshipfulness."

"If you want to keep breath in your body, you'd better put a sock in it."

"*See*? Did any of you hear *that*?" Frank said, and gesticulated to the others in the room, who paid no attention whatsoever. "It's the bleedin' aristocracy, tramplin' all over the proletariat!"

"Frank, you can't even spell proletariat."

"But I can spell, 'pint'."

Ryan flashed him a smile. "I always knew you were a genius."

EPILOGUE

One week later
Frankland Prison, Durham

Arthur Gregson had been told to expect a 'special' visitor, that day.

As far as he was concerned, if it wasn't Pamela Anderson, then he wasn't interested. Life in prison would never be 'good', but it had greatly improved since the death of the man who'd been a thorn in his side for years. Without Ryan, suddenly, the world seemed a brighter place, and even the food tasted better, especially when he could stomach an occasional interlude with the dinner lady in the canteen, just to tide himself over and give her the cheap thrill she was looking for.

As former Detective Chief Superintendent of the Northumbria Police Constabulary and sometime lieutenant in one of the largest criminal cults in living memory, he'd come to expect a certain standard of living, and had cultivated a habit of command. In Frankland, the shift in power had been a shock—and so had the regular beatings and solitary confinements, to try to prevent somebody planting a shiv in his kidney as thanks for having been the man to put them behind bars, once upon a time. Gradually, over the years, he liked to think he'd worked a bit of the old razzmatazz. It was amazing what money, drugs and other contraband could buy; chiefly, *safety*, with respect coming in at a close second.

"This way."

One of the screws, a man they called 'Winkler' because he bore a slight resemblance to the actor who played The Fonz, showed him into one of the meeting rooms and uncuffed him.

"Can I have some water?"

"Yeah, I'll get it for you, right after I've cooked up your lobster thermidor."

Gregson glared at him, and settled back to await his mystery guest. Ten minutes ticked by, and he was starting to become irritable.

"Oi!" he shouted out. "Is anyone coming, or what?"

Another five minutes went by, and then the door opened.

"It's about bloody time—"

The words curdled, as he caught sight of the man standing in the doorway.

"Surprised to see me?" Ryan said, and stepped inside with Frank following closely behind.

They gestured to the empty chairs.

"Mind if we join you, Arthur?"

"You—you were *dead*."

363

"Reports of my death have been greatly exaggerated," Ryan said, with a lazy smile. "You just can't get the help, these days, can you?"

He folded his arm across his chest, which was clad in a form-fitting white cotton shirt, rolled up at the sleeves. His sling had been removed the previous day and, although his arm still ached, he was making a solid recovery.

"I know it was you, who ordered the hit," he said, and his eyes flashed with anger, just once.

"I don't know what you're talking about."

"I spoke to the ringleader," Ryan said. "Janet wasn't happy to give me your name, at first, but once I told her you were one of the most diseased rats in the constabulary, she changed her mind." He paused, and took a sip of the water provided to him by the prison officer who looked a bit like someone from *Happy Days*. "Janet's a stickler for justice, you see," Ryan continued. "It's her own warped kind, of course, but she especially doesn't like bent coppers, so we could agree on that, at least. She sends her regards, by the way."

Gregson's mouth twisted into a smile. "You've got no proof," he said.

"We'll find it, never fear," Frank said. "Besides, where's the rush? You're not goin' anywhere fast."

"You can shut your mouth," Gregson growled, and then turned back to Ryan. "Come here to gloat, did you?"

Ryan shook his head and leaned forward, looking the man dead in the eye. "I came to warn you," he said, very softly. "If you ever threaten me, my family, or anyone else I love, ever again, I'll come for you, Arthur. There won't be a locked door that could hold me back."

"I've got all the time in the world," Gregson threw back, and his hands curled into fists. "Time's all I've got, Ryan. Days and nights of thinking about how I'll kill you."

"Well, we've all got to have a hobby," Ryan said, and rose to his feet. "I'm off for a walk along the beach. You remember the feeling of sand between your toes, and the breath of the sea on your face? You'll never feel that again."

Gregson pushed back from his chair and hurled himself across the table to make a grab for Ryan, eyes dark with hate.

He didn't make it far.

Frank's fist connected with his cheekbone and sent him sprawling across the floor.

"Nobody tries to blow me up and gets away with it," he said, and straightened his tie.

"Ready to go?" Ryan asked.

Phillips cast a beady eye over the man lying on the floor, and then nodded. "Aye," he said. "Let's find some better company."

Jack Lowerson was whistling as his car pulled up on the kerb outside his home in East Boldon. The sun had entered its Golden Hour, and he thought about calling Charlie to ask if she and Ben might like to go for a walk along the beach, before remembering it was probably too late for the little boy to be heading out.

Perhaps at the weekend?

He decided to ask Charlie about it, and began thinking of other places they might like to visit. There was Minchella's ice-cream parlour, Colman's fish and chips, the little train at Marine Park in South Shields—and then, of course, the wide, sandy beach.

He could imagine Charlie, with the wind in her hair.

He could imagine chasing Ben over the sand, or building sandcastles together.

He could imagine it all too well, and, what was more, he felt no fear about any of it; only a sense of contentment, as if a jigsaw piece had finally clicked into place.

He let himself inside the house, and nudged the door shut with his hip, tossing the keys from hand to hand before dumping them in the bowl on the hallway table, where they clanged against another set of keys.

Jack took a couple of steps forward, then frowned and looked back.

There was another set of keys in the bowl.

That could only mean—

"Jack?"

His head whipped around, and he saw a slim, tanned woman with blonde hair streaked by long hours spent in the sun. She looked the same as before, and yet completely different, at the same time.

"Mel."

"Yes," she said. "I'm back."

DCI Ryan will return in

BELSAY

If you would like to be kept up to date with new releases
from LJ Ross, please complete an e-mail contact form.

ACKNOWLEDGEMENTS

As always, my thanks to you, Dear Reader, for choosing to follow the adventures of DCI Ryan and Friends. Their stories are a joy to write and, little did I know, ten years ago, that I would continue to find such pleasure in crafting the characters I dreamed up on a train journey that took me along the coast, past Lindisfarne.

I would like to extend a personal 'thank you' to all the staff at The Alnwick Garden and, in particular, The Poison Garden—including Dean, who was so generous in sharing his knowledge of the incredible plants he and his colleagues look after so well.

Finally, to my husband, James, and my children, Ethan and Ella—thank you for all your love and support, you are the reason I am able to do the work that I do.

Until the next time…

LJ ROSS
SEPTEMBER 2024

ABOUT THE AUTHOR

LJ Ross is an international bestselling author, best known for creating atmospheric mystery and thriller novels, including the DCI Ryan series of Northumbrian murder mysteries which have sold over ten million copies worldwide.

Her debut, *Holy Island,* was released in January 2015 and reached number one in the UK and Australian charts. Since then, she has released more than twenty further novels, all of which have been top three global bestsellers and almost all of which have been UK #1 bestsellers. Louise has garnered an army of loyal readers through her storytelling and, thanks to them, many of her books reached the coveted #1 spot whilst only available to pre-order ahead of release.

Louise was born in Northumberland, England. She studied undergraduate and postgraduate Law at King's College, University of London and then abroad in Paris and Florence. She spent much of her working life in London, where she was a lawyer for a number of years until taking the decision to change career and pursue her dream to write. Now, she writes full time and lives with her family in Northumberland. She enjoys reading all manner of books, travelling and spending time with family and friends.

If you enjoyed this book, please consider leaving a review online.

If you would like to be kept up to date with new releases from LJ Ross, please complete an e-mail contact form on her Facebook page or website, www.ljrossauthor.com

Scan the QR code below to find out more
about LJ Ross and her books

If you liked *Poison Garden*, why not try the bestselling Alexander Gregory Thrillers by LJ Ross?

IMPOSTOR

AN ALEXANDER GREGORY THRILLER (Book #1)

There's a killer inside all of us...

After an elite criminal profiling unit is shut down amidst a storm of scandal and mismanagement, only one person emerges unscathed. Forensic psychologist Doctor Alexander Gregory has a reputation for being able to step inside the darkest minds to uncover whatever secrets lie hidden there and, soon enough, he finds himself drawn into the murky world of murder investigation.

In the beautiful hills of County Mayo, Ireland, a killer is on the loose. Panic has a stranglehold on its rural community and the Garda are running out of time. Gregory has sworn to follow a quiet life but, when the call comes, can he refuse to help their desperate search for justice?

Murder and mystery are peppered with dark humour in this fast-paced thriller set amidst the spectacular Irish landscape.

IMPOSTOR is available now in all good bookshops

LOVE READING?

JOIN THE CLUB...

Join the LJ Ross Book Club to connect with a thriving community of fellow book lovers! To receive a free monthly newsletter with exclusive author interviews and giveaways, sign up at www.ljrossauthor.com or follow the LJ Ross Book Club on social media:

#LJBookClubTweet

@LJRossAuthor

@ljrossauthor

Made in the USA
Las Vegas, NV
01 April 2025